£.1.50

CW00544392

Books by Richard Kearney

Fiction and Poetry

Walking at Sea Level

Sam's Fall

Angel of Patrick's Hill

Non-Fiction

Touch: Recovering Our Most Vital Sense

Imagination Now: A Richard Kearney Reader

Radical Hospitality: From Thought to Action
(co-authored with Melissa Fitzpatrick)

Twinsome Minds: An Act of Double Remembrance

Reimagining the Sacred: Richard Kearney Debates God

Anatheism: Returning to God after God

Navigations: Collected Irish Essays 1976-2006

Debates in Continental Philosophy:
Conversations with Contemporary Thinkers

On Paul Ricoeur: The Owl of Minerva

On Stories

The God Who May Be

Strangers, Gods, and Monsters

Desiderio et Dio (co-authored with Ghislain LaFont)

Postnationalist Ireland: Politics, Culture, Philosophy

States of Mind: Dialogues with Contemporary Thinkers

Poetics of Modernity: Toward a Hermeneutic Imagination

Visions of Europe:
Conversations on the Legacy and Future of Europe

Poetics of Imagining: From Husserl to Lyotard

The Wake of Imagination:
Ideas of Creativity in Western Culture

Transitions: Narratives in Modern Irish Culture

Modern Movements in European Philosophy

Dialogues with Contemporary Continental Thinkers:
The Phenomenological Heritage

Poétique du Possible:
Phénoménologie herméneutique de la figuration

For critical praise of Richard Kearney's previous books, visit:
https://rb.gy/eaouyg

SALVAGE

ARROWSMITH
PRESS

Salvage
Richard Kearney

ISBN: 979-8-9863401-7-3

Boston — New York — San Francisco — Baghdad
San Juan — Kyiv — Istanbul — Santiago, Chile
Beijing — Paris — London — Cairo — Madrid
Milan — Melbourne — Jerusalem — Darfur

11 Chestnut St.
Medford, MA 02155

arrowsmithpress@gmail.com
www.arrowsmithpress.com

The forty-ninth Arrowsmith book
was typeset & designed by Ezra Fox
for Askold Melnyczuk & Alex Johnson
in Times New Roman & Poster Gothic Cond ATF

Cover art, Simone Kearney
Ink drawings and ink script, Simone and Sarah Kearney
Inside cover map of Brigid's Island, Anne Bernard

In Memory of the People of Oileán Bhríde

From Port na bPúcaí

Bean ón slua sí mé
Do tháinig thar toinn
Is do goideadh san oíche mé
Tamall thar lear...
Beadsa ag caoineadh
'N fhaid a bheidh uisce sa toinn

I am a woman from beyond
Who came over the waves
And was swept into the dark
For a spell abroad...
I will be keening
As long as water remains in the sea

SALVAGE

a novel

RICHARD KEARNEY

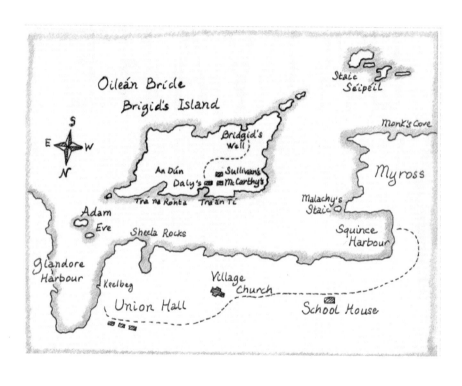

Prefatory Note

This is a story of the last inhabitants of Brigid's Island, West Cork. Originally known as *Oileán Bhríde* by its native Irish speakers, it was renamed Rabbit Island by the Royal Ordnance Survey in the 1830s. It harbors an ancient healing well, dedicated to Saint Brigid, which pilgrims visited throughout the centuries. The pilgrimage was abandoned in the last century when Brigid was removed from the Liturgical Calendar by Church authorities who deemed her too pagan and primal. But several of her wells, scattered throughout Ireland, remained; and one of these was on Brigid's Island, now reduced to a trickle in a collapsed cave. So many storms and strangers have come in across the sea over the years, along with swing tides, porpoises, migratory birds and clouds. Nothing is ever mute on Brigid's Island, and local neighbors in the townlands of Ardra, Myross and Cooscroneen, still relate old memories of the place, like trawlers' nets full of stray and quivering things — tales of fishing and farming, grief and resilience, love and calamity. (The Great Famine broke out on the nearby headland of Myross a hundred years before this fictional account unfolds.)

This story is the flotsam of such voices—washed ashore, overheard, handed down, imagined. Salvage of an island.

Tír gan teanga, tír gan anam.

On Irish Usage

I have chosen to use much Irish in this text, to acknowledge that the last inhabitants of Brigid's Island were native Irish speakers. Though all the characters in this story are fictional, they are inspired by people who were amongst the last to use Gaelic on a daily basis in this part of Ireland. For this reason I have included as many Irish phrases as possible, providing English translations in the text where I thought it important. But on most occasions it is the sound and music of the language that matters. I have kept the local Munster Irish spelling and accents where possible, generally guided by consultation with the classic Irish-English dictionaries by Dineen and de Bhaldraithe, and with Irish scholars Joseph Nugent, Seán Cahill and Manchán Magan. I have italicized most words in Gaelic apart from local placenames. Given the important role that diacritical accents play in pronunciation, here are some examples of the phonetic emphasis of key words in the book, where *í* is pronounced as 'ee,' *á* as 'aw,' *ó* as 'oh' and *ú* as 'ooh.'

Trá an Tí (beach of the house) — Thrawn-tee

Dreoilín (wren) — Dreo-leen

Púcaí (fungi or spirits) - Pooh-kee

Súitú (sucking-out sound of the shoreline at night) — Suet-two

Oileán Bhríde — Ill-awn Vree-deh

CONTENTS

I

BRIGID'S DAY
January-August 1939

Gaínéad-gannet

Maeve rose with the sun to meet her father. A cold mist crawled over the shores of Brigid's Island as morning light pierced through the clouds.

Michael Sullivan was already busy in his Brú, a lean-to hut at the back of the house. He'd left the door on the latch and scarcely looked up as Maeve entered.

'*Conas taoi?*' he asked, eyes glued to a scalpel slicing through a stalk of kelp.

'*Go maith,*' she replied, sidling past shelves laden with dried plants and sea wracks. She approached the wooden worktop where her father was cutting fronds into strips before suspending them from the rafters.

Maeve inhaled the last fumes of the oil lamp burning low as dawn crept through the windows of the hut. Nearing the table, she ran her thumb along dried stalks hanging like tobacco-stained fingers from the roof. *Ruálach*, small button weed with long-tailed leaves. *Láracha*, dabberlocks with dark purple wings. *Feamla*, sticky bladder wrack with wavy edges. She fondled a bouquet of kelp feeling the blistered moonscapes of skin against her hand. Caressing the dappled surface, she inhaled the sea-lady smell. All ingredients for her father's cures, which he was busy preparing for Brigid's Day. Only four weeks off with much to do.

'Can I help?' she asked.

Michael put down the scalpel and turned to his daughter. Blue eyes bluer than a mackerel's back. 'You can if your Mam lets you. But you know right well she'll want you at Mass.'

'I've a cold. Can't you hear it?' She coughed a small cough and patted her chest. 'I'd catch my death in that drafty church. And I've always told you I hate Father Kehoe.'

'You should hate no one, Maeve. He's a good man and kind to your mother.'

Maeve knit her brow and shuffled. 'Maybe. But he has bad breath. I could hardly speak during my last Confession.'

'What's smell got to do with it?'

'Everything. It's worse than rotten herring and his voice rises like a curlew when he talks of the Virgin Mary. Higher than John McCormack singing Macushla.'

Maeve was happy her father was amused, his shoulders rippling in a mute chuckle. She moved closer and eyed his work. 'Besides, Father Kehoe says what you do is all *piseógs*. Nonsense and make-believe. That's what I heard him tell Mam.'

'When was that?' Her father raised an eyebrow.

'Last time he sailed over for the Stations. Before Christmas.'

'Well, it's little Christmas now and he'll have other things on his mind. A full church for his sermon on the Epiphany and every parishioner kneeling before him.' Michael turned back to his work. 'Except me.'

'And me,' Maeve added, coaxing another fake cough as she tightened her scarf about her neck. 'Why go all the way to the village when we can have our own epiphany here?'

Michael nodded and smiled, glancing over at the lamp where a tiny blue flame still guttered and danced. He took a match and lit his pipe. A plume of sweet smoke filled the air. Then, reaching over to the font on the wall, he dipped a finger in the water and sprinkled a drop on Maeve's head.

'That'll do you now, chase the cold away.'

Maeve raised her hands to her hair before glancing towards the door where a smell of fresh soda bread wafted in from the adjoining house. Mam would soon be over with a plate of scones. Maeve's belly rumbled, but she knew she'd have to pretend she wasn't hungry. Too sick to eat or sail to the village. She didn't want to join Mam and her brothers, Connie and Seán, as they crossed the bay in the yawl for Mass; she wanted to stay here on the island with her father and the cures. Maeve longed to know more, to learn all the remedies listed in her father's book, the black sealskin ledger he kept on the shelf. She was the only one he'd told about the cures, saying that the 'old knowledge' was secret and that you had to be the seventh son of a seventh son to understand them. The fact that he was the third son of a fourth son didn't seem to bother him, nor that Maeve was his third child and daughter; he said it was as close as made no difference. Native savvy would do the rest. That's what he told her. But maybe he was teasing? Maeve could never tell. But she was sure he had the gift, and that's what mattered. And she knew he was sure she had it too.

He always said she had a special way with things since she was little, listening and looking deeply in ways no others did. Her brothers were jealous of her, her classmates too. No denying it. She saw and heard things differently, learned quick, could smell rain on the wind and was left-handed. *Ciotóg.* And even though others mocked her for that, especially at school on the mainland, her father took it as another sign. With her curly black hair and wild blue eyes, she was curious and daring since the day she was born. He sensed it from the start. He had no doubt his daughter was chosen, called, rare. And that's why he'd promised to pass on the gift. Beginning of spring, first day of February, when the pilgrims sailed over for the healing. Yes, it would be her turn soon: to help with the cures, recite them in Irish. To answer the call of the young Brigid. To play *Bríd Óg* on Brigid's day. *Lá Fhéile Bhríde*.

Maidin mhaith. Eileen Sullivan bid good morning as she entered the smoky hut. Carrying two mugs of milky tea and a basket of hot buttered scones, she was followed by the dog, Bawn, who brushed against Maeve's legs before she had time to shoo him away.

Michael and Maeve took the mugs and drank, though Maeve declined the scones, complaining of a sore throat.

'Poor *leanbh*,' said Mam, putting a hand to her daughter's forehead. She left it there for a moment, looking Maeve in the eyes before declaring, 'No fever. You're well enough for Mass.'

'Ah, would you leave her, Eileen?' Michael took a sheepskin rug from the chair and handed it to Maeve. 'She can wrap up in this and stay with me.' Then he turned and looked kindly at Eileen, taking her by the waist and holding her close. 'Isn't she safer here than coughing her lungs out with a load of holy Joes in that big damp church? Father Kehoe has enough disciples. She'll be better off with me.'

'Alright so,' Mam gave in with a sigh. 'But if she's not right by tomorrow we'll call for the doctor. If she misses Mass she's not missing school. She'll need proper medicine.' Mam fingered a blister of dried bladder wrack on the table. She put her nose to it, sniffed and turned away like a cat from sour cream, before facing Michael. 'And don't be filling her mind with notions now. *Bríd Óg* and *púcaí* and all that stuff. She's still a child with a life ahead of her....'

'I'm fourteen.' Maeve protested, rising to her full height.

'You're a child, like I say. You're my child and I won't see you wasted. You're the best in your class, Miss Collins says so, and Father Kehoe can help you….'

'How?' Maeve frowned.

'To grow.'

'Grow?'

'Yes…in faith and the teachings of the church. You need the faith if you want to get on. We all do. You know that, Maeve. Or would you rather stay here while your brothers and friends get on in the world — learn good English and get real jobs? Soon as they pass the Inter, Seán and Connie will be off to the mainland. Like all young islanders. They've said so. We'll miss them. But they'll have my blessing. There's no future for you here. Irish charms will get you nowhere. You need proper learning, you need the faith.'

'But I have faith. *This* faith.' She pointed to the water font and hanging fronds. 'I've faith in the cures. In Brigid. She'll look after us.'

'It's true enough, the girl's right.' Michael took Eileen in an embrace, wrapping his arms about her as he tapped her back with his big brown hands. Mam couldn't help a little laugh before pushing him away and turning to Maeve.

'Right then, for today. But once you're better, I want you at Mass with the rest of us.' She wrapped the sheepskin over Maeve's shoulders. 'Be sure to keep warm, and have the pollock pie ready when we get back.'

'Thanks, Mam,' said Maeve, hugging her mother before closing the door behind her.

Maeve smiled. Father Kehoe's Masses were long. None of the islanders would be back before dusk.

Once Mam and the others had left for the mainland, Maeve and her father worked away on the cures. Warmed by Mam's tea and the cast iron burner at the back of the Brú, they cut and sorted plants and wracks, storing them carefully in bottles and bowls, while singing together a chorus of charms:

> *Anair icorca glanbda*
> *Andess ingel gle amra*
> *Is miamh maiden dhomb*
> *Duileasg Lioc an Eigir*
> *Agus creamh an Sgoth*
>
> *The finest food is red seaweed*
> *Dulse taken from the Rock of Eigir*
> *And the wild garlic of Sgoth*

They chanted the charms in Gaelic, knowing the sounds were part of the healing. For Irish had powers unknown to English.

Shortly after midday, Michael realised he was missing a crucial ingredient — *craobhraic*, samphire — a potent shore plant popular with the pilgrims. Many came looking for a cure against the Sadness — it was that time of year — and Michael needed an ample supply. He knew the best place to harvest was the cove of Staic Séipéil, a craggy shale rock a mile to the south. It was a good hour's sail there and back.

'Are you well enough for a quick run?' he asked Maeve, reaching for his cap. 'I'd not want to leave you here on your own. How's your cough?'

'The sea will do me a power of good.' Her face lit up. 'I'll wrap up well.'

It was chilly at sea this time of year and it wouldn't do to catch a real cold. Maeve knew her father knew she was acting. But her mother was different. And Maeve felt bad. A twinge of guilt tightened her throat. She couldn't help it. Mam loved all her children and only wanted what was right for them. She really believed in Father Kehoe, that his Masses made people feel better in life, more able to cope with loss and disappointment, to find peace and grace in the Church's prayers and salvation in its teachings. Maeve had learned all this in her Christian Doctrine classes at school, in preparation for Holy Communion and Confirmation. It was part of her, whether she liked it or not, and now she'd lied to her mother and broken the Ninth Commandment.

Her father had little time for all that. He was another sort altogether, a loner and dreamer, a rare survivor of the old Gaelic ways. Maeve knew that. Some said he was a trickster, 'off with the fairies' half of the time; and one of the neighbors, Tadhg McCarthy, even called him mad. Mean things were said and there were few left now still believed in the cures, on island or mainland, apart from the loyal pilgrims who came every year to the island's well. Michael Sullivan was still their man. A great sailor and healer. *Fear Maith an Oileáin*. But no follower of Father Kehoe. Different worlds, different faiths.

Maeve chose to believe in her father, in the Gift passed on through generations. She felt it in her bones. But what if they were wrong? What, God forbid, if Father Kehoe was right?

Maeve rose from the cutting board and rolled the sheepskin under her arm. '*Ar aghaidh linn*. Let's go.'

'Alright my girl, but you'll need more warmth.' Michael

reached for his Harris tweed coat, thick and strong against the elements, the best bit of salvage he'd ever gleaned.

Maeve raised her hands, threading them through the arms of the coat, held open by her father, before rolling the sleeves up and fastening the buttons to the neck. The tweed tails fell to the heel of her boots and the pockets were filled with extra scarves. Maeve felt like a prize ewe! Ready for all weathers.

Michael and Maeve tethered Bawn in the yard and walked from the Brú to Trá an Tí, the small sheltered beach beneath the houses where the island families — Sullivans, Dalys and McCarthys — moored their fishing yawls and kept lobster pots and herring nets safe from the storms.

Michael pulled in the mooring while Maeve placed two wicker baskets at the stern, large enough for a fill of samphire and kelp. Not only would these and other shore plants replenish the stock of cures but, mixed with mule dung, they'd also serve as fertilizer when they set the potato drills in March. Stepping aboard, Maeve moved to the bow — her favorite spot for watching gannets — while Michael secured the mizzen and fixed the oars in the oarlocks.

They were soon rounding the west cliffs of the island, heading due south to Staic Séipéil. Once out of the lea of the land, Michael hoisted the mainsail, reefing it close to ease the gusts. The bow scudded through the waves as wind filled the canvas like a bloated belly. Maeve pulled the tweed tighter about her. Her father's favorite coat salvaged from an English steam trawler that had foundered off Baltimore in a westerly gale. It broke up on the rocks two miles shy of Sheeps Head. All of three hundred tons. Rescue boats were launched from the island and though they did their best there was no saving her. Luckily the crew survived and once the storm subsided the salvage was mighty.

The island was aglow for weeks after, every family proud of its catch. The Dalys got black walnut chairs and the Captain's table; the McCarthys a box of gold fittings, five crates of rum and silverware from the Mess, while Michael managed to save the bosun's copper bell from the upper deck along with the tweed coat and other valuables. It was a grand time, when the island rejoiced in the gifts of the gales — *gaotha móra na sí* — and everyone was happy for a spell. Then scarcity returned and the lean ways of offshore existence. Scant farming and fishing in season. Maeve was only five when the steamer went down but she never forgot the bright lights in the neighbors' windows, the feel of the Harris tweed coat and the brief swell of hope before winter returned.

A flick of spray stung Maeve's face. She licked salt from her lips and thanked Brigid for the coat, pulling the collar up to her chin.

Gulls wheeled overhead, swooping down in hopes of stray morsels, as high before them rose the Carraigroan rocks, each layer darker and thicker than the next, until they passed the strait into open sea. A favorite spot for lobster pots.

Michael was keen to get to Staic Séipéil, still a good half mile to the south, but Maeve begged him to lift the pots. Just a quick hoist to see what was there.

A white buoy bobbed on the swell, marking the Sullivan's string of traps. Michael knew the exact bearings: where Malachy's Staic masked the coastguard house to the north with a straight line running east to the Galley head. The white and yellow buoys nearby belonged to the Dalys and McCarthys.

Michael would often lift Dan Daly's as a favor, bringing him back any catch he landed. Best of friends always. But he never lifted Tadhg McCarthy's; and Tadhg McCarthy never lifted his. Rivals from youth, they hid it well; living on an island you had to get on. Today Michael would keep to his own.

Terns were out in force, dipping, circling, fussing. Michael shipped oars and bade Maeve balance the boat as he leaned over the gunnel and began hauling the timber traps. He piled the ropes, one coil after another, onto the deck. Fifteen fathom each rope, three from surface to bottom and one for every pot after. Maeve moved down from the bow to peer over her father's shoulder as the slatted cages rose from the deep. White ghosts peering up. She counted the pots as he hoisted them aboard, stacking them high beside tackle and floats. A full score of lobster and two fine crayfish, their long spiney whiskers flicking the air.

Michael clicked his tongue and Maeve did the same. Would they try for more at some other good spots? The Rónseach off to the West? Or the Mudrach under Monks Cove? Or maybe drop a new line off the Rómhór by Reen? Maeve was eager, but Michael shook his head — no time for that now; he dropped the cages back into the waves, fastening lead weights at each fathom to keep the ropes straight and the glass buoys tight. Maeve marveled at the savvy of it all, twirling an edge of scarf between her fingers as, above her head, light leaned thinly in from the east.

Tacking southwest to Staic Séipéil, Maeve spied a gannet diving off the Belly Rock. Its giant grey-tipped wings — seven feet at full stretch — buckled and tucked as it plunged from the sky. Hardly a splash, then nothing at all; before the bird surfaced again full of fish, hoisting itself back into the air, potbellied, wide-winged, triumphant.

Maeve loved gannets and could watch them all day. Hunters from the mainland paid six guineas to the council to harvest the eggs on the rocks off the coast. All the way from Rosscarbery to Bantry. Precious prey; but Maeve liked them flying free.

Nearing the Staic, Maeve heard a snorting to starboard and leaned over to watch a bob of seals surface and roll before vanishing again in the boat's wake. *Madraí na farraige*. Dogs of the sea. Brigid's own.

Entering the cove, the wind lulled. Michael wet a finger on his tongue and raised it high, testing the breeze, before lowering the sails; he then inserted an oar at the stern and sculled slowly towards the beach.

A clatter of gulls greeted their arrival. They moored by an outcropping, and stepped ashore careful not to wet their boots in the winter sea. Clumps of samphire grew abundant on the shale ridges of the lower rocks and it didn't take long to fill two baskets. The stalks were green and straggly, sticky to the touch with a lemony smell. Crisp and spicy on the tongue, Maeve chewed a handful before filling her creel. Delicious plants, not to be mistaken for sea fennel nor maidenhair, which also grew along this shore but had nothing of the same flavor — or healing powers against the Sadness when mixed with the *púcaí poill*.

Job done, they left their harvest on the shore and climbed a shingle path to the bluff. A patch of wild grass peppered with campions and purple vetch awaited them, the surrounding ocean stretching all the way from the Galley Head to the mighty Stags. They stood and gazed while Michael told Maeve about how this rock once harbored a chapel where ancient monks tended a cemetery for shipwrecked souls off the local coasts, including Spanish sailors from the Grand Armada, three hundred years before.

'Nothing's left now, not a single grave,' Michael sighed. 'But some say it's still haunted. Growing up we'd hear voices crying out on winter nights, rising up from underground caves, longing to return to the world. *Púcaí aon oíche*, they called them, spirits of one night, and like *púca* mushrooms they rose in the dark and vanished during the day. Same name, *púcaí,* for strange creatures that came and went. One moment there, gone the next. Moving between two different worlds, playing games with your mind.' Michael pointed to the ground and laughed. 'Right tricksters, you could never be sure.'

Returning to the boat, Michael confided to Maeve how he'd once fallen into a hidden cave here as a boy, only to find it was gone the next day when he returned with his friends. 'Black caves' he called them, unlike 'white caves' like Brigid's.

As they sailed home in a broad reach, Maeve wondered about the different caves as her father lit up his pipe, filling the air with a haze of sweet tobacco. In open sea, they both sang a song for the coming of spring, lifting their throats towards the sky:

> *Tig an geimhreadh dian dubh*
> *Gearradh lena ghéire*
> *Ach ar lá 'le Bhríde*
> *Gar dúinn earrach Éireann*
>
> *Here's the dark hard winter*
> *Cutting with its sharpness*
> *But on Brigid's day*
> *Ireland's Spring is close*

As they harvested more cures during the following weeks, Bawn was always with them. He loved hunting for gulls' eggs on the cliffs and rolling in slick algae on the south shore of the island. Covered in filth, he'd leap into waves and yelp like mad until

Maeve threw sticks for him to retrieve. If he was half shepherd, Michael Sullivan swore, he was half seal.

The dog was black as a cormorant, but Michael called him *Bawn*, meaning *white* — 'for devilment' — presenting the collie to Maeve for her birthday. Maeve laughed but Mam wasn't pleased, saying if it was Maeve's dog it was Maeve's to mind — feeding, tethering, walking, worming. Her father helped her train the pup well — long leash for sheep, short leash for fowl, fish-skins for breakfast, beet peels for tea; seal oil to loosen burrs from the pelt and a swipe of the blackthorn to scold him when bold. There were more canny lessons as the dog grew. Like calling him to heel by blowing through tightly knit thumbs and cupped palms — high pitch to halt, low to retrieve — or making bird calls with pressed lips and tongue: trills and twitters for sparrows, wails and hoots for teal, tu-whits for snipe, tu-whoos for chuffs. Maeve learned every cue; and Bawn was quick to follow.

The dog scarcely left Maeve's side, accompanying her through the fields and bracken, sniffing out hidden herbs and roots, and showing how, if humans speak the world, animals smell it. Bawn led the hunt with his snout, one moment snuffling deep in vetch, another perking his head into winds, flaring the air for some special waft. Michael had trained him to find certain cures — plants and sea wracks, flowers and saps, but above all the coveted fungi. Bawn was mad for the *púcaí* and learned how to track the different kinds: webcaps near the marshy reeds, scallycaps around horse dung, slipperjacks at the edges of meadows. But most precious of all the *púcaí poill* — white caps with sweet nipple crowns and blue-green stems which Michael used against the Sadness. Not to be confused with flat-scaled brownies. Both kinds grew near Brigid's Well and were lookalikes until you got close. White caps smelled earthy and healed; brown caps smelled mealy and harmed. Not to be mixed or mistaken. Michael taught Maeve to tell the difference.

On long foraging walks, when Maeve got back from school, Michael taught her other things too. If she was to play young Brigid for the pilgrims, Maeve needed to know more about the holy healer, ancient tales of her feats and cures — things Maeve would never learn at church when priests spoke in English of the great Catholic saints.

'She could still the wind and rain,' Michael told Maeve, speaking of Brigid as if she was standing there beside him. 'In fact, you see, she *is* the wind and rain, the very power of land and sea. She did cures with all kinds of things, simple things that grow beneath our feet, like madonna lilies and mushrooms — *Bia Bhríde*, 'Brigid's food — special plants which change our minds, and alter the way we see the world. Some said she could turn water to beer at the solstice and make lost objects appear in the bellies of birds and fish; she used well water to cure the sick and made babies grow in their mother's wombs.' Michael waved a hand in the air. 'Imagine that! What would Father Kehoe say?' And he told Maeve other Brigid stories too, about how she became Abbess of Druim Criaidh where she lived with men and women called *anamchairde*, soul-friends who kept a flame alive when she died, a fire in a cave that never burned out. Until the Irish church turned English and Brigid was considered 'pagan' and stripped of her sainthood. Most of her holy wells vanished after that, but on a few offshore islands the 'old knowledge' survived and Brigid returned with special cures.

When Michael had finished his litany, he turned to Maeve and said slowly: 'Maybe our island's the last of these?'

Maeve nodded but wasn't quite sure. When her father recounted tales like that, she couldn't always tell what was real or imagined, what was history or legend. Did Brigid really exist as a person, or was she more a power of the soul, a force of nature, a thing of the mind? When she asked her father, he said it didn't matter and smiled. When she asked her mother, she shook her head and said it was foolishness. Maeve was struck that the McCarthys and Dalys had removed Brigid straw crosses from their hearths and that Father Kehoe never spoke of her at all. While Seán and Connie just laughed and called her 'Biddy the Banshee.' But their mockery, Maeve suspected, came from other things too: hurt and jealousy about all the time their father spent with her — teaching the charms and foraging cures — when he could have been fishing and farming with them, or helping them with school work to pass their exams and move to the mainland. Connie and Seán never left off teasing Maeve about being a *ciotóg*, wagging their left hands in the air and naming her 'black magic Biddy.' Maeve held her peace and never fought back. They were older and stronger, and she knew where their meanness came from. Things would be better, she hoped, once Brigid's day was done and her father gave them attention again. It wouldn't be long now. A matter of time.

As the day approached, there was much to be done. The well needed dressing with flowers and the boat cleaning up for the pilgrims. Maeve picked snow drops from pots in the yard and pulled furry brown bull rushes from the wet marsh. She cut branches from the holly beside the Brú, the red berries and green zig-zag leaves brightening up the bouquet. Brigid's day was the first of February, beginning of spring and a new sowing season. But not everyone was content. Tadhg McCarthy accused Michael of doing cures for 'the money,' fooling poor mainlanders with his tricks and yarns. Connie and Seán got surlier by the day, Connie crossing his father in the yard — at sixteen he was six foot tall

— saying the whole business was a waste of time and refusing to help with the painting of the boat, while Seán complained there'd be more money using the yawl to catch lobsters than ferrying pilgrims across the Sound. But it was Mam who resisted the most, bursting into the Brú and interrupting their work.

'There's evil on the wind,' she warned. 'A fierce reek, bitter and foul — don't you smell it? The birds have gone dumb, not a sparrow in sight. Even the gulls have fled out to sea and I just found a dogfish in the water tank. This morning, below on Trá an Tí, there were swarms of jellyfish washed up on the strand. Soft and blue, like still-born babies. And the ship's bell rang outside the door, even though there was no one there.'

Maeve disliked seeing her mother distraught but was relieved her father could calm her down. He had a way with her when she grew anxious like that and had an answer for everything. The smell was from the midden where he'd mixed thong weed with dung to fertilize the potato drills ahead of the March seeding. The dogfish was surely a trick by the boys — forever baiting Maeve — while the tolling bell was just a gust of wind. What's more, blooms of jelly fish were a good sign, meaning spring herring would be running soon. 'There's nothing to fear,' he assured Eileen, taking her in his arms and rocking her gently. 'It'll all be grand. It'll all be grand.'

Maeve made a promise that when Brigid's day was over she'd do whatever her mother said.

When the day came they were up before dawn. The morning air was damp as Maeve and her father crossed the island from the house to the well. Maeve pulled her scarf tight about her head, glancing at the grainy sky before calling Bawn to heel as he scampered off into bracken and scrub. Passing the boat beach, the air cackled with gray crows swooping down onto the herring nets. Maeve shooed them away and cursed them to the devil. *Nach mórán diabhal sibh*!

'No bother,' Michael called over his shoulder, closing his collar against the chill. '*Ná bac leis*. Step on it, we've work to do.'

Maeve pushed her curls under her scarf and brushed flecks of mud from her coat. She could see her own breath on the air as she pinched her cheeks for a bit of warmth. She'd want to look good and healthy for the pilgrims. In a few hours she'd be sailing with her father to the mainland to fetch them. But first they had to check on the well, the place where all the healing took place.

Brigid's Well — *Tobar Bhríde* — was in a cave at the edge of the island, facing the sea from the south shore. As soon as they arrived, Michael and Maeve fished tallow candles from their pockets, lit them and stepped into the chamber. The holy spring flared into view — a small stream trickling into a pool. Placing the candles on a raised slab of stone, they laid out the bouquets of island flowers. Pink sea thrift, red berries, snow drops. Michael took a handful of shells from a meal bag hitched to his waist and gave half to Maeve. They sorted them into four neat rows — periwinkles, cockles, limpets, cowries.

Maeve heard whispering when she pressed her ear to a large whelk shell, before passing it to her father.

'A ghost?'

'A *púca*!' he winked.

Maeve plucked a straw Brigid cross from her bag and placed it on the flat rock as her father removed currant cake and a jar of honey from his coat and poured it gently over the crust. She shut her eyes and breathed through her nose. Honey was for special days, and when it mixed with the waft of her father's tobacco, it smelt grand.

Maeve fidgeted with an oyster shell in her pocket and thought of the pilgrims who'd soon be arriving. She made bets with her father about what they'd be wearing. Fancy black hats or colored cloaks? Linen shirts or velvet scarves? Would the men sport boots to the ankle or knee? Would the ladies' shoes be laced or latched? Would some have odd socks or shirts hanging down? They'd know soon enough. Pilgrims from as far away as Bandon and Schull, they'd come, as they came every year, hitching up hems to tread through clumps of heather and vetch. Some mocked them for their pagan faith but they paid the fare and believed in the cures. They'd be there in no time, just as soon as Maeve and her father sailed to the mainland to fetch them.

Michael stood tall, candle in hand, a lock of raven hair over his brow. He recited a charm:

> 'Look after us, Brigid, in the year ahead.
> Keep us safe at sea, fill our nets with plenty.
> And heal all those who come for the cures.'

He placed a palm on Maeve's shoulder —

> 'And your blessing on Maeve here beside me.
> Our own young Brigid on this holy day.
> Grant her the gift you granted me.
> *Beannacht Bhríde.*'

They set to work then clearing a space on the slate stone for the currant cake and holy water bottles. Maeve cut the crust into equal portions and laid it out in small piles for the pilgrims. She added a mix of samphire and *púcaí* to each piece and thought of her mother at home making breakfast for Connie and Seán, before they rowed to school in the village. Maeve should be going with them, of course, but this was her special day.

Michael pulled the ledger from his sack and recited a list of cures aloud — *sceach gheal, cliath, fual bó, lusrán.*

Maeve repeated the names, listing the pilgrim's common ills — ulcers, arthritis, nerves, the bad lad. She also rehearsed how to sprinkle well water on their heads and hold out the linen *brat* for their touch.

'Will I be able for it?' Maeve looked at her father, believing she would, but wanting to hear him say it again.

'You will, faith,' he said. 'And won't I be standing beside you?'

Then Michael took his daughter's hand and, coaxing it open, lifted a silver chain in the air before lowering it into the flat of her palm. It coiled like oil into a lamp.

'For *me*?' Maeve asked, staring down at the gift.

'Yes, for you.'

'Where did you get it?'

'In the belly of a fish.'

'You did not,' she laughed, shaking her head.

'I did so.' He tipped his cap. 'And this was how. The day you were born, your mother took a turn. Breach birth and a storm so bad the doctor couldn't make it from the mainland. I gave her a cure and a drop of the water and by the time the storm was over she was right as rain — she woke to find you lying in her arms. Soon as she was grand I gave thanks to Brigid and the next day hauled a salmon off Malachy's Staic.' He stretched his palms wide. 'Big as this and that wasn't all. When I filleted the creature I found this inside.' He nodded to the chain in Maeve's hand. His eyes shone. 'Two miracles in one day. Imagine!'

Maeve gazed at the necklace, threading the shiny chain

through her hands, before looking back at her father. Was he telling the truth or teasing again? She couldn't tell, but the gift was real.

'Don't lose it now,' he said. ''Twill keep you safe.'

Maeve put on the necklace and walked with her father around the cave — three times, east to west, sun-wise, though there was no sun. *An deiseal.*

They chanted the charm as they circled the space before dipping their fingers into the pool. Then they made the sign of Brigid — hands to chest then shoulders and crown — snuffed out the lighting tapers and stood for a moment in silence, listening to each other breathe.

Walking back from the cave, Maeve glanced out to sea where a steady swell was beginning to rise. White terns dipped over the Carraigroan rocks, screaming hungry cries.

'Wind's getting up.' Michael plucked at a blade of grass and tossed it to the wind.

'But we'll still go, won't we?' Maeve felt a bitter breeze on her face.

Michael walked on, squinting down at the toes of his boots. 'Your mother might be right, you know. Maybe you should stay home after all?'

Maeve stopped in her tracks, a lump in her throat. 'But you promised!'

Michael gazed at the sky, checking the clouds. 'Would you not wait here with your Mam and Bawn? I'd be there and back in no time.'

Maeve tugged hard at her father's coat. 'You swore Brigid would mind us, you did.' Her eyes flashed. 'Were you lying?'

'I was not.' Michael Sullivan thumped his chest. 'Come on so.'

They sailed to the mainland shortly after midday. It was less than a mile from the Island to the pier of Glandore. Entering the bay, Maeve felt a fresh wind rising from the east as a black cloud rolled through the sky. Not a gull to be seen. But they couldn't stop now. Her father was right. They'd have the pilgrims on board and be back to the island in no time.

Once docked at Glandore, a dozen passengers crowded round the boat, paying Michael a sovereign a head.

Maeve stood at the bow, mooring in hand, counting the passengers as they stepped aboard.

One two three four. First a woman with a baby carrying a food basket and blankets. Then Mrs King, the wife of the Bank Manager in Skibbereen, who looked quickly about her before choosing a seat at the stern and removing a blue velvet hat, sliding three silver pins into her hair. She came every year for the healing. Maeve stared at her loveliness, all groomed and graceful, smelling of rose water.

Five six seven eight. Two elderly couples, arm in arm, helping each other over the gunnel, bearing holy water bottles and shiny votives for Brigid's Well. Baubles, blue ribbons, red-berried holly. They chuckled and nudged each other as they put hankies over their noses against the reek of shellfish seeping from the bilges.

Nine ten eleven twelve. Three middle aged men and a bullock of a red-headed young fellow followed up the rear, all dressed in their Sunday best. The men's boots were laced, the boy's latched.

Everyone seated, her father at the helm, Maeve loosed the mooring and hoisted sail. In no time the yawl nosed out from Glandore harbor, heading due west towards the island. Michael spun the tiller to port and hauled the mainsheet while Maeve winched up the jib, tying the halyard to the forehead cleat. The yawl leaned gingerly into a tack and was moving at a fair clip when the air filled with darkness. It came of a sudden as if someone drew a lid across the sky. Michael looked up and slackened the sails. 'Weather's turning,' he shouted. 'Hold on to your hats and we'll all be grand. Brigid save us.'

They were doing three knots when the squall struck: a giant gust swiveling in from the South, sheering off the Sheila rocks and belting them broadside on. The boom swung wild as the hull tipped down and shipped water. Michael winced as he braved the blast. The sails flapped like mad bats before tightening again to a narrow tack.

Passengers cried aloud, bailing madly with whatever could be found — bait buckets, fish boxes, drink bottles, upturned hats.

'Main sheet!' roared Michael as a second squall struck. He yanked at the tiller and rose to his feet while Maeve plunged forward and loosened the jib. The rigging screamed as gusts ripped the sails. A howl out of hell bore down from the left. *Gairm ón dtaobh clé*. Two squalls in a row meant more to come. And sure enough, before they knew it, a giant black wave powered in from the east, pitching Maeve onto the deck. Michael veered windward to balance the boat, but too late; waves were already flooding the hull. No matter how hard everyone bailed, the boat listed, and listed again.

'God save us.' A man from Drinagh sank to his knees, arms raised. 'We're all going down. We're all going down into the hole.'

Things flew in all directions — water vials, candles, rosary beads, caps — as bodies rolled over and back, grasping at oars and clutching the mast.

'Stay back, Maeve,' cried Michael, seizing a rope and wrapping it firmly round a bait barrel. Desperate eyes watched him fling the crate into the waves, while Maeve clasped the helm, heart flapping like a hooked trout, as one pilgrim after another tumbled into the sea. There were howls to Brigid and the Blessed Virgin. There were mouths wide open, stunned by the cold, as Sunday shirts ballooned in the waves.

Maeve watched appalled as Mrs King slid slowly into the swell where she floated in a surf of petticoats, clinging to an oar until a wave-burst whipped her away. Poor creature. She screeched like a gull, and when the next wave broke she was gone.

Michael cupped his hands and yelled to Maeve, but all she could hear was wind whizzing through the stays, beating the masts. They struggled to save the few still afloat — the red-headed boy, the young woman and child — guiding them towards bobbing barrels and ropes. But the waves just kept rolling in, until the yawl's prow reared up towards the sky and the swell pulled her down into the hole, dragging the mother and boy in its wake.

Maeve grabbed her father as they fell into the sea. White thunder pounded their heads until they surfaced again, gripping each others' coats, desperate to keep afloat. All around them souls cried out, paddling the water like animals, weighed down by winter boots, darting wild glances north and south, as one after another their heads were sucked under by the surf.

'Swim home!' cried Michael. '*Buail abhaile.*' But Maeve wouldn't go. He pushed her away but she wouldn't budge. She clung to him fiercely, cycling the waves with her arms and legs as they sank together beneath the swell, until all Maeve could see was a blast of bubbles glutting up from his mouth. She flailed in his arms, she kicked and she punched, until their bodies finally parted and Maeve rose slowly, steadily upwards, to the light.

Maeve struggled to her elbows, only to fall back onto the sand. She tried to call to her father, but saltwater clogged her throat.

'You're breathing.' Someone was shaking her, wiping hair from her face, pushing an ear right up to her mouth. She knew by the smell of the shawl. Her mother.

Mam lifted Maeve in two strong heaves, pulling her onto her hands and knees, then further onto her legs and feet.

More voices.

'There! Over there!' Maeve craned her neck to see Áine Daly and the McCarthys scurrying along the shore.

'She's alive, thank God,' cried Mam. 'But soaked through, she'll catch her death.' She threw her shawl over her daughter. 'I'll take Maeve home. You go on. All of you.' She nodded to her neighbors, waving toward the headland. 'Find Michael! Find Michael!'

Back home, Maeve curled up in a blanket and collapsed onto the settle by the fire. Mam wept into a pan of warm milk and poured a kettle into a bowl. She dipped a flannel in hot water and wrapped it around Maeve's feet. Then she put a mug in her hands.

'What happened, child?' She spoke softly.

Maeve said nothing.

'What happened? Where's your father?'

Silence.

'Speak, for God's sake!' Mam raised her voice. 'Speak!'

Still Maeve said nothing. She moved her tongue and opened her mouth, but no words came.

Next morning Dan Daly and Tadhg McCarthy rowed out from Trá an Tí and picked up nine of the thirteen bodies. It was strangely calm. Maeve watched with Mam from the top of the cliff, looking down over the Sound, as the men hooked floating corpses with gaffs and hauled them dripping into the boats. They scoured the sea from Carraighilly to Glandore, but no sign of more bodies. No Michael Sullivan. Only waves, grey waves.

New boats were launched from Myross and Reen as the hunt went on for the rest of the week, combing the coast all the way to Rosscarbery. On the sixth day, another corpse was found floating off the Bithínach — a sheep farmer from Manch, oldest pilgrim aboard. And on the seventh day, another was washed up on Trá na Rónta beneath the Dún. Maeve and Mam were searching the cove with Bawn, when they heard Tadhg cry out, 'Over here!'

They scurried along the tide line to find a hand sticking up from the sand: waxy white fingers with long bruised nails. Tadhg, dray horse of a man, fell to his knees and scooped the body free. Maeve looked away before looking back. A head with silver hairpins. Bruised eyes, blind sockets. The work of crabs and dogfish. A foul smell filled the air. Maeve grabbed her mother's sleeve. It wasn't him.

That evening, Tadhg rowed Mrs King's corpse to the mainland and handed it over to her husband and three children, standing mutely on Myross pier. Tadhg pocketed the silver pins. He was sorry for the family's loss, but salvage was salvage. If Michael Sullivan risked lives for a sovereign, Tadhg deserved a few bob for himself.

The search went on for another two weeks. Mainland crews shunned the Sullivan family, some swearing it was madness for Michael to have brought people out in such a gale. All for the fare and pagan cures. Maeve tried to hide from the hatred in their eyes.

Things tapered off slowly as one boat after another went back to fishing and trade. Connie and Seán returned to school on the mainland. But Mam, who'd always encouraged Maeve's schooling — while her father wanted her on the island — wanted to keep her home until she spoke again. But Maeve knew she was also terrified to be left alone in an empty house. So all day, when the men were out fishing and the youngsters at school, Maeve and her mother worked away with the island women — Áine Daly and Nóra McCarthy — weaving sheaves of corn into tiny rafts which they set afloat on the waves every night. Each thatched float was stuffed with beeswax and mutton lard, with a candle atop; and when the flame went out, custom had it, a body would float up. The women watched and waited, but no corpse surfaced.

First week of March, a month after the drowning, two coast guards escorted Mam and Maeve all the way to Bantry to identify a body washed up on the Whiddy rocks. But it wasn't Michael.

Back on the island that evening, Maeve sat silently by the fire, ignored by her brothers, as Mam went to bed without a bite. But in the middle of the night, the house was woken with terrible cries. A long low moan rising in the dark. *Diadhánach.* The sound of a cow torn from its calf. At first Maeve thought it was coming from the neighboring fields, but she soon realized it was inside the house. A bitter, drawn-out keen, calling and calling. 'Michael, my Michael? Where are you, Michael?' It was Mam, raving about a hag with claws and pollock eyes dragging her husband down into a hole. *Tonn Clíona*. Witch of the waves. Brigid's reaper.

Maeve rushed to the bedroom and took her mother in her arms, trying to lift her up from the sheets. But Mam just continued to moan, staring at the roof, eyes darting to and fro, as if searching for something in the rafters. Terror flooded her face like a neap tide over sand. She just kept calling. The lowing of a vacant womb.

Watching, Maeve realized how much her mother had loved her father and could not live without him. She understood, she felt it, and wanted to do something; but she knew she couldn't help Mam any more than she could help herself. And as time slipped by, Maeve felt increasingly adrift, as if she was looking through the eyes of an oilskin, staring out from a faraway world where she'd disappeared after the drowning. She still hadn't spoken a word. If she couldn't speak to her father, she didn't want to speak at all.

One morning, as she milked goats in the yard, Maeve heard the neighbors without grasping what they were saying; their words hovered in the air, skittering by her, meaningless. Unable to connect with the world outside, she became helpless before the fears of her own mind: recurring fantasies that her father had made it ashore but forgotten who he was and wandered so far north that people didn't recognize him and put him in a Mental Home, without name or birth certificate to say where he came from. Or that he'd felt such shame leading pilgrims to their death, he could not face anyone again — not even his own family — and had walked all the way to Cobh and taken a steamer to America. America. Like his great grand-uncles Gearóid and

Pádraig Sullivan before him, who'd escaped to Massachusetts during the Bad Times when the crops went rotten beyond in Myross — fleeing the black fields where the whole thing started, where the first hundred died and a hundred thousand after. Maeve could see those same hills now from the corner of her eye: heathered mounds across the bay with serried drills like sunken ribs, furrows running through bracken and fern, ragged bones breaking up through the soil. But worst of all — the very worst — was thinking her father might be off in some foreign land with a whole new family and another daughter walking by his side.

Trapped in these reveries, Maeve heard a murmuring inside her brain, a sound coming at her sideways, out of nowhere — *glór an dtoabh clé.* As if her mind wasn't hers anymore, but somebody else's, and she was living at a distance from herself. A ghost of herself trying to crawl back inside. She longed to reach out and feel living things around her again; but how could she feel anything with the hands that had pushed her father away, those arms that flailed as he struggled to save her? Every time she tried to surface, Maeve found herself sinking deeper into the hole, her eyes clogged with weed, her throat full of stones. And worse, when she tried to pray to Brigid, begging for speech, for taste and for touch, her tongue still cleaved to the roof of her mouth. She wept but no tears came. She was all dried up. Without faith. Without words. The Brigid of her father was no more than a sound. *Bríd.* A name she could no longer say.

On Ash Wednesday, tenth day of April, Father Kehoe sailed over from Squince and sat down with Mam by the fire. Maeve watched unseen from the loft, hiding away at the top of the stairs.

The priest seemed smaller on the island than in his pulpit, and older too, with his thinning hair and wire-rimmed glasses.

A Saint Christopher medal hung from his neck and his voice was soft. He spoke English as always.

'How are you, Eileen?' He took Mam's hand. 'And the girl? How's young Maeve?'

When Mam didn't answer, the priest put a small crucifix in her fist.

'That's enough now, good woman. Poor Michael is gone. You have to accept it. Hard as it is, it's God's will.'

Mam looked up, stroking the crucifix as if it were a cat. 'I know, Father. I know right well, but you don't understand, it was a wicked day.' She laid the iron cross on her lap, and started to rock back and forth. 'I'm afraid, Father. Terribly afraid, that we'll never find the body. Never lay Michael to rest. And I fear for Maeve too, that she'll never come back. I know she's alive but she's not really there. Not a single word from her mouth since that day; and scarce swallows a bite. Was it some *púca* crawled out from the sea? Who was it at all?' Mam paused between breaths. 'There was evil on the wind that day. I smelt it, Father. Bitter and rank. I knew it in my bones and begged them not to go. All that carry-on about *Bríd Óg*, young Brigid with a healing Gift. But what Gift? And what healing? What blessing? What cure? What damn bit of good did it do them at all? Michael or Maeve or anyone else? All the poor creatures on that Godforsaken boat!'

Mam pushed both arms down on her chair and was about to rise, but sank back again, swiping the air with a weary wave.

The priest leaned over and patted her arm. 'It will be all right, Eileen. You're a good woman'

'She had no business in that boat, Father. Young Maeve. She should have been at school with the rest of them. I told Michael that, but he paid no heed. And where is she now, the child I knew? And where is *he*, the man I loved?'

Mam stopped and glanced about her, listening carefully, not wanting Maeve to hear what she was saying. She lowered her voice. 'My Michael. My man. My own *fear maith*. Though we bickered at times, we knew lovely things too. There was no one like him. He made me laugh. Even that last morning when I told him not to go, he hooped his arms around me and squeezed me tight, singing sweet things right into my ear. But he wouldn't listen, no matter what. And may God forgive me, Father, but I cursed him that day. I did. A terrible curse I can never forget. "If you sail now, don't ever come back." I said that to him, Father, right to his face. My last words as he walked through the door.' She looked to the latch then back at the priest. 'Now he's gone.'

Mam glanced up at the empty stairs, but did not see Maeve's shadow on the landing. 'And my Maeve. She's gone too now and I don't know if I'll ever get her back.'

Mam stared blankly into the air as Father Kehoe went to fetch cups and saucers from the dresser and returned to the hearth. He took the kettle off the iron crane and, banking the fire, set it down beside the embers before wetting the tea and pouring two cups.

'Take this now, Eileen. It'll do you good.'

Mam took the cup and laid it down, before going on. 'It wasn't right, Father, the way the gale came from nowhere.' Her face lifted and strayed, busy fingers rubbing knots on her knuckles. 'When I heard the cries rising up from the sea I knew it. I rushed to the neighbors and called for help, but the Dalys were off saving nets from the rocks; the McCarthys were sheltering cattle; the boys off at school. By the time I ran to the cliffs the boat was upside-down in the bay. It was over.'

Father Kehoe lifted his cup to his lips and held it there for a moment, pondering, before placing it soundlessly back on the saucer. 'You're not to blame, Eileen. Nor Michael.' He spoke quietly. 'It's God's way, you know, not ours. You must put your trust in the Lord above. He'll take care of you now. No more of the Brigid business. And no more talk of pookas and cures. It's all talk, Eileen. Superstition. Let well enough alone. I'll see to it, there'll be no more pilgrims. It's not right and it never was. Good woman, you've a family to look after. Think of that now and forget the rest. Two grown sons needing to be fed, and a daughter saved from the sea. We must give thanks for small mercies.'

'But what will I do with her, Father?'

The priest moved his cup to one side.

'Keep her close to you, Eileen. She needs you more than ever. And soon as she speaks let her back to school.'

Then he sank to his knees before the fire, pulling a Rosary from his pocket and stretching the beads between his hands.

Mam followed suit.

'First Sorrowful Mystery. The Agony in the Garden.'

Above on the landing, Maeve stood mutely still before retreating to her room.

Maeve was angry with Father Kehoe and her mother. She felt for her mother, she really did, and knew the priest was doing his best. But how could they speak like that about her father, saying his cures were only talk and nonsense? What did they know about his ways? Or the drowning? She wished she'd marched down the stairs and faced them, there and then. But the cat got her tongue and she said nothing. Not then nor the day after, nor the weeks that followed after that, slowly as ewes following ewes. She didn't want to hurt her Mam more, making matters worse with her anger. And she knew Father Kehoe would never change. *Riamh*. It was useless.

So she bit her tongue and sought comfort with Bawn — her closest companion during those long April days, while her brothers and peers were at school on the mainland. Whenever Mam took her daily stretch — dozing for an hour after tea — Maeve would slip out for walks with the dog, following him over cliffs and shores, hunting after this cure or that. And as they foraged the fields, she often imagined she could scent what he was scenting — tart pungencies of stem and root, mild fragrances of scale or spore — each odor egging them on. At times it seemed they couldn't let off, or didn't want to, as they followed little passages through vetch and briar, tracking gullies and waterways along ditches and dips, always veering towards the well. It was as if every plant they harvested, every fungus they foraged, every stream of water they crossed, was coaxing them home to the underground cave. But Maeve turned back every time they got close; still too much pain. She'd stop and think, doubts rising like bile in her gut. What if Mam was right after all? What if Brigid had swept her father away? And the pilgrims and cures were cursed? Maeve swallowed the lump in her throat. No. It couldn't be. Her father had told her — Brigid was good and healing would come.

One day scouring the shore for mussels, Bawn disappeared behind a ridge of rocks. When he didn't return, Maeve went after him only to find him digging in weeds. His snout was burrowing in a mound of kelp, coiled in a heap exposed at low tide. As she approached, Bawn began to whine, louder and louder as he pawed and scraped, nosing and mouthing at a covered shape. A patch of cloth shone through the weed. It caught Maeve's eye in a sudden flash. Woven thread. Grey-green stitch. Harris Tweed.

Maeve turned away and ran home through the fields. She

couldn't think, she couldn't stop, tears blurring her swollen eyes, the pang in her chest too deep to breathe. She found her mother hanging woolens in the yard and cried — 'a Mhamaí, a Mhamaí!'

'You've your voice back, love,' smiled her mother, not yet knowing what Maeve had found. 'You can sing again. You can go back to school.'

Maeve never actually saw her father's body. Given its three months at sea, it was wrapped in sheets by the neighbors, covered in oils and beeswax, and brought straight to the church on the mainland. Mam insisted on a proper funeral: solemn Mass with Father Kehoe in the village followed by a burial in the parish cemetery. Maeve did as her mother and brothers wanted — how could she not? — but as they lowered the coffin into the ground, she sang aloud to her father in Irish: *Solas Dé ar d'anam go deo.* May the sun shine on you forever.

As the church recovered her father, Maeve let him go. And got her voice back.

Shortly after the burial, Maeve finally returned to the well. It was her first time back since the drowning.

Her body trembled as she crossed the marsh leading south to the underground cave. Recurring worries snagged her soul. If Brigid saved lives, like her father said, why had he and the pilgrims died? Why was she the only survivor, cast back on the shore without shoes or speech? And why was Brigid, hailed as 'Mary of the Gaels' for centuries, dismissed by Father Kehoe for her 'pagan' ways? Once revered as a saint of healing, with holy wells scattered through the land, equal only to Patrick and Columba, why was she now deemed an old wife's tale? *Piseógs* and pagan fantasy. What did it mean? How could it be? She didn't know, but she didn't turn back.

When Maeve reached the cave her body froze. A pour of cold ran the length of her spine. Big timber crates were wedged in the entrance, broken barrels blocking the way. Who did it? she wondered, heaving and pulling at the stacked wooden slats, yanking them free, plank by plank, until she managed to make a breach big enough to enter. She crawled on all fours through the open gap like a vixen slipping back to its den.

Once inside Maeve stood and blinked, finding her bearings. She put her hand to the wall of the cave, feeling its rugged edges. The air was cold and musty. Her eyes strained to make out shapes as the shrine stood shrouded in a swell of shadow. She approached the well, gently touching the wet stone basin. The moist moss cooled her bruised fingers. Everything was just as before. Same as the day of the drowning, except for the faded flowers. Nothing else had changed. Painted shells, rosary beads, medals, tapers. And a faint smell of stale tobacco.

Diadhánach. The dark sad lowing at the pit of her being. She couldn't help it. She could no longer enter this sacred space and find her father standing beside her, smoking his pipe and teaching her cures, cheering her up, telling her tales, reciting rhymes to make her laugh. Those times were gone. Her father was gone.

Maeve slipped off her shoes and approached the stone boulder beside the pool, feeling the pebbled ground beneath her feet. Lifting the Brigid cross, she stared at it in the half-light before pressing the rough straw to her lips, holding it there for a moment, pausing before she kissed it, hesitating to make a blessing. How could she? Pray to the one who had left her bereft? She couldn't. Not now. There were no words. The cave was empty. The pool motionless. Even her sighing found no echo from the walls. She stood and waited for what seemed like ages, until a faint sound of water began to rise from the base of the well. A mere trickle at first, dripping slowly, one drop at a time; it kept coming, louder and louder, surely and irresistibly, as it turned into a stream. The pool was filling with water. She could hear it and see it. Sinking to her knees, Maeve plunged the Brigid cross into the basin and held it under for several seconds, pushing it down into the well, as if drowning a hapless animal. She did this again and again, hunched over the water, thick black curls bobbing over her face, her whole body heaving, until she finally pulled the thatch back out. Shaking it dry, she made the sign of Brigid, tapping herself four times — forehead, mouth, shoulder and breast. Then cupping water in the palms of her hands she sipped and swallowed deeply.

And she stayed there like that, alone in the dark, until it all came back. Every detail of that morning. Dressing the altar and sorting the shells, doing *an deiseal* and donning the necklace, quizzing her father on sickness and cures, inhaling the fumes of sweet plug tobacco. And as Maeve knelt there, eyes closed, she felt the nugget in her chest melt and her moan became the bold clear call of a copper bell ringing inside her. *Guth gluair áib uma.* She heard it before she knew what it meant. The words spilling out of her mouth.

You have the gift. Buail abhaile. You have the gift. Buail abhaile.

By the time Maeve left the cave, night was falling. She patted Bawn, waiting by the entrance, and inhaled the salt sea breeze, feeling a calm in the late April air, a new kind of ease loosening her chest, as if she was protected by the skin of the sky. To the east the moon was rising over the ocean. A pale red penny, shadowed by a fleck of gannets. While westward the Fastnet lighthouse cast casual beams over the waves.

Before returning home, Maeve dropped into the Dalys, who lived beside the Sullivans.

'The well,' she said, entering the kitchen without knocking. 'The well is blocked.'

'I know.' Dan rose from his chair to greet her.

'I had to break in with my own bare hands. Look!' Maeve held out two bruised wrists. 'Who did it?'

Áine stepped forward, wiping her hands on her apron. 'Father Kehoe. When he came to visit your Mam after the funeral. You were still sick. He gathered us in McCarthy's yard and went on about the First Commandment. Strange gods and the rest of it. He said no one should go to the well anymore, that the Brigid business was over. The old ways gone. Superstition and idolatry. Pagan nonsense. Turning God into pookas. They were his words.'

Dan's face stiffened as he rubbed a wrinkled neck. 'He had Tadhg block it with driftwood and he'll do it again when he hears you've undone it. We're under strict orders. No one's to visit.'

'I hate Father Kehoe.' Maeve buried her head on Áine's shoulder, inhaling the smell of soda bread and herring.

'I know, child,' Áine muttered. 'But if it's cures you want, there's more than the well.' She pulled Maeve back and cocked her head. 'Isn't your father's Brú still full of them?'

Maeve raised her face. 'I know, Áine, but Mam would die. She locked the door after the drowning. She swears it's cursed.'

'Sure, I know, but your mother isn't herself these days.' Áine peered at Maeve with big eyes. 'You know that, *a leanbh*. And she never had any time for the cures. She's not from the island. She adored your father but never understood his ways.' Áine's

voice slowed to a whisper. 'Look here, girl. Why not slip over to
the shed when your Mam's having a stretch, tomorrow maybe?
She won't mind if she's asleep. Here, a spare key.'

Maeve felt a latch lift in her heart. She thanked the Dalys
and went home.

Next day, Maeve returned to the Brú. Stale smells greeted her as
she stepped inside. Dried fungi, oiled wood, fish scales, rotting
algae. She shut her eyes and saw his eyes, blue as the blue of
a mackerel's back. She felt a pang in her chest. *Athair*. Father.
Teacher and healer. *Fear Maith an Oileáin*, chief of the island,
ferryman and fisherman, maker of brews and master of the old
ways. Beloved of pilgrims. Her dear departed father.

Maeve moved to the work board and ran her thumb along the
timber edge. When her eyes fell on the lobster crate, her throat
tightened, remembering how he lifted her onto it as a child so
she could peer over his shoulder as he worked away on the remedies. Always promising it would be her turn one day, to learn the
healing, try the cures, receive the Gift on Brigid's day.

Then she spotted her father's notebook, the black ledger where
he kept the cures. She touched the sealskin spine, smooth and
shiny as a living skin, and wondered why her father so often read
its pages but rarely let her do so. Now he was dead. And Brigid's
day had come and gone. Her lips tightened. She fretted: if she
had the Gift like her father said, then why not read the cures
for herself? If it *was* folk nonsense, what harm could it do; and
if it was true, it could only do good. Maeve took the book and
placed it on the oak table. She hesitated, recalling her father often
saying it wasn't the words but sounds that mattered. Cures were

to be chanted or sung and delivered with water and a touch of the hand. Doing was more than reading or writing. Doing and believing — that was the way. That's what he taught.

Propping herself on her father's stool Maeve opened the first page. She craned her neck and leaned closer, her shadow crossing the scribbled paper. The book was divided into four parts: Plants, Algae, Fungi and Fish. Each part had rows of names and charms, neatly written in Irish and English. The Irish was in a loose hand, the English in squat block letters. Maeve's heart leapt as she struggled to make out the entries. She knew she shouldn't be doing this, but her eyes raced ahead anyway. She started with the plants, feasting on every word. Detailed cures for ailments using nettles, clover and kelp. These were familiar; but there were others she'd never heard of before. *Cliath*, a wattle cure for broken bones. *Turscar*, rotting sandwort for mumps. *Gonomil orgomil* for hearing. *Bainne bó bleachtain* or cowslip for nursing mothers. There was even a special charm for period pains: *beir bran ar leor meor*, which only worked if you recited the words in the right order holding a sprig of hawthorn. All in the sound, all in the touch. Like her father said.

Then she turned to the third section where her gaze fell on a list of fungi. Each column included precious kinds with sketches of where they grew on the island. Michael Sullivan was a devil for lists, and Maeve Sullivan took after him. She ran her finger slowly down the columns, saying the names out one by one. Her face flickered with excitement.

Púca méaracán. Cave mushroom or fuzzball. Also known as toadstools. Good for sleep and dreams. And for getting rid of bad memories. Found in wet black soil beside Brigid's Well and along the creeks by the Sheep staic.

Púca cosa. Stink-horn fungus for back pain and joints. Often found growing in the cow pasture and south marsh. Especially in August. Also known as *adharc an phúca*, the pooka's horn. They spring from an egg-shape in the ground into a pike with a honeycomb top. When they bloom the cap becomes an ugly knob covered with sticky wetness. Smells nasty. Flies love it.

Púca cáire. Puffballs growing on the bark of birches behind Daly's goat pen. Also known as *cáis an phúca*. The spongey white flesh looks and smells like old cheese. Some call it *cáise phúca* or the pooka's stream. Great for bladder and period pains.

Púca poill. White liberty cap. For the Sadness. Very common in Soldier's Field, especially early in the morning around cow pats. In season in autumn, lasts for up to a year dried and bottled. They grow in circles and are called *cupáin drúchta,* cups of morning dew. Also known as *fás aon oíche* as they pop up overnight and disappear in no time. You know they're there when the lambs are dancing in the fields. Sheep never get enough of them. And their milk is sweeter after. Does wonders for the Nerves in a hot cup of tea.

Púca feoil. Flesh mushroom for appetite and tiredness. But careful. Mind these fellas. Too many can give terrible cramps. A man from Mallow turned blue and died when he ate a dozen in a kidney stew. They grow in dangerous places, beside cliffs. Mostly on the Dún in winter. Stay shy or use scarcely.

Finishing the list, Maeve sighed aloud, fumbling the pages as she closed the book. She felt relief mixed with joy. She bit her lips for fear she might laugh; she couldn't help it but didn't want her mother to hear. Placing the ledger to one side, she glanced at a low shelf where glass jars lined the wall, each containing samples of the different fungi. But without labels. She couldn't tell which was which. She'd have to forage afresh. But she'd have the notebook and work from memory — recalling her father walking the fields, saying the names as he bottled each cure, slipping them carefully into his sack. She put a hand to her mouth. *Ciúnas. Is binn beál ina thost.* The closed mouth is sweet. Not a word to a soul. She was on her own.

It was already June, and though Maeve was speaking again, there was no more school until September. Seán and Connie were back on the island all day, helping the McCarthys with the cattle and crops, when not out netting and lobstering with Dan. The McCarthy twins — Joan and Nance, three years older than Maeve — were busy packing up, heading for work as domestics on the mainland. Meanwhile, Maeve returned to the Brú whenever her mother took her rests. She reread every page of the book and had learned many remedies by heart by the time Áine called with a job.

'Listen, Maeve,' said Áine. 'McCarthy's cow has red water.'

That morning Nóra McCarthy had spotted blood in the urine of their black and white Friesian. The one called Nelly after the McCarthy grandmother who'd passed away the same day the calf came into the world, the death groans in the bed echoing the lowing out in the yard.

Joe Casey the vet sailed out from the village and declared that the disease was picked up from ticks in the reeds, and that it was a lot worse than the hoof-rot he'd treated last time with a dab of the blue stone, same stuff he'd used for potatoes against the blight. Joe gave Nelly a jab in the rump, making her bellow louder than the time she was mounted by the bull swum over from Squince. But it did no good.

Áine recounted all this with a glint before nodding sagely west to the Brú. Maeve knew what she meant.

Once inside Maeve set to work. Sitting at the work top she opened the ledger and followed the remedy for cows with red water. She pressed six bulbs of bladder wrack into her father's tobacco tin and mixed the paste with a shred of milkwort — *lus an bhainne*, the little sisters of the seven gifts. The more she stirred the more the colors changed, now dark as the copper door bell, now bright as the band of a goldfinch wing. But knowing there was still something missing, Maeve dipped her finger in the water font and made the sign of Brigid — heart to forehead to shoulder to mouth — before sprinkling a few drops onto the paste. Then raising the container with both hands she read aloud the words on the tin:

Petersen's Pipes and Pipe Tobacco. Ireland's Premier Tobacconist.

First light next day, Maeve stole from the Brú and slipped the potion into Nelly's feed. And by tea time she heard cries coming from the field — 'The cow is down, the cow is down.' She ran out to find Nelly lying on the flat of her back, breaking stinky wind out one end, a steaming tongue hanging out the other. The entire McCarthy family looked on in dismay. Maeve clutched her neck chain, terrified she'd murdered the beast. But within minutes Nelly was rearing her head and rising up onto her fore legs. And in no time, there she was, standing tall before them, foursquare, dribbling gob, right as rain.

When Tadhg McCarthy saw Nelly padding up the field he honked like a goose as Nóra declared it a miracle. Maeve was learning quick. The thin line between poison and cure.

When Áine heard what happened, she came and took Maeve by the hand. 'You've got it so. You've got the Gift. I can see Michael smiling from above.' She put a finger to her lips. 'Not a word to your Mam.'

'Not a word.' Maeve nodded.

Though Áine had raised three girls of her own — Máire, long gone to Liverpool, and the twins, Joan and Nance, soon leaving for Cork — she treated Maeve like one of her own. Unlike Mam and the other islanders, Áine still half believed in the cures. She knew her plants and offered to forage with Maeve in the afternoons when her work was done.

Áine scuttled along on short little legs, and though she was forty and Maeve fourteen, they strode the fields together like sisters. Áine had a nose for bad plants and was a sheer devil for rooting out weeds — anything toxic to cattle or fowl, that bloated bellies and swelled throats. Ragwort above all. The yellow fellas. *Buachalán Buí*. Whenever she spied a bunch on a hill, their bright yellow locks swaying in the breeze, she'd bend right down and yank them from the earth, as if she was pulling teeth from old gums. Maeve protested at first — she loved the gold rosettes and the striped orange and black caterpillars that nibbled at the stalks — but she soon let Áine have her way. There was no staying her passion for killing plants fatal to living creatures; and though the yellow fellas were top of the list, there were other evil culprits in tow: bog asphodel with creeping stalks; hairy hogweed with foul smelling sap; cow parsley with bitter-fern leaves; groundsel weeds with flimsy florets. But nastiest of all, Áine swore, were the flirty bluebells with round fleshy bulbs. 'Wicked bodies in angels' dress,' she called them. And when

Maeve asked why the loveliest plants were the wickedest, Áine shook her head and winked: 'If your father learned you the good weeds, I'll learn you the bad.' She shrugged and puffed. 'Put that in the cure book — and don't forget the difference.'

It was Áine saw Maeve through the long summer days, accompanying her to the north cliffs where they'd chatter away while gathering roots. And, one time, Maeve stopped and stood agog as Áine got down on all fours, hands and knees thick in vetch, to pick a clump of nettles from the edge of the Dún — a sixty foot drop to the rocks below — making sure not to touch the toxic fur as she folded the leaves into butterfly wings and tied them tight in neat piles. 'They sting awful but cure like gods,' she said. 'A cup of nettles, boiled in salt water, does wonders for the joints.'

As they were packing the nettles in the tobacco tin, folding them in layered rows, Bawn sniffed a scatter of fungi by a nearby cow pat. Liberty caps, *púcaí poill*, powerful against the Sadness. They picked them one by one, careful not to damage the gills or break the slim blue stems.

'Why did Mam call me a *púca*?' Maeve looked up.

'When was that, child?' asked Áine.

'After the drowning, when Father Kehoe came to visit.'

Áine stood with her hands on her hips. 'She meant no harm, but I don't really know. Maybe she was afraid? Fearful the fright of the drowning had changed you. That some spirit had taken you off and left someone else behind. A changeling, like the old stories.' She placed a palm on Maeve's shoulder. 'But you're back with us now, aren't you? Full of talk and mad for the cures.'

'But why do people fear the *púcaí*?' Maeve walked on, swatting vaguely at a cloud of flies.

'I suppose because they're good and bad.' Áine reached for

a liberty cap and raised its slender stem in the air. 'See this one here. Small little thing. It can make you sick or make you sound. It all depends how you use it. That's why mushrooms and spirits have the same name. They go either way. It's hard to tell. They both rise up from the ground at night and are gone before you know it. Coming and going without rhyme or reason.' Áine's look strayed then brightened again. 'And that's why you need your father's book, Maeve. To tell the difference.' She spread the black gills on the palm of her hand. 'These wee creatures can change your mind, make you see things you never saw before. That's why *púcaí* love to play, appearing to us at special times. Holy days that are good for cures. Like Brigid's day, when winter becomes spring. Or John's day — *Púca Sheáin* — when the light turns back. Or All Saints when the crops are ripe and we light bonfires and put candles in turnips with fiery eyes and spit on blackberries before the devil gets them. *Púcaí* are little tricksters at heart. They save us or they fool us. They spin us or they heal us. It's all about how you *see* them. It's all about where you go.'

Maeve peered at the cap in Áine's hand before raising her head and looking out to sea.

'My father knew how to use them, didn't he?'

'He did, faith. But you must be careful, Maeve. His ways are disappearing now and the old knowledge with them. There aren't many left who understand these things. Secret things of the secret healers. *An t-aos Sí* and the *sidhe draoi*. It did Biddy Early and Biddy Cleary no good. We know that. Poor creatures. Some things you need to keep to yourself. Be mindful who you talk to.'

Maeve listened to what Áine was saying. She'd be careful right enough, but felt more set than ever to try out more cures.

After Nelly, Maeve tended other animals on the island. She

gave Dan's lame nanny goat a mix of scutch grass and silver-weed. She fed a paste of green *lusrán*, picked from the hedge behind the Brú, to the chickens with flu. She nursed a gander's wing with a binding of thong weed and mended Bawn's septic paw with a lotion of bran, salt and cleavers. Maeve followed recipes in the book, and always added a drop from the well.

When most of these worked, Maeve felt bold enough for people. She started with the neighbors, treating Nóra McCarthy's period cramps with alaria and Dan's headaches with samphire. Not everything worked, she had to admit — she'd no luck, for instance, with dulse and cow's urine for Tadhg's croup, *fual bó*, a tricky one — in fact he got worse; but she reckoned that might be because she didn't like him. She really couldn't be sure and was often bewildered as she tried out new remedies, wondering what was her own part in it all and what was nature's. Was it practice or charm? Chance or grace? The old knowledge or bodily tides? Was it all in her head, a matter of faith; or nature's own way of healing her own? Brigid or the weather? She'd have to find out.

Shortly after the Feast of Gallus — first of July — Maeve was heading from the house when she heard someone mentioning her mother's name. She hid behind the gable and listened to the neighbors hanging clothes out to dry.

'Twas too bad Eileen lost him.'

Maeve recognized Nóra McCarthy.

'Michael was a good man, but Eileen never let up, always at him, picking and poking, griping and whining.'

Sheets flapped in the wind.

'Now he's gone and she's got her comeuppance.'

'May God forgive you, Nóra,' Áine Daly protested. 'I'd like

to see you if you lost your man. It's hard for Eileen on her own with the children. And harder the second time.' Pause. 'Like some curse: her mother drowned and she still a child. If 'twas you, Nóra, you'd be a sight.'

'Maybe I would, but we've all lost someone. Everyone has crosses to bear. Storms and ailments and boats that never returned. And no one else moaning like Eileen. A sourpuss from the day she was born. She was mad for Michael — no doubt about that — but was never happy since she came to the island.' More flapping and fussing with sheets. 'And young Maeve, poor creature. It's a wonder she survived at all. Spat back from the sea like a bad oyster. Like her mother before her. Two bad oysters. *Drochdhubh drochéan.*' Nóra paused. 'Maybe Michael's better off beyond?'

Maeve's blood rose but she held her tongue. Without a word, she stole back home where she was met with the splatter of churning and the thick smell of cream becoming butter. Her mother at work. Best cook on the island, everyone said, her cakes and soda breads the envy of all. Maeve stood by the kitchen door and stared as Mam pulled the churn shaft up and down, nodding away to some tune in her head. Beside her on the dresser lay a crock of buttermilk and a thin pile of muslin for wrapping the wads of butter once the kneading and salting was done. To keep off the bluebottles. Maeve strode to the center of the room and put her left hand to the churn.

'Stop it,' she said, rounding on Mam. Her blue eyes narrowed. 'Is it true about your mother?'

Mam lowered her head, shaping the yellow-white paste into pats. A cloud of flies buzzed around the churn.

'I want to know,' Maeve said, prodding her mother's arm.

Mam pulled back, flicking a look at her daughter before

speaking slowly.

'I didn't know.'

'You didn't *know*?'

'I didn't know myself for years,' she stammered. 'They kept it from me, they did, until I married your father. Then they told me. Aunt Nelly told me. She'd fostered me after my own mother died and my father had gone to the poorhouse with drink. She only told me the eve of the wedding. The drowning was an accident, she said. It happened when I was a child. I couldn't believe it. I remembered nothing.'

'But why keep it secret — all this time — from me, and from the boys?'

'Why? And what good would it have done, tell me? It was a curse. And your father's drowning more of it. I felt it in my bones. Things like that can't be told.' Mam paused for a moment. Her face stiffened. 'Your father had secrets too, you know.'

Maeve locked her mother's eyes. 'The cures. I know. I read the black book'

'Of course you did,' Mam smirked. 'Do you think me a fool, child? Do you think I don't see you slink off to the Brú, locking the door for hours at a time? Reading those pages. The wild hungry look on your face. Reciting the cures. Cutting the plants. I've watched through the window. 'Twill do you no good. All that Brigid carry-on. You must stop it Maeve. It was your father's business. Not yours.'

'But he wanted me to know, to help with the cures, to pass on the Gift. That's what he told me before he died — '

' — Enough, child,' Mam winced. 'It won't end well. You lost your voice and almost your life; and it's a lucky thing you're here at all. Can't you just be good and settle back home? Come back to me, Maeve.' Mam hung her head before raising it slowly. 'It's bad enough losing your father. I'll not lose you.'

Mam kept moving her mouth without saying another word. She returned her hand to the shaft of the churn but did not move it up or down; she just left it there on the iron rod as the half closed window banged in the breeze.

Maeve sucked in the buttery air and was about to reach out an arm, but Mam brushed her off with a flick of the wrist.

'Sooner you're back at school the better.'

Maeve walked from the room without saying another word. Her heart hurt but her step was swift. Her mother was letting go.

That night Mam woke again screaming things Maeve and her brothers had never heard before. Foul curses. Bitter wails. She cried out for her long-dead mother, for Michael, for someone to help. No one slept a wink. First light, the Dalys were summoned and Dan rowed to Squince to fetch the doctor from Union Hall.

As it happened, he was out on a case, so Dan brought back the dispensary nurse, Mary Donovan, instead. She placed the silver bell of a stethoscope against the gulley of Mam's chest, listening carefully, before giving her medicine from a bottle blue as a dunnock's egg. One spoon at night; two in the morning. But it didn't seem to work. In fact, Mam got worse. And three days later she attacked Tadhg McCarthy.

Maeve knew Tadhg had it coming, dropping by for Michael's old nets, with drink taken. Tadhg was the meanest soul about and had already filched most of the Sullivan's tackle, leaving only the nets and pots. Their father gone, Connie and Seán were helpless to resist. Within months of the drowning, Tadhg had appointed himself *fear maith* of the island.

When Maeve heard the ship's bell ring, she'd let Tadhg in and led him to the bedroom where Mam sat staring out the window, pulling at a spool of lamb's wool. Thinking to humor Eileen, Tadhg stood by the doorway, shifting from one foot to another like a cart horse, as he recited a litany of Michael's old feats — casting for herring and splicing ropes, mending moorings and fileting cod. But halfway through the recital, Mam leapt from the bed and grabbed her pot. 'You'd steal the spit from a widow's gob,' she roared. 'Get out of my sight, you gombeen scut, and never darken my door again.' She struck him with the chamber pot and knocked him out cold.

Tadhg came to soon enough, sidling out the door muttering every kind of filth. But for all the glee it gave her, Maeve knew her mother had gone too far.

That evening, Maeve stole out to the Brú to find the recipe for 'the Nerves.' The one she'd seen her father use on Granny Daly after a fit the previous summer. Leafing through the notebook, she found the cure and set to work. She took a jar of *púcaí poill* from the shelf and mixed the gills with a frond of nettle, grinding them down in the Petersen tin before adding a dash of water from the font. Then, closing the lid, she kissed the shiny container and hoisted it high in the air. *May the púcaí heal her.*

Next morning, Maeve slipped a dose into Mam's cup, filling it to the brim with tea. When she brought it to the bedroom, her mother lay motionless, exhausted by the assault on Tadhg. Her hands were fisted up under her sleeves as if she'd forgotten she had fingers; until they peeped out, one after the other, like claws from the shell of a hermit crab.

'It's for you, Mam.' Maeve served the tea and opened the window for air.

Mam lifted her head, crows' feet softening around her eyes, her nose wrinkling slightly as she stole a sip; then another, then whole mouthfuls slowly, thirstily, as Maeve's worries melted and she began to feel the heat rising up through the soles of her feet, and further up again through her chest and throat, until she could almost taste the hot tea in her own mouth, as if she were the one drinking.

Once Mam had emptied her cup, she sat up and smiled at Maeve, her features brightening as the world returned to her eyes.

'Thanks, child,' she said, asking for cornbread and butter and eating more that morning than she had for weeks. When Seán and Connie returned from potting that evening, Mam was down on the beach in her Sunday best to greet them.

Next day, Mam cooked the family favorite for dinner: salted pollock pie with cream and mashed potatoes. And as Maeve watched her serve out the steaming dish, she wondered how the potion had worked. She knew Mam never had time for the cures — she cursed them at every turn — but this one seemed to succeed nonetheless, behind her back, as if triggering some physical readiness inside her, a yearning of the body to get well even if her brain didn't know it. Like some inner tide flooding back from illness to health. The swing of a current from eddy to flow. Coming and going. A turn of the soul, at the right time and season. Was it all about time turning and returning, like sea weather, without why?

In the August days that followed Maeve continued to practice more cures, each time matching fresh plant ingredients with remedies recorded in the black book. She used dandelion tea for Áine Daly's boils and red clover for Mona McCarthy's chilblains;

she eased Connie's ear ache with sea pinks and had middling luck with lemon balm on Dan Daly's indigestion; though she had no luck at all with sticky willow on Nóra McCarthy's lumbago. Maeve was still fiercely shy about her work, careful never to be seen as she slipped a few drops into someone's teacup or bowl when their back was turned. She watched and waited, to see what happened. She listened and learned. No one got worse and those who got better got better — fair progress, she reckoned. Mam sometimes asked Maeve for more of 'that tea'; but Maeve knew she didn't need it as long as her mood continued to improve.

As late summer spilled over the island, sunlight stole into the kitchen through the small squares of the windows, filling the house with color and life. Ditches were in full bloom again, ablaze with foxgloves, ox-eyes and red-belled fuchsia. Each evening the air was alive with the piping of barn swallows and long-tailed swifts flown all the way from Africa; while mackerel and whitebait shoaled right onto the shores until you could almost catch them with your hands. The smell of frying fish filled the yards between the houses and almost everyone seemed to be getting on, even the McCarthys. There were mutterings of good times returning.

Maeve too felt better each day. She was glad to see her mother rise from the bed each morning, baking scones and doing small jobs about the house, while she herself foraged for plants with Bawn under blue skies, sorting them after in jars and pots. Everything was settling when one calm evening — August 15 — Connie came back from fishing with a clay pipe in his hand. He had found it snagged in a salmon net and knew right away it was their father's. No mistake. Maeve warmed the pipe between her palms and wept quietly as she placed it on the top shelf of the Brú, beside her father's other things, the tobacco tin and the black book. Her consolations. She still read the ledger most days, following the curly writing, attentive to the tiny accents — the rising *síntí fada* and elusive *séimhiú* — each shift of sound a key to native savvy; for she knew the cures worked only in Irish.

But as days passed and the evenings shortened, she found herself thinking of other books too. Printed books she wanted to read. Proper books. Public books. School books her teacher Miss Collins would give her once she returned to class in September. Library books she could share with school mates. Maeve was proud of the cures, of her father's calling; she'd not let go of that, ever. But she also longed for something else now. Something not on the island, not in the Brú. Another kind of learning. Less lonely and hidden, less secret and unspoken. Tired of being on her own for so long — missing her father, shunned by her brothers and minding Mam — Maeve wanted to be with friends her own age again, people she could talk and dream with. Bawn was great company but Bawn was a dog. She wanted more. She longed to return to life on the mainland.

II

ACROSS THE SOUND
September 1939-October 1940

Craobhraic ~ samphire

First week of September Maeve went back to school. Mam was there to see her off with Seán and Connie in Dan Daly's yawl. She stood on Trá an Tí and watched as they weighed anchor to sail to Squince. From there it was a mile walk to the village.

Miss Jane Collins greeted Maeve warmly, placing a hand on her shoulder as she ushered her to a seat at the front of the class. Maeve inhaled the familiar school smells of wood polish and pencil lead, leather satchels and glue-bound copy books. She felt a bit awkward at first with her threadbare gansey and scuffed boots, but she was happy to be back with her teacher and classmates and had no problem switching back to English. The island was the last place in the townland where people still spoke Irish, though Mam and her brothers chose to speak more and more English, especially since the drowning. It was the language of the future, as Miss Collins and Father Kehoe agreed. But her father had always used Irish and believed the cures only worked in that tongue, as did Maeve, for whom it was the language she still lived and felt and dreamed in. She couldn't help it. But with six years of schooling behind her, she was also fluent in English. Despite her strong guttural accent, she exchanged easy greetings with the other girls as she walked to the desk at the front of the class. Only to find a newcomer already in the seat beside her — a tall, imposing stranger with golden hair tied back in a plait.

During Composition class, Maeve was dipping her pen in the inkwell, holding her quill between finger and thumb, when she felt a sudden dig in the ribs. She looked up to see the new girl with a bold grin, pretending that nothing had happened. Maeve's chest ached, but she didn't want to make a fuss, not on her first day back; she just wanted to continue copying the phrase that Miss Collins was writing on the blackboard, a short sentence in beautiful copperplate. *In the future, telephones will work by dial.* Having missed so much school since the drowning, Maeve was hungry to apply herself, to catch up with everything, impress her teacher. But when she gazed down at her copy book, she saw ink had spread all over the page. The phrase she was copying was ruined.

Though her ribs hurt badly, she managed to place her nib back in the ink well. Maeve was tough, long used to bullying from her brothers on the island; but this was different. This was a girl sitting innocent beside her with perfect hair and blackberry eyes. All Maeve knew was what Josie Hayes had whispered walking into school that morning: 'Would you look at fancy pants, Helen Flynn. Thrown out of Bandon Grammar and still thinks she's the bee's knees.' And there she was, class hardly begun, ruining Maeve's writing and bruising her ribs.

Maeve turned and stared at Helen Flynn, expecting her to apologise. But when all she got was a brazen glare, Maeve dipped her pen in the inkwell and flicked a blob right onto her blouse.

Helen Flynn let out a cry.

Miss Collins, still at the board, swung around and faced the class. 'What's this?' She folded her arms and peered at the girls. 'Was it you, Maeve Sullivan?'

Maeve stood up from her desk and nodded.

Miss Collins's kind face tightened, hazel eyes narrowing as she rested her chalk on the ledge of the desk and strode down the aisle in her long woolen skirt. She took Maeve's hand and led her to the door.

'Out,' she said. 'Out to the yard. You're not on your island now, young lass.'

Maeve bit her tongue as she left the room. Her lips quivered. Jane Collins had never spoken harshly to her before. Maeve adored everything about her teacher: the way her voice rose in a sing-song city lilt, how she dressed in fine pleated skirts and adored books and rode her bicycle through the hills like one of the Celtic queens she spoke about in class. Maeve wanted to go back in and tell her what Helen Flynn had done. But she couldn't; she wasn't a squealer.

Out in the yard, Maeve stood and shivered. She buttoned her gansey against the chill blowing in from Ardra and wished she was in the Brú, sitting beside her father as he smoked his pipe and filleted his fish, surrounded by hanging wracks and plants. Sailing to school that morning, Maeve had so looked forward to being with Miss Collins and other girls again, and here she was now standing in the cold.

After a while, Maeve looked up and saw swallows flocking on the school gable awaiting their flight back to Africa. *Aon, dó, trí, ceathair.* And beside them, a yellow tufted warbler perched on a hawthorn bush by the road, its beak surrounded by the pink-tipped petals of small white flowers. A seasoned traveller blown all the way across the Atlantic, like the terns flung south on winds from the Artic. All sky-borne fliers, light of wing and high of pitch. *Bíonn súileach scéalach*: wanderers with the best songs. Unlike the crows and cormorants who clung to local ditches and rocks, black hooded, full-bellied, lazy. Like curates tucked in their choir stalls. Funny, she thought, how different birds dwelt wing to wing in the same place.

At morning break, all the girls were let out. Some ran up Donovan's lane towards Castle Ire looking for sparrows' eggs, while others played with skipping ropes by the school gate. But most clustered around Helen Flynn at the end of the yard, queuing for slices of lemon cake left over from her father's grocery. 'Daddy sells special pastries and just bought a rotary phone,' she boasted to her school mates. 'You can come and try it anytime.' She stole a quick glance at Maeve, standing by the chestnut tree, but pretended not to see her.

Josie Hayes and the other girls ignored Maeve too, whispering behind her back. All class of mean things. *Ciotóg*. Biddy the islander. Little wild girl whose Daddy let pilgrims die for a bob. Believer in *piseógs* and *púcaí*, black magic and fairy wells.

Maeve clenched her fists and vowed to learn everything she could from Miss Collins, to pass her exams and one day live in a house with books on polished shelves and a big oak desk with copper nibs and inkwells — and have no need for the Helens of this world.

After the break, the Master, Dan Maloney, appeared at the door, fat and bearded, with large jug ears. He held a holly cane in one hand, a brass bell in the other. Girls and boys stood in separate lines as he called their names and each replied — 'Present' — before filing into adjoining rooms. Maeve feared she might get a hiding from his holly or be kept back after school. But when her name was called and she stepped forward, Miss Collins took her by the elbow and said, 'Come in now, girl. You'll be alright.'

Maeve and Helen didn't speak for the rest of the week. Even though Miss Collins insisted they continue sitting together, they never said a single word nor looked each other once in the eye. Sometimes Helen motioned Maeve aside so she could go to the toilet or fetch something from the coat rack. Other times she'd stretch across Maeve's body for a pencil or dip her pen into the two round wells, set in holes on either side of the desk, as if everything was hers. And once she took Maeve's foolscap copybook, pulled back the blue-lined pages and sniffed — like a cat sniffing fish — before closing it with a frown. But Maeve said nothing, not wishing to make another scene or distract Miss Collins from her teaching.

At Friday Catechism, Miss Collins stood at the front of the class and clapped her hands for attention. Maeve thought she was God's own creature, standing there in her pressed cotton blouse and auburn hair curled tight in a bun.

'Saint Brigid,' she said, brushing her skirt with both hands. 'Today we'll learn about Saint Brigid. I hear there's been talk, and its important to get things right.' She held up a book called *Lives of Ancient Irish Saints*. 'I am writing a lesson on the board now and I want you all to copy it down.'

Miss Collins leaned forward for a piece of chalk before walking up to the black board. She wiped the board clean and, with the volume open in one hand, wrote out long sentences with the other. She moved slowly, adding curlicues and flourishes to each line. The girls bent their heads and transcribed the fluent letters.

Brigid was a Celtic goddess of three wisdoms — poetry, healing, and smithcraft.

She was called an 'ancient bride of nature' and later became a Christian Saint. She was known as 'Mary of the Gaels.'

Brigid was a mixture of legend and history.

According to legend, she existed from the beginning of time, and was present at Jesus's birth, placing three drops of water on the Savior's brow to make him fully welcome on earth.

According to history, Brigid was born in Dundalk in the middle of the fifth century, her mother a slave and her father a chieftain. She was sent off to a Druid in Tipperary who fed her milk from a cow with red ears and taught her many wonders.

Her first miracle was when she gave her cow's butter to beggars and the butter was restored ten-fold. She healed with herbs and natural elements. For centuries she was revered as a holy patron of midwives and blacksmiths, travellers and orphans, fishermen and brewers, harvesters and poets.

She could make wells rise up by planting a staff in the ground. A few of these wells still exist in Ireland and are known as Brigid's Wells.

Miss Collins turned from the board, placing the book and chalk on the desk.

'Brigid's Island — *Oileán Bhríde* — is one of those places.' She smiled at the class, then nodded at Maeve. 'As most of you know, that's where Maeve Sullivan comes from. Any questions?'

After a silence, Helen Flynn raised a hand.

'But was she *real*, Miss?'

'What do you mean?

'Saint Brigid. You said she was partly a legend. Does that mean she was partly pretend, a fairy story, something people made up?'

'Legends can be true too, in their way — if you believe in them. If you have imagination.'

No one else put a hand up.

'Do you see?' Miss Collins continued 'Do you understand now, Helen Flynn?'

Helen stole a glance at Maeve before looking at the other girls.

'No, Miss. I don't.'

A sly giggle ran through the class followed by a long silence. Maeve wanted to ask Miss Collins to say more about what she meant by imagination, but she didn't. She felt her teacher — hard on her earlier, sending her to the yard — was now on her side, while most of the class were on Helen's. She didn't want to make things worse by asking about this 'imagination' that Helen Flynn was clearly missing. Maeve was sure her father had plenty of it, and that she did too; but she also believed that Brigid was more than that — someone that made a difference in the world, helping heal people through plants and water and natural things. She'd learned new things from Miss Collins' book — the butter multiplying and Jesus' birth and the wells rising up from the staff in the ground — but she was puzzled by other things: Brigid existing before time and also being born into time, the daughter of a slave. How could she be both? And how could Miss Collins be so strict with Maeve one moment, and then speak so kindly about her Island the next? Things were complicated enough, God knows, without asking more questions in front of Helen Flynn and the other girls. Maeve knew she must humor her classmates, just as she'd dealt with her brothers on the island. If she was the only one following Brigid, she still needed friends. She had to get on.

After school ended, Maeve found herself surrounded in the yard.

Josie Hayes blocked the way. 'So tell us, Biddy the Islander, tell us about your spells.'

Maeve clutched her satchel and said nothing. She looked left and right, then up at the canopy of chestnut leaves arching over the school wall. A lone raven, perched on a high branch, kept guard.

'You're a mad little witch.' Josie grabbed at Maeve's bag, trying to snatch it away.

Maeve clung firm as if protecting a baby. She tried to push through the circle but the girls banded closer.

'Fancy yourself a healer, do you?' Nell Nagle piped up, shoving her face right up to Maeve's. 'Like your father before you. Isn't that right, isn't it? And look what happened, God forgive ye. Where are all the holy Joes now? All for a shilling. All for Brigid. My Mammy says it's one big scandal. Black magic, lies and backwardness. That's what she says.'

Maeve set her teeth, and pushed forward, staring Nell in the eye. The other girls recoiled for an instant, leaving a gap wide enough for Maeve to break through. Nell and Josie tried to grab her as she went, but Helen stepped back to let her pass.

Back on the island Maeve walked with Bawn to Trá an Róin, a cove on the tip of the north shore. She headed for the *leachtana*, a mound of stacked flagstones where the boats were stranded in summer for loading with seaweed. She perched on a flat lime-stone slab at the edge of the pile, one of her father's favorite places to sit and stared at cross tides moving between the rocks. She eyed the evening sun and waited for her breathing to settle. It calmed her to watch the currents making curious shapes and noises with the waves. The little churning circles or *coinnicí* which could ease you into a daze if you stared long enough.

The turbulent unsteady *tápholl* where swells met and went in opposite directions, a special moment when the tides turned. She loved the sucking sound of the waves pulling pebbles from the shoreline before swishing them back in again. *Súitú*, the islanders called it, and she could listen to it all day.

Perched on top of the raised stone, Maeve closed her eyes and let the Irish words slither off her tongue. These sounds, all these different terms for the sea — was she the last to utter them? Now that her father was gone and her Mam and brothers were turning to English, she feared she'd be speaking to herself before long. All the islanders were the same now, eager to forgo their own tongue and learn the language of the mainland, where there was trade, education, a future to be had. Her father had taught her the riches of Irish, key to his cures and stories, just as Miss Collins had taught her good English, and Mam and Father Kehoe the prayers of the Church. Did she have to choose between them? Could she keep her *blas* without being mocked? Relish the sound of *súitú* while succeeding in English at school, as Mam wished? How could she honor her father *and* her mother? The Fourth Commandment — not easy to keep.

By the time Maeve opened her eyes, the tide was licking at her toes. To get home, she had to take off her boots and wade with Bawn through the shallows to dry land. She did not share her thoughts with her family or speak about what had happened in class.

On the Feast of Guardian Angels, second of October, there was commotion in the school yard. Miss Collins raised the hem of her skirt and hurried across the gravel during break, muttering something to Master Maloney who was standing by the gate. She gave a quick nod, cupping her mouth so the pupils wouldn't hear. The Master removed his thumbs from the lapels of his jacket, where they were neatly tucked, and stroked his rusty beard. The teachers' heads dipped as if staring into a hole in the ground, whispering at a great rate, before the Master tapped his cane on his boot, turned heel and shuffled towards the coal shed east of the gable. Miss Collins followed with a hand on her throat.

Josie Hayes, who overheard everything, sidled over to the other girls and announced — 'Rats! In the coal shed! Nan Casey had her finger bit while out having a smoke. They said the rat was big as a badger and it's not safe to fetch fuel for the furnace. We'll all be wearing coats for a while.'

The Master sent Nan home for a bandage, but not before he boxed her ears. Miss Collins protested but the Master would have none of it. He called for the vet, John Deasy, who arrived with a bag of poison and three wire cages. If the poison didn't work, Deasy said, the traps would. Rats were as wily as ferrets these days but a quick dunk in the water barrel and the little creatures would be off with Holy God.

The class clustered around the vet, keen to witness the coming torture, when Maeve stepped forward.

'Don't,' she protested. 'Please don't. They're only in the shed to shelter from the rain.'

'Little rat girl!' Josie Hayes mocked, and everyone laughed.

And before anyone knew it, Helen Flynn and the other girls were pulling Maeve by the sleeves towards the shed. They bayed and hollered and were about to push her through the door when Miss Collins intervened.

'Enough now, enough!' she cried, shooing them off with a wave of her hand. Then she placed an arm around Maeve and escorted her back to the school room.

Cockcrow next day, Maeve arrived early, a good hour before class. She slipped into the coal shed, east of the schoolhouse, and waited in the dark sooty space. Not a sound apart from a slight creaking of the door, moving back and forth on its hinges, and a flutter of dried leaves against the coal scuttles. Nothing stirred as Maeve stood, not moving, breathing in odors of turf and coke. Musty, underground smells, like Brigid's cave. And for a moment she imagined a soft whoosh of surf. *Súitú.*

After a while she spoke to the rats — '*Amach libh anois, mas é bhur dtoil* ' — 'Off with you now, please.'

And taking the Petersen tin from her sack she sprinkled drops of well water onto the floor, repeating three times, '*Amach libh anois.*' Then she stood back and watched as an entire family of rats stole silently from the shadows and scuttled out the door.

Maeve replaced the tin in her sack and was returning through the yard when she felt a pair of eyes on her back. Someone was hiding by the chestnut tree.

'I saw you.' Helen Flynn stepped from the leafy shadows.

Maeve stopped and turned.

'Saw what?'

'The rats. I heard you speaking. What were you saying? Those funny words?' Helen's lips twisted. 'And what's in the box?' She squinted, poking at the tin in Maeve's sack.

Maeve hesitated. Helen had done her nothing but harm since they met. Just one day ago she was rallying the class against her and telling Josie Hayes she was fed up sharing a desk with a '*ciotóg* from Biddy's Island.' Ever since the ink business, Helen and her gang had mocked Maeve for being left-handed;

but Maeve knew their cruelty wasn't really about her hands or the dirt under her nails or the wild curls hanging over her face; it was about the drowning. Half the village still blamed her father for risking the pilgrims' lives in a storm; and Maeve was her father's daughter. She felt a dull shaming gaze when she entered the school each morning; it was in the air and it wasn't fair. No other girl was bullied or shunned. Not Josie Hayes for being foul-mouthed and scatterbrained; nor Nell Nagle for having a birth-mark the size of Bandon on the side of her face — God help her; nor Helen Flynn for being fired from Bandon Grammar for bad behavior or having warts between her fingers which she covered with paint and plasters. And yet Helen too was a stranger, arriving suddenly from another school. She and Maeve were different in different ways, Helen a class above with her posh accent, Maeve a class below with her guttural tongue — two outsiders needing acceptance in the group, and only room for one. That one was Helen. The ire was stirred and directed at Maeve. Helen had won the girls in the class. So what could Maeve do but win Helen?

'Why did the rats go?' Helen raised her shoulders and let them fall.

Maeve didn't answer at first. She just stood there, looking west to the field.

'You know you can die if they bite you.' Helen screwed up her face.

'You can die from lots of things,' Maeve replied.

'Rats are dirty, you know that.'

'Like your warts?'

'What warts?'

'The ones between your fingers.' She reached for Helen's hands and opened them.

Helen pulled back, covering her fists with her sleeves.

Maeve waited several minutes, watching Helen slowly weep, before speaking again, more softly now.

'What's wrong with you?'

'I hate them.'

'I know.'

'You don't know anything about me.'

'I know that you need *me*.'

'*You*? Need you for what?'

'To make them go away.'

Helen removed her hands from her sleeves. She looked puzzled. 'Go away? How?'

'The way I made the rats disappear.' Maeve nodded to the empty door.

Helen's eyes widened. 'Really?'

'Really.'

'Forever?'

'Yes.'

'Would you?'

'I might. If you ask nicely and let me alone.'

Helen nodded and after a pause took a step forward.

Maeve took Helen's hands in hers, bending her head to examine the warts. She ran the base of her thumb across the tiny fleshy tufts, rough and wrinkled as a sow's nipples, while Helen gushed nervously. She confessed to Maeve how she was always picking at the horrid little things, making them bleed so much her parents had taken her to the doctor in Skibbereen; and how, when that did no good, she'd followed Nell Nagle's advice and rubbed the warts on pebbles and left them in a brown paper bag at Reen crossroads so the person who found them would catch the warts instead. But nothing worked.

Maeve listened calmly before looking Helen in the eye. 'Come to the island.'

'When?'

'After school tomorrow.' Maeve turned to leave. 'Meet me at five on Squince strand.'

When Helen arrived at Squince the next day, Maeve was waiting by Dan Daly's yawl.

'For Biddy's Island, are you?' Dan lifted a curious eye. He shook Helen's hand and laughed, pulling his head back like a spirited horse.

Maeve watched as Dan hoisted Helen's slim frame into the boat, his sinewy neck going taut as he lowered her carefully into the stern, making sure her pleated skirt didn't touch the dirty nets. 'Watch them clothes now.'

As Dan rowed out, Maeve sensed Helen's skittishness. They still hardly knew each other and this was, Helen admitted, her first time in a boat. In her fifteen years she'd never been to sea. Her lemony smell was sharper than usual and when her hands began to shake, Maeve reached over and touched them, letting her know they hadn't far to go. A column of cormorants looked on from the mussel-clad rocks, like gardaí siochána watching them pass. Whiffs of slurry blew in from Myross headland, mixing with odors of tar and stale shellfish seeping up from the bilges. Helen was white.

Halfway to the island, Maeve sighted a swarm of jellyfish and leaning over the side, peered down at the pale pulsing discs, their organs trailing lilac strings. Helen did likewise, letting her hand drift in the wake.

'Don't touch them,' Maeve warned, 'they sting.'

Helen pulled her fingers from the water, nesting them under her armpit.

Dan rowed steadily, letting the odd grin crease his features as he took in both girls huddled at the stern. He manned the oars proudly, as if he'd been a ferryman all his life, though he'd only taken over the job when Michael Sullivan passed away. Maeve was glad it was Dan and not Tadhg McCarthy who'd succeeded her father. She hated the way Tadhg had nabbed whatever he could get after the drowning — the Sullivans' nets, pots, tackle and moorings. But he didn't get the ferrying — that was Dan's now with the handy transport of herring and lobster in season and the odd few crossings of doctor and priest. A small income to supplement the farming.

Nearing the island, a westerly breeze whiplashed the waves, making the fuchsia dance about the houses. Once ashore, Maeve thanked Dan and led Helen straight to the Brú. She avoided the main house, fearing Mam might make a scene; she was still up and down these days. Besides, they hadn't much time. Dan would be rowing back to Squince with lobster for the market soon.

When Maeve opened the door, a dark shadow shaved their heads. Helen ducked, covering her hair. 'What's that?'

'*Sciathán leathair*. Bats,' explained Maeve, patting Helen's head. 'They're friends.'

'Like the rats?'

'Yes, but with wings on.'

It was dark in the hut with only one small window looking out on the Sound. A single shaft of sunlight fell across the earthen floor. There was a tart smell of bladder wrack hanging on strings from the rafters. Maeve wiped the stool with her sleeve and passed it over to Helen. Her first patient from the mainland.

Helen rubbed her hands tightly. She gave a nervous moan before sitting down.

'Shush now,' said Maeve, placing a palm on Helen's shoulder as she set to work. She uncluttered the work top, removing coils of hemp, a rusty iron clamp and some old brass fittings, placing them onto an upper shelf. Once she'd cleared the space, she took her father's filleting knife and sliced a blade of duilleasc, placing the purple leathery strips beside a bunch of dandelions which she crushed until a pale milk oozed from the stems. She then opened the tobacco tin and brushed the ingredients inside.

'What?' Helen pinched her nose, gawking at the mush in the tin. 'I have to swallow *that*?'

Maeve smiled, coaxing Helen back to the stool.

'Watch,' she said, parting Helen's fingers until the warts were fully exposed; then dipping her thumb in the paste she rubbed it onto the fleshy lumps. She spent a few minutes on each, whispering gently in Irish — *imígí libh, imígí libh* — as if she was talking to living creatures; and when she'd finished she bent down and kissed them.

'Don't!' cried Helen, pulling away. 'They're ugly!'

'No, they're not,' Maeve replied. 'They're part of us. Hurt bits that heal if you bless them.'

'How do you know?'

'Because my father told me.'

'And how did he know?'

'Because he learned it from Brigid.'

'*Saint* Brigid?'

'Yes.'

'But she died,' protested Helen, 'hundreds of years ago. Miss Collins told us.'

'A bit of her died, but a bit still lives. She comes back whenever someone heals.'

'Like now?'

'Yes, like now.'

'And how can you tell?'

'Because my feet go hot and I hear special sounds.'

'What sounds?'

'Irish sounds. Island sounds. Like bees buzzing, flames licking, shells cracking, waves falling. Special sounds.' Maeve's eyes shone. 'You think I'm off with the fairies, don't you?'

Helen lowered her gaze and didn't answer.

Maeve raised a finger and closed Helen's eyes.

'Don't look now. Just listen.'

'*Eascair Leigheas Mothaím Cneasú.*' Maeve spoke the words slowly before going silent.

Helen waited.

'Do you hear something?' asked Maeve after a bit.

'No.'

'Waves?'

'No.'

'Bees?'

She shook her head. 'Nothing.'

'Well, can you *feel* something?'

'Like what?'

'Like fire in in your hands.'

Helen shrugged. 'No.'

'You have to try, Helen. It won't work if you don't have faith.'

Maeve reached for the Brigid *brat* hanging by the font and, dipping the wool in the water, brushed Helen's warts.

Helen opened her eyes. 'You're like Father Kehoe cleaning his chalice.' She cocked her head, beginning to relax.

'Maybe,' Maeve shrugged. 'But I don't talk Latin.'

'You talk Irish.'

'I do.'

'Why?'

'Because it works.' Maeve rolled up the cloth and replaced it on the hook. 'Irish words heal if you use them right. It's the sounds which matter.' She repeated the cure slowly: '*Eascair Ligheas Mothaím Cneasú.*'

'You believe that?'

'I do.' And at that moment, Maeve did believe. She believed everything she was saying, everything she was doing, all doubts dissolving like foam on a wave. 'And if you believe too, Helen Flynn, your warts will be gone when you wake in the morning.'

At school next day, they met under the chestnut tree and Helen opened her hands. 'They're gone. The warts are gone!'

Maeve smiled.

'Come to my house after school,' whispered Helen, making sure no one was listening. 'I've things I want to show you.'

No sooner in the door, Helen led Maeve to the parlor. Passing through the Flynn's hallway, lit by stained glass windows, Maeve found everything bright and clean compared to her own dark house. She couldn't help gawking at the brass umbrella stand stocked with ebony canes — so different from Tadhg McCarthy's knobby hawthorn and the Master's twisted holly. In the parlor Helen showed Maeve a collection of sculpted ivory birds kept in glass cabinets behind an upholstered sofa.

'Here, take this!' Helen opened the latticed panes and handed Maeve a carved toucan with long beak and plumes.

But before Maeve had time to touch it, Helen was already replacing the bird in the casement and ushering her towards the mahogany desk on the far side of the room.

'Look here.' She pointed to a gleaming wheel perched like an owl. 'Look at this!'

'What is it?' Maeve asked.

'It's a dial phone.'

'Like the one Miss Collins talked about?'

'Yes.' Helen stroked the neck of the phone as if it was a living thing.

'How does it work?' Maeve edged toward the phone, one step at a time, leaning in and pulling back slightly as if it might leap up and fly.'

'I'll show you,' Helen laughed. 'Come here to me!'

And taking Maeve's forefinger she placed it in the first of the ten finger holes on the faceplate.

'You start with the zero — see, each hole has a number — then you turn the dial.' Helen put her hand over Maeve's and moved it gently clockwise. 'This way.'

'*Deiseal*,' said Maeve.

'What?'

'Oh, nothing.'

'Daddy bought it last month. It's the only one in the village, apart from the Doctor's.'

Maeve stared at the 0. 'Is it a letter or a number?'

'Both.'

'And if I dial it?'

'You get the Operator!'

'Operator?'

'Yes. The lady at the Skibbereen Exchange. Marie Shanahan. Daddy knows her well and says she listens to all the calls. Every word. "Once you have the Operator, the world's your Oyster. Dublin. London. Boston. Madras!" That's what Daddy says. '

Maeve moved her finger from one small hole to the next, until she'd gone full circle and returned to zero. It reminded her of the day her father guided her finger into the mouth of an empty sea urchin. *Cuan mara.* 'Don't be afraid, there's nothing inside,' he'd assured her. And he was right. Only this was different. Helen's phone was no mollusk but a magic box with numbers that connected you to the world. Maeve wondered what her father would do if he was standing there beside her. Dial the Fish Market for the day's prices? Chat with the Skibbereen Operator? Make a call to old relatives in Boston?

Maeve removed her finger from the dial and ran it along the rim of the plate before raising the telephone to her nose. It smelled of nothing. Or if it did, it was completely drowned by the scent of brass polish and white water lilies spilling from a vase beside the table. No fumes of smokey peat here, no waft of damp clothes and seal oil, or cured fish and root vegetables. She touched the dial wheel again. Hard, cold, gleaming. Another world.

'Maeve's the best in our class,' Helen announced to her parents over tea, tapping her forehead with her forefinger. 'She's very brainy, even at English Composition — though she was born speaking Irish.'

Helen leaned over the table and patted Maeve's arm, as if she were her new pet. Then looking up at her father: 'And guess what, Daddy? Maeve's going to help me with Irish for my exams and I'll teach her how to use the telephone. Isn't that a good deal?'

'Yes indeed.' Mr Flynn raised an amused eyebrow.

'Good business?'

'Very good business. You're born to trade.'

Helen and her father laughed.

'And Maeve knows the name of lots of birds too — in Irish and English.' Helen glanced from her father to her mother. 'Tell Maeve about *your* birds, Mummy.'

'Well,' said Mrs Flynn dreamily. 'We have carved and feathered kinds.'

'Maeve just saw the toucan,' said Helen. 'But tell her about the real ones.'

Mrs Flynn placed her cup in her saucer. 'We have many winged visitors, you know.' She wiped her lips with a napkin and turned towards Maeve. 'We keep feeders in the yard. Helen and I give them leftovers. Especially lard and bread crumbs. They love it and come and go as they please. Finches and blue tits mainly.' Mrs Flynn thought for a moment, glancing out the window. 'But we don't like magpies, do we Helen? They steal everything.' She waved her napkin as if shooing the predators from her plate. 'My favorites are the starlings.' She gazed fondly at Helen beside her. 'Darling starlings. How they fly.' Mrs Flynn made a fluttering movement with her fingers over her chest. 'And they're clever too. They copy other birds, imitate their chirps.' She cupped a hand to her ear. 'Like our Helen. Quite the actress.'

Helen made her mouth into an oval and mimicked an English accent, 'Quite the actress.'

Mr Flynn chuckled. 'If only our daughter spent as much time studying books as going to the pictures in Skibbereen....'

'…We must keep an eye on the magpies,' Mrs Flynn interrupted, ignoring her husband.

'Devil's creatures,' Mr Flynn said jovially. 'I wish our cat did a better job.'

'Kitty is fine.' Mrs Flynn placed a hand on her husband's cuff, before turning back to Maeve. 'Now tell us about *your* favorite birds, Maeve. There must be lots on Brigid's Island?'

Maeve hesitated for a moment, rubbing the silver napkin ring on her lap as if it was a piece of salvage. Her hands trembled slightly. She knew all the island birds in Irish but not as many in English, despite Helen's boast. She clasped her hands under the table and thought of a few.

'There's the herring gull, *faoláin*. You know them, they're everywhere — on the beaches and boats, gables and cliffs. And the storm petrel, *gearr úisc*, which flits over the waves and shows up when people are in trouble. It's tiny with black feathers and braves all weathers. And then there's the gannet, *gainéad*, that can dive ten fathoms after herring and sprat. I could watch them all day. But my favorite is the robin. We call it *spideóg* because it's full of spirit, *spriod*.' She placed a hand over her heart. 'Robin redbreast — it feels our pain.'

Mrs Flynn stopped slicing the almond cake. 'How charming.'

'Charming indeed,' echoed Mr Flynn, sinking back in his chair before changing the subject. 'And I must say I'm delighted you'll be helping Helen with the Irish. She needs it. We all do. Our national tongue, after all. A precious thing. Pearse was a good man, and the Gaelic Leaguers, wanting to salvage our native ways, our Celtic soul. A noble dream. Though one has to admit, Dan O'Connell was right. The way forward *is* English. No trade and travel without it. Two-thirds of the world speaks it now, you know. And O'Connell knew it too. No fool. The liberation of Catholics came through English. Impossible otherwise. And look at us now. A free Catholic country, second to none, with better English than the English themselves. Father Kehoe would agree. Ultramontane, I grant you, with a twist of Jansenism. But a small price to pay for freedom, don't you think, a bargain in order to practice the faith.'

Then he turned to Maeve, not wishing to offend. 'But don't get me wrong, young lady, I too cherish Gaelic, our ancient heritage. A timeless treasure, not to be lost. And lucky for us, Maeve, there are people like you left to speak it....'

Helen interrupted, pushing her plate to one side. '...and to use it for *magic*!' She held up her hands to her parents. 'Look! Maeve made my warts go away! She spoke to them in Irish — and now they're gone. See!'

'I see, indeed,' said Mrs Flynn, surprised.

'Quite the doctor!' added Mr Flynn, raising a heavy eyelid.

Maeve removed her napkin from her lap and placed it back on the table. She loved listening to Mr Flynn talk — with big words like *ultramontane* and *Jansenist*, whatever they meant — but she didn't like the idea of English replacing Irish like that. The future replacing the past. No. And she was upset that Helen had shared her secret, though she knew she couldn't say anything now. If she mentioned the cures she'd have to talk about her father; and she really wasn't ready for that. Not yet. Right then, she didn't want to think about the drowning or her mother's moods or the bitter storms that battered her island. Sitting there amidst the Flynns with their fine talk, neat clothes, foreign teas and spicey pastries, she just wanted the moment to last.

After tea, Helen brought Maeve to her bedroom.

Though Maeve was small — at five foot four she was smallest

in her class — Helen swore she'd make her grand. So grand no one would care if she was a *ciotóg* living on an offshore island. She sat Maeve down in front of the dressing table and adjusted the gilt mirror.

'Close your eyes, open your mouth and see what God will send you.'

Maeve obeyed as Helen popped a peppermint onto her tongue.

'Now to work!' She set to straightening Maeve's wavy curls with a tortoiseshell comb before rubbing crimson lipstick on her mouth. Then she sauntered to the wardrobe where she fussed with the racks before removing a tailored gown. 'Mummy bought it in Cork. Cashes. The best. Try it!'

Maeve changed from her plain flannel skirt into the frock, while Helen acted out little scenes from *Gone with the Wind*. Miss Collins had brought the class to see the picture in Skibbereen and Maeve was happy to play along now with Helen's antics, amused at how perfectly she took off Scarlett O'Hara. And she laughed out loud when Helen went on to mimic voices of posh local Protestants, BBC radio announcers and Nell Nagle's moans about belly cramps. Maeve loved it all and didn't even mind when Helen took off her own sing-song accent, calling her 'Biddy the islander!' She just stood there in the borrowed dress, dazzled by Helen's blackberry eyes as she danced about the room like a girl with bees in her hair.

Right then Helen could do no wrong. And Maeve wasn't the least bit shy when, after all the carry-on, she flipped Maeve's hand to slip on a dress bracelet and tickle the scar on her inside wrist, a candle burn from her childhood.

'My father said it was a fingerprint of God,' Maeve nodded down at the purple mark. 'And that you find it on special kinds of fish — John Dory, bream, horse mackerel, haddock. God's favorites. Christ was a fisherman — like my father.'

'Yes, your father was a fisherman and you're a fisherman's daughter.' Helen aped an island lilt. 'But it's not fish we're after now, Maeve Sullivan, is it? Nor fishermen, nor Christians. It's fine rich handsome gentlemen!'

And wrapping an arm around Maeve, Helen twirled her in a circle until they were both gone with the wind.

That evening, strolling back along Myross road, Maeve found herself humming Helen's phrase — *Close your eyes, open your mouth and see what God will send you*. She couldn't get it out of her mind and didn't quite know what to make of it. Have fun? Eat up? Act the maggot? Trust God? But it didn't really matter. What mattered was it made Maeve feel giddy for the first time in a long while. Her father had always made her laugh with his teasing riddles and Gaelic rhymes; now it was Helen's turn.

When she reached Squince bay there was damp in the air. Maeve pulled up the collars of her woolen coat and waited for Dan Daly, due at six but late as usual. Standing on the strand, she fished Helen's tortoiseshell comb from her bag and tapped it gently against her Adam's apple, as if she was playing music with her throat. Helen Flynn. How she'd changed in a few short days. From schoolyard bully to best friend, in the turn of a penny. All so sudden. A little miracle. But what had made the difference? Maeve wondered. Did the healing of the warts turn Helen's heart and make her really believe in the cures? Or was she just being nice so Maeve would help with her Irish and homework — it was true she was first in the class and Helen was terribly scattered. Or perhaps Helen meant it when she said Maeve was really pretty? She'd never thought much about her looks before, not until

Helen had sat her down before the mirror, straightening her curls and blackening her lashes until she saw someone else staring back at her, a stranger she'd never seen before, some glimmer of secret loveliness waiting to show itself, like a covered moon peeping through a cloud. Perhaps it was the same loveliness her father said he saw in her mother the first time they met walking the hills of Myross? Maybe one day, Maeve hoped, she'd be as beautiful as her mother was then.

The sound of splashing interrupted her thoughts. Young lads from the village were skimming stones on the tide while local boys baited cobblers in pools. Above them, the dipping sun leaned west and the sky spread wide as if levelled by a rolling pin. Maeve stood and watched the light dulling in the bay, bluey green becoming purple grey. A brace of mallard made their way north towards Rineen, wings creaking like hinges, while in the distance a purl of smoke drifted into the air above the island.

Now that Maeve had been to Helen's house, she felt stronger returning to her own. She knew Mam would scold her for being late, but she didn't care; she'd tasted the sweetness of another kind of life and was excited by the idea of doing lessons with Helen every day after school. She pressed her satchel to her belly, feeling the shape of the copybooks against her skin, like little creatures growing inside her. She might be a *ciotóg* without a father but nothing could stop her now. She'd practice cures on the island and pursue her studies at school. She'd follow her father's way and learn to write like Miss Collins. For a moment everything seemed possible.

Standing on Squince strand, Maeve looked across the waves to the blur of gorse headland. Brigid's Island. Her island. So far and near at the same time. Half a mile and a stone's throw. She was tempted to swim it, like she'd done many times — she knew the winds and currents, the difference between the *misruth* of tides and the *táphall* of turning waters; she could handle any weather; she feared nothing. But Dan would be there in no time, to ferry her over and take her home.

Sunlight spilled through the half door, scattering white splotches onto the walls. Mam looked blankly out the window.

'The food's packed,' said Maeve, tucking the currant bread and tea bottle into the wicker creel. Bawn sat at her feet, tail thumping. 'Seán and Connie are waiting by the boat. We have to go now, Mam.'

Mam pulled a black shawl over her head and said nothing. Dullness clouded her eyes. It was back, Maeve knew. After months of improving, her mother had darkened again as winter grew bitter and the year turned. Black shadows crossed her face as the anniversary loomed. First of February. One year on.

Waiting for her mother to budge, Maeve felt puzzled. Why hadn't the cure lasted? Why did healing work for some and not others? Was it Maeve's fault for not mixing the ingredients right, with her father no longer there to guide her and his hand-written notes so hard to read? Just one year since they'd gone to the well, preparing the cave for the pilgrims, and the passing on of the Gift — but did Maeve really have it? The gift. Or had it passed away with her father? Seeing Mam turn dark again, Maeve wasn't sure. And here she was now, badgering her family to revisit the well. It had taken days of persuasion, and a bribe of pastries from Flynn's grocery, to get her brothers to man the boat. And to convince her mother to join them.

'The boys are ready on the beach.' Maeve repeated, tugging at Mam's coat. 'They won't wait.'

Mam bunched her hand into a fist and lifted it to her throat, touching it once, twice, before lowering it again to her chest. Her glassy stare didn't alter as she smoothed her woolen dress several times and gave a quick nod, while Maeve opened the door and they stepped out into the light.

Before leaving the yard, Maeve bent and stroked Bawn, kneading his ears until his tongue hung out and his hind paw peddled the air. 'We won't be long,' she consoled, feeding him a crust and tethering him to the door. 'You're the devil on picnics, you know that. A right scavenger! Look after the house now.' Then rising to her feet, Maeve took a tallow candle in one hand, the wicker basket in the other, and escorted her mother down to the yawl.

Pure blue, not a crease in the sky. Seán had insisted they row around the west rocks, rather than walk the four fields across the island to the well. He and Connie wanted to pull the nets on the way. Seán was eighteen — three years older than Maeve — and could hold his own with a pair of oars. He rowed hard, shoulders all sinew as he pulled back and forth. Connie sat with Mam in the bow, holding onto her arm for fear she might slip overboard, while Maeve sat at the stern peering down at the churning wake. Its foamy crests coiled like ropes.

No one spoke as they rowed. Mam hadn't said a word all week; and Seán and Connie were sullen and cold; they'd never forgotten that if they were Mam's favorites, Maeve had always been their father's. They avoided her at every turn and rarely caught her eye. They lived separate lives from their sister, like dogfish and lobsters — never to be found in the same pot together.

When the yawl reached Carraiganam — where the nets were

set on a line of floats — Mam refused to let the boys stop. She grimaced and stared, insisting they continue to the cave. Seán and Connie reluctantly obeyed, casting a flinty glance at Maeve. It was Maeve's idea to make this trip and they were not happy to be dragged along. Bad enough to lose their father without having to be reminded. Brigid's day was a miserable day.

Maeve did her best to ignore her brothers' ire. She eyed a brace of shearwaters shaving the water, and wished Helen was sitting beside her — to see all this. The birds, the floats, the rocks, the well. But Helen couldn't stomach the sea; and, besides, Mam hated sharing Maeve with anyone since the drowning. She'd lost her man; she'd not lose her daughter.

Once landed at Brigid's cave the Sullivans heaved the boat up the shore. The tide was flooding, spume licking the sand like calves' slaver.

'Can we have cake now?' asked Connie, poking Maeve's basket. He spoke in English, something islanders never did at the well.

'*Fan nóiméad*, wait a while,' Maeve replied, ignoring Connie's barb. No time for a quarrel. There was more important business to attend to. She balanced the basket on her hip as she rummaged inside for candles. Then she walked to the cave with her brothers while Mam looked blankly on.

The three of them had little trouble removing the boards from the entrance — Tadhg was remiss at keeping it blocked — but when they'd cleared the way and looked about, they discovered their mother was gone.

'Where are you, Mam?' They called and called again, but there was no sign of her anywhere. They looked by the boat, beneath the cliffs, along the shore, all over; until they spotted tracks in the sand leading around to the side of the cave.

And there she was: squatting against a flat slab of rock, her head in her arms, shoulders bunched as if giving birth. Behind her, a smooth surface of granite rose up until it disappeared into lichen and furze. They waited as Mam raised a hand and ran it down the initials on the stone. The twelve names. Only twelve, though thirteen had drowned. Twelve names followed by a zero. A blank circle. After the drowning, Tadhg McCarthy had cut the initials of each recovered corpse onto the rock, except for Michael Sullivan who remained lost all those months. When his body was eventually found, Tadhg had forgotten to add his name, or had simply not bothered.

Maeve rushed to help her mother to her feet but she reared back, clutching her shawl as if it was a precious robe Maeve was trying to steal from her. Mam recoiled like a spooked animal, her spine pressed hard to the rock, palms splayed flat against its surface. Then she raised her fingers slowly and placed them on her head before sliding them down to her mouth and throat, removing her scarf as she did so. And as Mam rose and bent, furling inwards like an accordion, her shoulders rubbed against the rock as though she was trying to wipe the names out, to pretend they never existed, that the drowned were still alive and her man was standing beside her. But she soon stopped moving and sank down onto the sand, mouth opening and closing, like a beached fish. She stared at the sea.

Maeve followed her mother's gaze to the ocean; but all she could see was sunlight torn to ribbons by the waves.

Mam stayed like that for some time, not entering the well, not taking her eyes from the sea until a gull-like cry sprang up from her lungs. 'No,' she wailed. 'I'll not go, I'll not go in. I'll never darken Brigid's den. The bitch took him from me and I'll never forgive her. She swallowed him alive and never gave him back.'

'We're not going in either,' Seán and Connie agreed.

But Maeve stepped forward and removed her shoes. She clenched a candle and entered the cave.

All dark, Maeve fished a match from her pocket and lit the taper before placing it on the raised slab. Then she did the *deiseal*, as her father taught her, circling the space three times clockwise, her hand touching the flickering walls, from smooth and damp to brittle and dry.

Approaching the well, she brushed the shells and rosary beads to one side, and wiped the grime from her hands. No one but Maeve had visited the cave since the carving of the names. The odor of burning tallow wax, mixed with the whiff of bladder wrack, made an incense sharper than anything she'd smelled in Church. Wet moss glistened in the candlelight as tiny rivulets of water trickled down into the trough.

Maeve pulled one of Mam's medicine flasks from her pocket and, making sure it was empty, plunged it gently into the well. She waited as it gurgled and gulped, a soft pulse entering the container as air escaped and bubbled to the surface. The glass of the flask was so blue she could hardly see the water inside when she raised it to her eyes; but it was heavier. It would do. She stole a quick sip before tucking the bottle back in her coat and joining her hands in front of her throat. And then she felt it. The soft drowsy hum flowing up through her veins, warming her body and making her tremble.

'Come back,' she spoke to the flame on the rock. 'Come back to us, Brigid.' The candle fumes smelled of honey and tobacco. She drew a long breath and held it in her belly until she could hear her own heart beat; then she breathed out again, like she was breathing her father's breath.

Back outside, Maeve straightened her coat and walked straight up to her dazed mother. 'It's all right, Mam. We can eat now.'

The four Sullivans moved from the cave to the tide line, until the water licked their feet. Maeve stared at the sky and guessed three o'clock. She unpacked the wicker creel, laying out the soda cake and uncorking the bottle. Pouring the milky tea, she managed to slip a drop of the water into Mam's cup, handing the other mugs to her brothers. No one said a word about it being the anniversary of the drowning, as if the only reason they'd come was to celebrate the first day of spring. Maeve sang her father's song, the words soft and easeful.

> *Anois teacht an earraig*
> *Beidh an lá dul chun síneadh*
> *Is taréis na Féile Bhríde*
> *Ardóidh mé mo sheol....*

> *Now that spring comes*
> *and the days stretch longer,*
> *I will hoist my sail*
> *after Brigid's day.*

She'd seen a demon cross her mother's face, but it was calm again now. No more cries. No more curses. Maeve looked at Mam looking at her sons drinking their tea and was almost happy for a while.

As spring stretched towards summer, Maeve spent as much time as possible on the mainland. Her visits to Helen's were now daily during the school week; but she missed her friend at weekends when she had to look after Mam on the island. Her brothers were always out fishing with Dan these days, every chance they could get, avoiding the house where Mam's moods were worsening again, making things miserable for everyone. The calm after the picnic hadn't lasted, and Maeve was still obliged to take care of all the basic things like cooking and cleaning, scalding the churn and salting the butter, feeding the chickens and penning the goats, separating the potatoes into waxy and floury, early roosters and Kerry pinks, home guards and golden wonders. It seemed endless, and the more cabined she felt on the island, the more she looked forward to the Flynns' happy house — the long chats with Helen in her bedroom, the delicious smells and hot water baths, the telephone calls to the Skibbereen operator, the gramophone music and radio songs. Maeve loved it all and couldn't get the latest tunes out of her head. Vera Lynn and Gracie Fields, Marlene Dietrich and the Ink Spots. She and Helen spent hours sitting by the mahogany transistor radio imitating the songs and wondering why such sweet music was always followed by awful war reports from the BBC News. And when they weren't chatting and chanting they were helping Mrs Flynn out in the grocery store — weighing coffee and spices, wrapping dried fruits and pastries in brown paper bags — and then dressing up afterwards in Mrs Flynn's capes and kimonos as Helen primed Maeve's hair and painted her nails every color under the sun, swearing she'd make her the loveliest lass west of Bandon. And then it was Maeve's turn to dress Helen, enthralled by the quickly shifting hues of her face as it varied between pallor and rouge with every different garment she tried.

Going to Flynn's after school during weekdays cheered Maeve up no end. She'd grown attached to Helen's special ways — her agility and playfulness, her mischievous wit and restive charm; but above all she loved the fact that Helen *believed* her. Helen was the only person, besides Áine Daly, who she could confide in about the cures. It didn't bother Maeve that Helen teased her about 'black magic'; what mattered was that, since the curing of her warts, Helen seemed to trust and need her, making her feel less lonely in the world, less strange in her thoughts, less possessed by a claim to follow the call, minding sick people and mending harm. One of Maeve's secret fantasies was that one day she might share the cures with Helen too so that, when the faraway war was over, they might travel the world and be healers together.

Mondays were the special time for Irish. That was the bargain and they kept it. Maeve sat with Helen in the parlor — while Mr and Mrs Flynn worked in the grocery — and taught her brand new phrases each time. Maeve began with words for sea and weather. *Tápholl* for the calm between two turns of a tide, when currents met and changed direction; *Buáilteog* for a shaft of light on the wrong side of the sun, announcing bad weather; *Tine shionnáigh* for a special light by the shore on dark nights when the slick of fish and seaweed met. And many more. But Helen was less interested in sea words than in learning Irish curses and jokes. She loved reciting bold phrases like *Go n-ithe an chráin mhíolach thú*: 'May a flea-ridden sow eat you alive!' Or *Go bhfana an bhuinneach choíche ort*: 'May you suffer from runny pooh.' Or Helen's favorite of all, which she had Maeve repeat several times until she'd learned it off by heart: *Clúmh ar do pholl, míola id chraiceann is gearb ar do ghabhal*: 'Hair on your bottom, lice on your skin and scabs all over your itchy crotch!' And there were other saucier sayings Maeve uttered in Irish but told Helen she could not translate — teasing things about lovers' lusts that islanders always kept to themselves. Helen would whine in protest, but Maeve wouldn't yield. When it came to Gaelic, she was in power. And Maeve could be bossy too, saying she'd only teach Helen curses if she also learned blessings. Since they both loved dogs, their preferred one was *saol gadhair agus sláinte an bhradáin chugat — croí folláin agus gob fliuch*: 'A dog's life and a salmon's health to you — a good heart and a wet mouth.' Such phrases wouldn't be much use to Helen in her grammar exams, but they amused her no end.

The more Maeve taught Helen Irish, the more she longed to share her island. She wanted to bring her to Brigid's Well and teach her how to harvest wild roots and sea weeds, to introduce her to Bawn and stroll the cliffs of the Dún and the shore. But there were always obstacles. Anytime Maeve asked Mam if Helen could visit, the answer was no. *Níl ciaróg agus fuiseog in nead céine* — beetles and larks don't nest together. And when Maeve protested that it wasn't fair — that she was invited to Helen's every week but could never invite her back — Mam threatened to forbid her going to Flynn's altogether. Maeve wondered what her mother meant by beetles and larks. Was it that Helen was rich with mainland English and she was poor with island Irish? Or that Mam was trying to protect her, fearful of her being hurt, of losing her? Or was she just jealous? Maeve didn't ask and she didn't fight. The mood in the house was bad enough and she didn't want to make things worse. It was still so hard with her father gone and loneliness creeping from every door. Connie and Seán shunned Maeve at every turn and thought only of escaping to America, while Mam sank further into madness.

The brothers finally flew the nest, one after another. Fly-away-Peter, fly-away-Paul. No sooner had Seán reached eighteen that April than he got a ticket in steerage to Boston — paid for by relatives on their father's side who'd fled the local hunger as youngsters and sailed from Bantry on a cargo ship. America was now rising from the Depression and there were new opportunities to be had in the cities. Within two months of his arrival, Seán managed to send enough money back for Connie to follow in June, first to Boston, then on to Dayton, Ohio. Connie wrote a postcard home saying he was delighted to be in the town where the Wright brothers had invented airplanes. But Maeve smiled when she read it, thinking it was another of Connie's yarns, like when, as a boy, he swore he saw Lindbergh fly over Brigid's Island on his way from Newfoundland to Normandy. Four thousand miles in a single seat engine, without stopping once. Connie's childhood fantasy. But when a second envelope arrived with the same Ohio postmark, Maeve realized it must be true: he'd gone to Dayton after all, and was working as an apprentice Air Force mechanic. She wrote back asking if he could make a trunk call to her at Flynn's. She sent the telephone number, but Connie never rang. In fact, Maeve never heard from her brothers again.

After the boys left, the skin on Mam's face grew rougher by the week. She rarely washed and withdrew deep inside herself, though she always wanted Maeve about the house. She began resenting any extra bit of time Maeve spent with the Flynns in the village and depended on her for every household chore, cleaning and cooking, milking and churning, and most of all — since her eyesight got poor — for reading aloud by the oil lamp at night. Especially the 'news from Connie and Seán': letters which Maeve herself secretly wrote and folded in an envelope with sender addresses from America.

The Dalys helped out as best they could. With the boys gone, Dan took on the ploughing of the Sullivans' two acres, while Áine took care of the poultry and sheering. They were tireless. Unlike the McCarthys who were never there when you needed them; and if any farming or fishing tool went missing, you knew where to find it. Things were made worse when meat and eggs became scarce after the chickens died of flu in late August, shortly after England took to the skies against Germany — there was more fuss over the chickens than the War — and soon there were only two goats and a few meagre crops to keep Maeve and Mam fed, along with the odd string of herring the Dalys sent their way.

Dan was a blessing during that long hot summer, often taking Maeve out in the yawl while Mam took her afternoon naps. Well trained by her father, Maeve could stomach high seas with no bother. She helped Dan bait the traps and hoist the ropes, binding crab claws with twine as she listened to his yarns about lobsters — how they could taste things with their feet, smell things miles away and talk to each other by peeing in each other's faces. Dan explained how people ate lobsters who ate urchins who ate kelp, holding a big blue lobster in one hand and a fresh urchin in the other. No matter how worried Maeve felt about her mother, Dan knew how to cheer her up. And though she sometimes smelt drink off him sitting windward, she knew she was always safe. Dan cared for her, unlike Tadhg McCarthy who made her quail with his shifty leers and sly moves, forever on the make for an extra half-acre of land, or a quick shilling from a bit of stolen salvage. Though he'd never crossed the line while Michael was alive, Tadhg found a new swagger after the drowning. He was younger and stronger than Dan. And Maeve feared the day he might be the last man on the island.

The day before returning to school in September, Maeve walked with Bawn to the top of the Dún. Surrounded by vetch and ox-eyes, she gazed at trawlers on the horizon, not quite sure whether their hulls were getting bigger or smaller, approaching or sailing away, as rolling waves rocked the masts and fulmar petrels crossed the bows. Standing on the crest of the cliff, she remembered the times she'd waited for her father to come home from long hauls — prow low in the water if the catch was good, high if it was poor — and she recalled how, as a child, she'd run down the beach to greet him as he'd hoist her up in his brawny arms and name every gleaming fish in the nets — haddock and hake, cod and ling, skate and turbot, John Dory and brill — as they sorted them into boxes and sang their favorite song:

> *Dance for your Daddy my little lassie*
> *Dance for your Daddy my little one*
> *You shall have a fishy on your little dishy,*
> *you shall have a fishy when the boat comes home,*
> *you shall have an apple, you shall have a plum,*
> *you shall have a pear, when the boat comes home.*

But as the sun dipped and a bitter chill wind blew in from the east, sweet memories were chased by black thoughts. Where had her father gone when he drowned? Down to the bottom with the yawl and gear, his blucher boots snagged on riggings and ropes? Down to the darkest pit of the sea to be eaten away by dogfish and crabs? *Madra éisc agus portáin.* Bottom feeders, quick eaters, they didn't leave much behind on the bone. And no way of knowing 'twas him at all were it not for the stitching on the salvaged tweed. Or was he carried by currents and tides to faraway rocks where gulls preyed on his flesh? God forbid! Maeve hated thinking such things, but the images kept coming as she stared out to sea, like riptides drawing her down into a hole.

Maeve descended from the Dún to the well and prayed to Brigid to rid her of such thoughts. Her father was dead and buried now; let him rest in peace, she begged, and not return like the ghosts of Staic Séipéil, darkly keening in the black of night, strange airs coming in off the sea. *Port na bpúcaí*. Like other drowned islanders before him, phantoms no one spoke of anymore, for what could one say? The wounds were too deep.

III

BETWEEN WORLDS
September 1940-July 1941

Púca poill–púca mushroom

'After you.' The boy stood aside to let Maeve and Helen pass into the hall. He was tall and intent, like Connie the day he left for America; only with a softer accent and fancier clothes. Starched collar, cotton shirt and tan leather shoes; and a strange whiff of iodine, like the kind Maeve smelled off the kelp in the Brú, only sharper, more antiseptic. She liked him from the start, especially his eyes, blue as a mackerel's back.

'Foreign,' Helen whispered as they entered the Rowing Club. 'He's the doctor's son.'

'Sounds English,' Maeve said.

'Yes, a bit.' Helen nodded. 'Josie Hayes says his father's a Dubliner who went to London and married an Englishwoman. They moved back to Ireland to escape the War.' Helen plucked a peppermint from her purse and slipped it to Maeve. 'Freshen our breaths.' She winked. 'Handsome, isn't he?'

'I suppose.' Maeve pocketed the mint. 'What age, do you think?'

'Eighteen, Josie says. And Josie knows. He'll be doing his Matric with the Salesian Brothers in Skib.' Helen gave Maeve a poke and a wink. 'Too old for you though. And way too tall.'

They hung their coats in the Ladies and took their seats at a card table. Maeve felt awkward, not used to gatherings like this. Keelbeg Rowing Club was the one place in the village where boys and girls could meet, in summer for gigs and dances, in winter for card and board games — bridge, chess, gin rummy, twenty-one. The games were organised on Fridays after class by teachers from the local schools, Catholic and Protestant; membership fees went to good causes like widower charities and homes for unwed mothers.

Maeve waved to Miss Collins, who was standing by the food table, decked with sandwiches and lemonade, chatting away to a Presbyterian teacher from Leap while the pupils bent over their game boards, more keen on competing than talking.

Helen took a chair beside the doctor's son and beckoned Maeve to join them.

'I'm Helen Flynn,' she announced. 'And you?'

'Seamus Kennedy,' he replied, looking up from his cards.

'This is Maeve Sullivan,' said Helen, coaxing her friend to come closer.

'How do you do?' Seamus Kennedy rose and shook hands, first with Helen, then Maeve, before sitting down again.

Maeve was taken by how polite he was. He had the hands of a girl with the grip of a boy. And that medical scent. She already had questions queuing in her head. Had he learned prescriptions from his father? Could he tell chemicals that harmed from chemicals that healed? Or pronounce the Latin names? Or dispense them?

'I live on the village square,' said Helen. 'My parents run the grocery and pub. Victuals, Wine and Spirits, to be precise. You can't miss it. Drop in if you need anything.' Helen nodded at Maeve. 'And my friend here, Maeve Sullivan, lives by the sea.

You can drop in anytime… for a *swim*.' Helen laughed at her own joke, elbowing Maeve, who looked away, embarrassed.

'Good to know.' Seamus grinned before picking up the deck of cards. He shuffled and cut. 'Shall we play?'

'What?' Maeve asked, getting a word in at last.

'Twenty-one.'

'My favorite.' Helen rubbed her hands. 'Maeve's too.'

'Is that right?' Seamus looked at Maeve.

She nodded, though she'd never played the game.

'And where do *you* live, Seamus Kennedy?' Helen tilted her head, taking cards from the deck and fanning them wide. She peeked cheekily over the top.

'The old Rectory. We've just arrived.'

'The Rectory,' Helen mused. 'Are you Protestant?'

'You're rather forward.' Seamus smiled. 'Actually my mother's Protestant, my father's Catholic.'

'Digging with both feet.' Helen laughed, then changed the subject. 'I heard you can drive?'

'Word travels fast.' Seamus fished a packet of Gold Flake from his pocket and lit up, the flame brightening his face.

Maeve watched him inhale. The dark blue eyes and lovely mouth. She liked how he managed Helen's brazenness.

Helen shrugged. 'My father owns a car — Austin 6 — but he won't let me drive.' She brushed away Seamus's smoke, pretending to be annoyed.

Seamus turned to Maeve. 'Your friend's not sixteen yet?'

'Oh she is, she's seventeen, but she hasn't her license.' Maeve tried to think of something else to say. 'She's a good singer though. And a great dancer.'

Helen looked up from her cards, tucking a Queen behind a

Knave. 'Maeve's a dancer too, so she is. Learned jigs on her island, foxtrots from me.'

'Do you live on an island?' Seamus tapped the dog-eared deck on the table and waited for a reply.

'I do, mostly.' Maeve tucked a cuff to hide her scar. 'Weekdays I go to Helen's after school. Weekends I'm on the island.'

'I'd like to live on an island. I love the sea. I love to sail.'

'Have you a boat?' asked Maeve.

'My father does. A ketch, two-master, great for these waters.'

'I know these waters well. My island's surrounded by them.'

'You've *two* homes so — island and village?' Seamus smiled. 'Like me in a way. Last year London, this year Cork.'

Maeve liked the idea of moving between places, but before she'd time to say so, Helen cast her cards on the table. 'Can we go for a spin in your car?' She gazed at Seamus, cocking her chin.

Maeve blushed, thinking Helen too brash. They'd just sat down. They couldn't leave now. What would Miss Collins and the others say?

'Where would you like to go?' asked Seamus.

'To the Pictures,' Helen said.

'In Skibbereen or Clonakilty?'

'Depends what you like. *Philadelphia Story* or *Stella Dallas*.'

'I've seen both,' said Seamus.

'Where?'

'In London.'

'So have I,' said Helen.

'Where?'

'In Cork. They've everything in Cork.' She mimed a snooty pout. 'But I'd go again, so I would. I *love* Katharine Hepburn.'

'I've seen neither,' Maeve confessed.

'We'll have to fix that, won't we Seamus?' Helen raised an eyebrow.

'I'll leave it to you,' replied Seamus, before turning back to Maeve and looking her in the eye; but not long enough for her to flinch. 'You know,' he said after a pause, 'I think you're the spit of Barbara Stanwyck.'

Maeve peered at her cards, red as the queen of hearts.

'The men are gorgeous,' said Helen to Maeve, not missing a beat. 'Cary Grant and Douglas Fairbanks. Fine looking fellas. But I don't want to ruin things. You'll see for yourself, Maeve.' Helen curled a lock behind her ear. 'So what'll it be?'

Seamus inspected his hand. 'Clubs for Clonakilty, spades for Skibbereen.' He slipped a card from the pack and placed it on the table. Face up.

Jack of spades.

'Skib it is.'

On the Feast of the Annunciation, Maeve and her mother sailed from the island and got a lift to Mass on Joe Hayes' cart. Passing the Co-Op at Reen, the stench of dung was so strong Maeve took a sprig of heather from her pocket and patted her coat. Few birds sang and the foxgloves seemed half asleep as they made their way to the church. The hedgerows were draped in a shawl of mist and the dogs along the way kept their heads down. Even the cows east of the Creamery were sitting flat in the fields as swallows flew low over their heads. Rain on the way. By the time they reached the church it was drizzling so thick they went straight inside. The men were already taking seats at the back while women and children headed for the front. Maeve and Mam sat in the middle.

Waiting for the priest, Maeve wished she was with her father in the Brú, with candles flaming and the smell of fresh tobacco, rather than this reek of stale incense. She recalled her father's old phrase about the curing shed — *Ar scáth a chéile a mhaireann na daoine*: a shelter to gather in each other's shadow. She still missed him so badly. Maeve peered down at her boots, shabby-looking beside the shiny patent shoes of the other girls. Everyone sported their Sunday best.

As she folded her hands and closed her eyes, she suddenly felt a faint heat on her skin: a gentle glow in the small of her back rising up the curve of her spine until it became a quick flame on her neck. She didn't look around. She didn't need to. She knew. Seamus Kennedy was looking at her.

As Father Kehoe approached the altar, Maeve felt a nudge and turned to find Helen standing in the aisle. She wanted to sit in beside her.

In nomine Patris, et Filii, et Spiritus Sancti.

Everyone bowed as priest and altar boys, in scarlet soutanes and surplices, intoned the Confiteor. Maeve loved the sound of Latin, which Miss Collins told the class was great for 'education.' You needed it for Law, Medicine and Religion. You couldn't be a doctor, priest or solicitor without it — the Three Wise Kings of every Irish town.

Confiteor Deo omnipotenti
Beatae Mariae semper Virgini
Beato Michaeli Archangelo

As Father Kehoe read the Gospel, Maeve pictured the scene in her head. The Annunciation of the Angel. Mary about her age with eyes dark as Barbara Stanwyck in *Stella Dallas*. Gabriel a handsome young fellow arriving out of nowhere, a cross between Seamus Kennedy and Douglas Fairbanks. Maeve could feel Mary's worry — 'she was troubled and pondered,' the Gospel said — but was glad she said yes in the end.

Dominus sit in corde meo.

The reading over, Father Kehoe put his lips to the Missal and, replacing the crimson page marker, made his way to the pulpit.

'Today's Gospel' — he peered at his people — 'speaks of a special kind of devotion. Holy devotion. Mary had a child without knowing another man. She conceived Jesus in purity. Through the Holy Spirit. And she did it because she herself was conceived without sin. Mary was immaculate.'

The priest folded his hands on his tummy as if he was the one expecting a baby. His eyes bulged behind full moon glasses.

'Now some people get confused, so they do. It's natural. But let me explain. The miracle was this: Jesus was born without sin. Like his mother before him. They were both sinless. Spotless. Mother and son. *Sine macula*. Immaculate.'

'And what about Jesus' granny?' Helen whispered to Maeve. 'Mary's mummy? Was *she* spotless too?'

Maeve shushed Helen with a raised finger.

'Immaculate!' repeated Father Kehoe, brushing a speck of spit from his lip. 'Mary is pure. She preserves morals and wards off temptation.' He stared down from the pulpit as if expecting the faithful to blush. 'On this special Feast today, may I say to all the young ladies here present — make the Virgin Mary your example. A woman conceived without sin. A woman who conceived without shame. Let her, and her alone, be your guide.'

Father Kehoe swung full circle and, his back to the congregation, walked from the pulpit to the altar.

Maeve touched her neck chain, thoughts buzzing like bees in a jar. She raised her head. What did Father Kehoe know? If Mary was the model, where was she when you needed her? Where was she for all the 'unwed mothers'? Where was she for the likes of Elsie Casey who'd worked as a maid for Captain Rynn in Rosscarbery only to disappear with child one day, never to return? Or for all the other poor unfortunates who, as Josie Hayes put it, 'let their drawers down and went the whole hog,' desperate creatures who had to give up their babies and wash laundry in the Convent of the Good Shepherd? Branded 'spoiled goods' after. Or, worse still, the fallen ones who never even made it to convent laundries, making their babies disappear all on their own or swimming out to sea altogether. The truly forsaken. The hopeless cases. If only they'd turned to Brigid instead, *Muire na nGael*. Their own Mary. That's what her father told her. Brigid was already in Bethlehem helping Mary give birth to Jesus when no one else cared. She was always there for unmarried mothers and unwanted babies. Wasn't she? Maeve put a hand to her belly, pondering. Was she there for the Casey girl? And for all the others lost to 'temptation'? Surely. Yes. She must have been there, warming their bodies with her woolen shawl, covering their heads with soft mist and clouds, blessing them with water, comforting them with her gentle winds. Surely, just like her father said. But she wasn't there when the boat went down, was she? She hadn't saved the pilgrims, had she? Why had she let her father drown? Why had she saved only Maeve?

As the congregation knelt, Maeve put a hand on her mother's

hand. Mam sat mutely beside her, not responding, not reciting any of the prayers, shoulders curved inward as she fingered her beads. The same intent look she'd have sewing by the fire, lace spread over the hollow of her lap as she guided thread through the needle's eye. Maeve felt a wave of pity and pride. In spite of her mother's sadness, there was loveliness yet in her high cheekbones and brown eyes — features her father always praised and which never shone brightly since the day he died. Wasn't she another kind of Mary, giving everything for love of a stranger? Devoted to a man who'd be taken from her? Going into exile, giving him children, loving him madly 'til the day he departed — and not being able to live without him.

Father Kehoe adjusted his chasuble and poured the cruets into the chalice. Water and wine. Poor ingredients. No maidenhair or fungi. Poor priest, Maeve thought, as he bent and touched the altar with his forehead, chanting the Sanctus. Holy, Holy, Holy. Poor people. If they knew what they were missing.

Maeve tapped her chest three times and counted the minutes to Communion, hoping Seamus Kennedy was admiring the curls she'd brushed twice that morning and the skirt she'd ironed with a wet hot pan. As the priest placed consecrated hosts on a paten, Maeve managed to glance around. And sure enough there he was, Seamus, sitting with his father a few pews back. So alike, the two of them — same high brow and Roman nose, same quiet confidence and calm. And the hands, so pale compared to the rough fists of the island men. And Doctor Kennedy's missing finger. Was it true, she wondered, what Mrs Flynn said about him losing it — his ring finger — in a car accident? And him still a grand healer, curing her slipped disc with deft shifting of bones and medicines from England? Glimpsing them there, father and son in the polished pew, Maeve wondered what they'd make of her own father's cures — nettles for rheumatism, bladder wrack for burns, fennel for asthma, watercress for croup? Maybe she'd get a chance to ask someday. But where was Mrs Kennedy? At the Protestant service in Ross? Digging with the other foot?

Maeve bowed as Father Kehoe lifted the Host and the altar boys rang their bells; before she knew it, she was stepping out into the aisle and following Helen up to the rails, behind the heels of her friend's gleaming shoes. And when Maeve knelt for Communion she found herself imagining something utterly strange: Jesus pulling a heart from his chest and placing it deep into hers.

'This is my body and this is my blood.'

She opened her mouth to receive the host.

'*Corpus Christi.*'

And when she rose from the altar there he was — Seamus Kennedy, oh so lovely — right beside her. Their eyes met. Her heart flared.

The Mass was ended.

Ite, missa est.

It was blowing hard when they exited the church, a bitter gale whipping in from the East. Father Kehoe stood in the archway as the faithful filed past, gripping his stole for fear it might fly off. Helen slipped furtively by, but Maeve got caught.

'How's Maeve Sullivan?' The priest leaned close enough for her to catch his meaty breath. She had a cure for that — meadowsweet — and vowed to slip some in his tea next time he visited the island.

Maeve looked around, buttoning up her coat as people hurried to buggies and hacks. There was no sign of Helen. Or Seamus. Only her mother walking towards her.

Then she spotted Flynn's brown Austin idling at the curb.

Mr Flynn lowered a window and kindly greeted Maeve and her mother. 'I wish we could chat,' he said, 'but we're lunching with the Kennedys.' Mrs Flynn sat beside him with Helen in the back.

'Eldon hotel, so we can't be late,' added Mr Flynn. He reached a hand through the window as Mam shuffled forward, brushing her palm down the side of her coat as if ironing out wrinkles before taking his hand.

Maeve held her breath, not sure what Mam might say.

'We're delighted with Maeve's visits.' Mrs Flynn spoke from the passenger seat.

'That's so,' said Mam with a half-smile, trying to hide her stained teeth and fastening her scarf against the cold. 'Safe journey.'

'I hope *your* journey is safe too,' said Mr Flynn. 'And shorter than Father Kehoe's sermon!' He smiled and spun the steering wheel, pressing firmly down on the pedal. 'Sorry we can't drive you to Myross.'

'We'll be grand.' Maeve breathed relief.

'Right so,' said Mr Flynn, tipping his hat while Mrs Flynn raised a hand to her mantilla, and Helen, with a wave, sank back into her upholstered seat.

Maeve waved at Helen and didn't take her eyes off the car as it sped up the Skibbereen road. She felt a bump in her throat and found it hard to swallow. In one hour's time, the Flynns and the Kennedys would be sharing Sunday dinner in the Eldon Hotel, while she and Mam went home to their island.

Maeve sat on Trá an Poul, resting after a long swim. She stared at her feet on the tide line, toes playing with the soft red dulse, then looked out to sea. Sun sky high. June glare. She masked her eyes against the glittering waves.

Something large stirred on the water, looming through the haze. A two-master ketch was mooring off the beach.

Chains rattled, followed by a splash; and before Maeve knew it a punt was being lowered from the deck and making its way toward the shore. Who was it? Rates men coming for the rates? Father Kehoe calling for dues? Pilgrims looking for cures, defying the ban after all this time?

She rose to her feet and was turning for home when she heard someone call — 'Maeve!'

It was Seamus. He had come with his family.

Maeve brushed her curls back, salty-stiff after her swim in the Sound, and buttoned up her shirt, a threadbare hand-me-down from the Daly girls. She didn't want Seamus seeing the freckles on her arms or noticing how small her breasts were.

As the boat touched shore, Maeve approached the bow and offered a hand to Mrs Kennedy, first up and ready to land.

Next came Seamus, waving Maeve gently aside. 'Don't get yourself wet.' He was followed by his young brother, Ben.

'*Fáilte romhaibh go hOileán Bhríde*,' she greeted them.

'*Go raibh maith agat*,' answered Dr. Kennedy in stiff Gaelic, stepping onto the beach after his wife and two sons. 'I apologise for my Irish. I was schooled before the new state. Just the odd phrase.' He bowed. 'But when in Rome do as the Romans.'

'This is hardly Rome, Doctor.' Maeve waved a hand about her.

'Maybe it is finer still,' said Dr. Kennedy. 'I hear there are places here as holy as the Vatican.' He smiled at the comparison, removing his cap.

Mrs Kennedy smiled too and asked Seamus and Ben to fetch the picnic from the stern of the punt. The sun beat down as the boys handed things over the gunnel. Herring gulls hovered above them, protesting the invasion.

Maeve held Bawn by the scruff of the neck, trying to stop him sniffing the visitors.

Everything ashore, Dr. Kennedy straightened his back and peered at the path leading up to the bluff. 'We'd like to picnic at Brigid's Well.'

Maeve was taken aback, surprised they knew about the well. She gave Seamus a look, wondering if Helen had said something.

'Is it far?' the doctor asked.

'Not at all. A few furlongs over the fields.'

'Could you show us the way?'

'Of course. There's a short cut through the pasture.'

'Excellent,' Dr Kennedy replied. 'The tide is ebbing, and time is tight.'

She nodded before leading the way.

The Kennedys followed Maeve along the sheep path, Bawn herding them on. They passed between the flowering shoots of the potato drills onto Gortadubh, the pasture of thick grass where Dan's piebald ponies grazed, swooshing hairbrush tails against flies. Seamus and Ben, sporting collarless shirts with roll-up sleeves, trailed several paces behind. Seamus warded off mock tackles from his brother with a mixture of annoyance and play.

Whenever Maeve looked back, Seamus looked away, but when she looked ahead, speaking with Dr and Mrs Kennedy, she could feel Seamus's gaze on her back, the heat stealing up the small of her spine through the slope of her neck to the tip of her head.

What would Helen think? Maeve wished she was here but was glad she wasn't.

Mrs Kennedy looked somewhat out of place in her light linen dress and sun umbrella. She moved closer to Maeve, until they were side by side. 'Thanks for showing us the way. If it wasn't for you we'd be wandering in circles.' A foreign lilt rustled at the hem of her words.

'I'm glad to help.' Maeve breathed in Mrs Kennedy's jasmine scent, and was soon responding to her many questions — about life on the island, weather in winter, farming and fish yields, what the islanders ate.

'We've lots of lobsters,' Maeve said, loosening up. 'Buckets of them. So many that when we empty the pots and row around the island they're already full again. They fetch a grand price on the Skibbereen market. Though we call them *bia na mBocht*. Poor man's grub.' Maeve tossed a grass stalk in the air. 'Some call them *francaigh na farraige*, sea rats, because they eat anything. Gobbling away on the floor of the sea. But I think they look beautiful.'

'I always found it strange' — Mrs Kennedy paused, taking in the vast blue sea — 'how so many died of hunger with all those lobsters and crabs to eat.' She sighed before moving on.

Maeve gazed at the ocean and thought of her people, all the folk from Myross, Ardra and Cooscroneen, way back when the potatoes rotted and the boats were sold off for whatever morsels money could buy. All the coasts stripped naked of mussels and clams. Not a frond of kelp or dulse to be had. One bare tideline as far as the eye could see.

The group walked on in silence until Mrs Kennedy fetched a book from her bag — *A Guide to British Flora and Fungi*. She handed it to Seamus who opened the elegant calfskin and leafed through the pages. He soon started naming plants he saw along the way — tufted vetch, meadowsweet, milk thistle, ragwort — matching each flower with the image in the book. Everywhere about them bracken and heather danced in the breeze as wild gorse exploded in grenades of yellow flame. Seamus plucked a flower from the top of a gorse bush and crushed it in his fingers. 'Coconut. Smells of coconut, see?'

Maeve leaned close and inhaled. 'Hmmm. I never smelled coconut before. Smells like gorse to me! I love it and, you know, it just keeps growing no matter how much you cut it back.'

'Like brambles,' said Mrs Kennedy, amused. 'Or montbretia. Invasive species. Imported from South Africa. Takes over everything. Weeds really.'

'I like weeds,' said Maeve. 'They last longer, even when you think they're dead.' Then spotting a ring of white caps growing near a cow pat, Maeve exclaimed: 'Púcaí!'

'Púcaí?' Mrs Kennedy frowned. 'What's that?'

'*Pucaí poill*. Look,' Maeve knelt down and cupped the stems in her hand. 'There, by your feet. Careful not to step on them. They're my favorites. *Bia Bhríde*. Brigid's food. They're grand for cures. Especially for moods.'

'What kind of moods?' asked Seamus.

'The Sadness mainly. And the nerves.'

'I'm afraid not, young lady,' interrupted Dr Kennedy with a knowing smile. 'They're poisonous, actually.' He borrowed the Guide book from Seamus and leafed through the pages until he found the right one. '*Psilocybe semilanceata*,' he read aloud. 'Toxic mushrooms found in large numbers in pastures, upland fringes and commons. The bell-shaped cap is olive grey with a central nipple. The wavy stem is slender with a distinct blue-green base.'

'That's it,' said Seamus, taking the book back from his father and bending down for a closer look, comparing the illustration with the real thing. He plucked a thin stem, turning it upside down. 'See, the blue at the root.'

'And the tiny hat,' chimed Mrs Kennedy. 'Charming. Like a bowler.'

Maeve knew they were wrong. All wrong. For years she'd seen her father use the dried gills of púcaí to comfort people suffering from the Sadness. It worked every time. They might poison the English, but they cured the Irish.

Maeve said nothing, not wishing to be difficult. She just walked on beside Seamus, reciting the Gaelic for each new flower he was naming from the Guide — *airgead luachra, lus na mban sí, slálus mór* — until they were like foreigners speaking different tongues to each other. Not another word about *púcaí*.

'Quite the scholars, aren't you?' offered Mrs Kennedy after a while. 'We're hoping to make a shrubbery in the garden this summer. Maybe you'll come and help us, Maeve?'

Maeve nodded and was about to say something about the healing power of meadowsweet — surely everyone could agree on meadowsweet? — when Mrs Kennedy grew anxious. She put a hand to her wide straw hat and looked up. A soft rumbling filled the air. What was it? she asked. Planes flying overhead? The Luftwaffe spying on convoys from Canada? Or friendly Spitfires — Mrs Kennedy stared at the clouds — 'Maybe it's my brother Will,' she mused, 'up in the sky, protecting us.'

But Maeve didn't look up, knowing well where the sound was coming from. A muffled thunder rose from the ground. The slow beat of underground drums.

'Cattle,' she said, pointing to a herd of bullocks cantering down the field. The Kennedys waited, not sure what to do as the herd of stocky beasts drew near, surrounding them.

Maeve stood and faced the cattle, raising her hands in a sign of Brigid. '*Amach libh anois — buail abhaile*,' she cried.

And the young bulls stopped straight in their tracks — every one of them — lowering their horned heads to the ground. Maeve stroked the tufted crowns before the bullocks turned and lumbered up the field.

'Thank God!' Mrs Kennedy stroked her pearl brooch. 'Thank God for you, Maeve Sullivan.'

'What did you do'? Seamus asked, eyeing the steer vanish over the hill.

'I made the sign of Brigid,' said Maeve, repeating the gesture slowly with her hands. 'Animals understand.'

Maeve led the visitors further south on the island until they came to the bluff above the cave. A sharp smell of sea wrack greeted them as they descended the sheep path in single file. When they reached the strand, Maeve pointed to the hole in the cliff. 'That's it,' she said. 'Brigid's Well.'

As the Kennedys unpacked the picnic by the cave, Maeve went to fetch water from the well.

'I'll help,' offered Seamus, accompanying her with a jug.

'Hot day,' she paused at the entrance and stared up at the sun.

'Summer solstice.' Seamus nodded.

'Close, John's day. We call it *Púca Sheáin*. Always great for the pilgrims. In the old days this beach was full of boats.'

'Don't they come anymore?' asked Seamus.

Maeve shook her head.

'Why?'

'Because they closed the well. I'm the only one comes here now.' She turned to Seamus. 'See those marks.' She pointed to the initials carved on the rock.

Seamus leaned in to get a better look. 'What are they?'

'Names.' She stroked the letters with her fingers. 'People lost crossing from the mainland. My father was the skipper. I was beside him. Everyone drowned.' She paused. 'Except me.'

Seamus stared at the marks.

'The sea took them.'

'I'm sorry.' Seamus reached a hand towards Maeve but didn't touch her. 'It must be hard.'

'It is,' she said, walking into the cave.

He followed.

They could see nothing at first. Sheer black after the blazing light.

'*Fan nóiméad*,' whispered Maeve. 'Listen.'

They both stood, all ears, until they could hear the faint trickle of water and see shapes slowly emerging from the shadows.

Seamus took a step toward the mossy slab. 'No statues?'

'No. Nobody knows what Brigid looked like. She's not someone you see. She's not someone at all actually, a particular person, though she's present when someone heals someone else. More like a power inside you or a presence around you, a feeling, like water or clouds or the wind.'

Maeve moved closer to the spring and put a finger to the Brigid straw hanging from the rock. 'It's all we've got.' She brushed her thumb over the rough thatch before bending towards the pool and scooping water into her palms.

'It's sweet,' she took a sip before offering some to Seamus.

He placed his hands under hers and sipped.

Maeve wondered what he was thinking as he drank. That his father's medicines were different than hers?

'You're right,' he said, lifting his lips from the bowl of her hands. 'It is sweet.'

And then she felt it — *scrimplini* — the little flame flashing behind her eyes as heat rose from the soles of her feet, up through the muscles of her back until it warmed the skin of her face.

She turned to Seamus and asked him to repeat the Irish blessing after her — *Moladh Bhríde* — as they stood there, breathing each other's breaths. Then they filled the pitcher and returned to the others.

It was a grand picnic. Pork pies, spiced beef sandwiches and carrot cake served with cutlery and lace napkins. The Kennedys knew how to lay it on. Maeve wasn't hungry but she ate anyway, never taking her eyes off Seamus, his mackerel blue eyes and dark black hair. She watched, and kept watching, hoping no one noticed, looking away and looking back, at the way his fringe fell over his forehead as he chewed thoughtfully and laughed between bites, the way he said please and thank you, and went into a little trance when he stared out to sea as if expecting to see someone appear on the horizon. Maeve knew that feeling too. She feasted on every gesture and move. She was drawn to him like a tide, a current or force that couldn't be stopped. Maeve finally lowered her eyes to the sand. Embarrassed. She tried to think of something else, of someone else. Maybe Helen was right, maybe Seamus was handsomer than Douglas Fairbanks after all.

After lunch, Dr Kennedy took a copy of the *Illustrated London News* from the picnic basket, and sitting on the strand with his trouser legs rolled, began to read out headlines to Mrs Kennedy. Uninterested, Seamus and Ben stripped to the waist and ran to the sea, diving head first into the waves and racing each other to Carraignanam. Maeve watched from shore as they ploughed the waves before scrambling up the black rocks where they shook like spaniels, laughing, before jumping back in. When they surfaced again, Ben was shouting. He'd struck a reef.

Dr and Mrs Kennedy were off on a stroll, so Maeve was alone as the boys came ashore. She helped Seamus examine Ben's injury: a deep gash running from the ankle bone to the toes. It was bleeding badly and, Seamus said, needed stitches; but there weren't any needles or sutures to be had. Leaving Seamus to rinse the wound, Maeve ran to the end of the strand and quickly returned with a handful of wrack. Bending down she wrapped coils of thong weed around Ben's heel, strapping the fronds tight as boot laces. She patted his foot. Neatly bound. Job done. 'That should get you home for now.'

Returning through the fields, Maeve asked the Kennedys if they'd like something to eat. 'My mother bakes scones for John's day.'

Seamus was keen to accept but Dr. Kennedy insisted they get Ben home for 'proper stitches.'

Maeve was hurt that Dr Kennedy treated her weed poultice so lightly but was relieved her invitation to tea was declined. She didn't really want the Kennedys visiting her dingy house cramped between the Dalys and McCarthys like a limpet stuck between rocks, without a dab of whitewash since her father died. Not to mention Mam's moods and the stench of dung in the front yard. And though Maeve was proud of the door bell — pure bronze — she feared Mam might make a show of that too, confessing it was salvaged from the wreck off Sheeps Head.

How Maeve dearly wished that her father was there — to

show them his yawl and talk about cures going back hundreds of years and feed them fat lobsters from his pots, heaving in the ropes like only a man who has sea in his bones can do. *Mianach na farraige*.

Back at the north beach, Seamus turned to Maeve as he hauled in the mooring. 'There's a regatta on Sunday.' He glanced through his fringe.

Maeve tried to think what Barbara Stanwyck might say to Douglas Fairbanks; but she wasn't Helen and they weren't at the pictures. She'd no real airs for that sort of thing.

'Thank you,' she said, 'but I can't. I promised to spend the night with Helen.'

'Helen could come too.' Seamus grinned, threading the mooring as he coaxed the dinghy to shore. 'You could both come.'

Maeve was surprised. 'I'll ask her.'

'Do that and let me know.' Seamus touched her arm lightly before helping his parents into the boat.

Having seen the Kennedys off, Maeve walked home through the fields. Her body was shaking from the touch. She hoped Seamus hadn't noticed.

Noon the following Sunday, Maeve and Helen gazed down from Glandore boat club onto the bay. A brace of One Oars were crossing the line.

'Seamus!' cried Helen out loud, waving both arms in the air, as Maeve stood and stared by her side.

Seamus shipped oars and reclined in his boat, acknowledging Helen's greeting as his feet trailed in the water. Union Hall had shaved it, Bantry a close second. Scarce a length between them. The rowing race was decided; the dinghy class still to go.

Maeve put a hand to her bushy hair, shielding it from the blustery wind. Clouds scudded across the sky, casting shadows on the tall masted Dragons slinking to and fro in the bay as two-master ketches loitered by the Race Buoy and a flotilla of motor vessels patrolled the start line. All so elegant and polished, Maeve thought, compared to the tar-stained yawls on her island, rubby dubby smattered on the hull, with never a chance for racing or sport. There were boats and boats.

Mr Flynn stood beside Maeve and Helen, talking with Captain Rynn, Commodore of the Yacht Club. The girls looked like slim volumes wedged between holders. Mr Flynn dabbed his face with a kerchief and congratulated the Captain on a fine regatta, before changing the subject to Hitler's invasion of Russia. 'All far away, granted, but one can never be sure how Jerry might turn. East or West, one never knows.' Mr Flynn inspected the crowd as if looking for German spies. 'Maybe England next? Or Scotland? Or Godforsaken Wales? And then what? Maybe ourselves, Lord forbid. Even Dev couldn't stop them!'

Mr Flynn did most of the talking as the Captain lent a lazy ear, half listening as he scanned the busy bay and cast furtive glances at the ladies lifting their hems as they entered the pavilion. Maeve saw how he held his grin a second too long, hooded eyes darting, taking stock, surveying.

After a break for refreshments, the dinghy race got under way. Maeve spotted Seamus behind flapping sails and gripped Helen's arm. It was the last event of the day with Union Hall and Glandore competing for the prize. Bantry and Castletownsend were already scotched — having lost the One and Two Oars — and Kinsale had no chance at all.

Maeve fastened her cardigan and leaned in close to Helen. The day had started mixed but was now turning frisky by the minute. A stiff breeze swept into the harbor as the young rivals rigged the fourteen footers — varnished and sleek — and made their way to the start line.

As the dinghies waited for the marshall's gun, Maeve noticed Seamus struggling with his sail. He was standing upright at the base of the mast, trying to free the sheet from a stay. Meanwhile Robbie Rynn, the Captain's son, was readying his vessel, fastening the halyards and trimming the jib to the port side. They were almost level now, Seamus sailing for Union Hall, Robbie Rynn for Glandore, gliding neck and neck towards the start buoy.

And then they were off. The flotilla tacked tight into rising wind, and by the time they reached the mouth of the bay, Seamus and Robbie Rynn were heading the pack, coasting along at a brisk three knots. Helen pulled nervously at Maeve as the boys rounded the rock of Adam, their vessels bobbing on big waves rolling in from the Atlantic. It was already gusting four to five. At each squall, the boats turned to weather, their bows plunging deep into crests and shuddering as they rose again, white spume scattering from sea horses racing around them.

Maeve peered at the darkening sky, nestling closer to Helen. Mr Flynn removed his Derby and stroked it nervously, while the Captain cursed the marshals for letting the race proceed in such wind.

Halfway, most boats had surrendered, going about and heading for home. Some spectators — including Miss Collins and the Presbyterian teacher — said they were wise. But no sign of Seamus or Robbie.

Maeve knew those rocks by heart, the blind side of Adam being visible from her island every day. Seamus would be passing the Sheela Rocks now, the same waves where her father went down. *Tonn Clíona*, treacherous swell, the fatal meeting of wind and tide. She squinted hard at the tip of Adam, waiting for Seamus's bow to appear, scanning every crest and rock.

Her hand clutched Helen's and it all came back. *Greim an duine bháite*. Was the boat shipping water, capsized, sunk? Was Seamus already going down into the hole? Maeve tasted salt at the back of her throat. Gripping her necklace, she repeated to herself: *Tabhair Seamus abhaile dom, a Bhríd*. Bring Seamus home, Brigid. Bring Seamus home.'

Within seconds, a roar rose up from the crowd. 'They're safe!'

Two boats were rounding Adam, gliding fast before gusting winds.

Seamus was a length ahead, goose winging level on an even keel, when Robbie hoisted a spinnaker.

'He's trying to catch him.' Mr Flynn doffed his derby.

'I know.' The Captain winced. 'But spinnakers in this wind? Madness! My boy's lost it!'

And before he'd finished his phrase, a roller struck Robbie broadside on.

'He's over!' Mr Flynn cried, as the upturned hull bobbed in the waves.

Within seconds, Seamus had swung about and gone into irons. Mainsail flapping, he skulled windward before diving headlong into the waves. He swam hard until he reached Robbie Rynn, buffeted by incoming waves, and grabbing him tight, kept his head above water. Then kicking strongly with both legs, Seamus swam back to his own boat and hauled Robbie onto the deck.

The dinghy was still in irons, main sheet clacking against

halyards and stays, but within minutes both boys were sitting on deck, sailing home, side by side.

Seamus reefed the sails and swung his vessel around to the north. They were surfing back in a single reach.

'They've made it!' The Captain threw his cap in the air, as cries of hurrah went up from the crowd.

But Maeve said nothing. She just kept gazing out at Seamus, steadfast at the helm, arm around his rival, keeping him safe as they headed for port. A storm petrel flew across the bow.

This time the boat came home.

Maeve continued to help Helen with her Irish on Fridays. As the Inter exams approached, they practiced for an hour after school in Flynn's parlor. Helen, sixteen that June and the oldest girl in the class, still couldn't get the *fada* accents right. Nor did she seem to care, preferring to act the maggot in front of the gramophone and play funny games with the telephone.

One Friday, bored with Irish lessons, Helen dialed the Holborn Exchange — trunk call — and handed Maeve the ear piece. And there it was, clear as day, the Golden Voice of Miss Jane Cain, London's famous operator, delivering Greenwich mean time to one-tenth of a second. Cool as a cucumber in the heat of war with Germany, announcing clean-cut calendars and putting booming Big Ben in the shade.

Maeve pulled the receiver close to her ear. How could one voice reach half the globe? World time in an instant. The universe at the turn of a dial — a circle beginning with 0 through which faraway people come and go.

'What time is it?' Helen interrupted.

'Sixteen hours, five minutes and two seconds—,' Maeve repeated Jane Cain's exact words. handing back the receiver.

' —to be precise,' mimicked Helen with a posh London accent, replacing the phone on the holder.

'Time for dinner,' called Mrs Flynn from the parlor.

'Coming.' Helen led Maeve to the table where they both sat down opposite her parents.

'The bridge. Look!' Mr Flynn raised a spoon and drew a semi-circle in the air before pointing to a print on the dresser. 'The twelve-arch bridge at Ballydehob. Pride of the West Cork Railway. See!'

Unfolding a napkin, Maeve peered up at the mounted black and white photograph. A row of mustached gentlemen stood beaming before a viaduct.

The picture, Mr Flynn explained, had first appeared in *The Eagle* after the opening of the new rail line from Skibbereen to Schull. Tenth of March 1922. Historic date for all West Cork. Twelve men, one for each arch, and right in the middle: James Flynn Esquire. Strong jaw, top hat, barrel chest. Mr Flynn's father, Helen's grandfather.

Helen rolled her eyes as her father recited his lifelong dream: to bring Cork Rail to Union Hall.

Maeve didn't like how Helen smirked when her father went on like that. She'd never mocked her own father, ever, and loved listening to Mr Flynn recount the famous feat of 'The Cutting' — thirteen men carving through Knockaneen to a depth of forty feet. Among them farm hands from Myross brought all the way for the job. Twenty-two days to clear the way.

'Now you know what Knockaneen means in Irish, don't you Maeve?' Mr Flynn dabbed his mouth with a napkin.

'I do,' Maeve obliged. '*Cnocáinín* means little hill.'

'Little hill,' echoed Mr Flynn. 'There you are. But you may be sure it wasn't "little" for the Myross men who dug through it, was it? No indeed! Nor to our Railway Board who had to ask Parliament for an Extension Bill.' He reached down and patted his dog, Scamp, so hard he cocked his snout in the air.

Maeve nodded without being sure which Parliament Mr Flynn was referring to. Dublin or London? History was one of her favorite subjects, along with Latin and Composition, and Mr Flynn seemed to know more about everything than anybody else she knew, including Miss Collins and Father Kehoe. She liked how he got all excited about the 'March of Progress,' puffing out his pigeon chest as he reeled off tales of the South Coast Railway. Of which he was Chairman, like his father before him.

Much to Helen's annoyance, Maeve asked Mr Flynn to repeat the story of the first four stages. Cork to Bandon, Bandon to Ballineen, Ballineen to Dunmanway, Dunmanway to Skibbereen. And while Maeve also wanted to ask when trains might finally reach Union Hall, Mr Flynn was already onto the story of the girder crossing the Ilen river at Bridge Street when the workers blasted through ten feet of rock, extending light rail all the way to Schull.

'Puts the Raj Rail of India in the halfpenny place!' He waved his hand, tipping a sherry glass onto the table.

'Oh, Florrie, look what you've done,' fretted Mrs Flynn. 'Enough of trains! My good tablecloth!' She poured salt onto the sherry stain. 'Let's just try and finish dinner in peace.'

'Enough of trains! Enough of trains!' exploded Mr Flynn. 'What do you mean enough of trains? My father lived and died for trains. And if it wasn't for the West Cork Railway we wouldn't be sitting here now eating roast beef and Yorkshire pudding!'

'Of course, Florrie,' Mrs Flynn sighed. 'You're right. But there are more important things than trains....'

'Such as?' Mr Flynn sat forward so abruptly the dog sidled off and collapsed in protest by the fire.

'Such as Mr De Valera speaking about the League of Nations on the radio.' Helen's mother did not raise her voice as she touched her hair, pulled tightly into a bun, and replaced her fork and spoon on the plate. She brushed her lips with her napkin before folding it into a silver ring and glancing across the table. 'Don't you agree, girls?'

But no one answered. Helen was keen to leave the table and Maeve didn't want to take sides. She liked Helen's parents equally and wanted Mr Flynn to go on talking *as well as* to listen to De Valera on the radio. Perched in her chair, she wondered what Seamus would think. Would he want to hear about the West Cork Railway or protest at De Valera keeping Ireland out of the war? After all, his uncle was in the RAF, saving England from Germany. Maeve pictured Seamus in one of those planes, slicing the silver clouds, brave as the day he saved Robbie from the sea. In fact, Maeve realized she had a whole list of things she wanted to ask Seamus. What was life like in London? Did Piccadilly girls look different from Cork ones? Was he happy with his move to Ireland? She imagined herself posing all these questions, though she hadn't laid eyes on him for a week. Not since the regatta; and she had no idea when she'd see him again.

'There'll be no politics in this house,' Mr Flynn boomed. 'Not English politics, not Irish politics, and certainly not the League of Nations. Trains brought Belfast to Ballydehob and that, my friends, is enough for me.'

He slapped a hand on the table and sank back into his chair. 'De Valera my eye!' he muttered, looking up at the chandelier. 'He can go to pot!'

Helen rose from her chair and followed her mother to the kitchen while Maeve decided to linger in the parlor, browsing through the bookshelves.

'Borrow anything you like, my dear,' said Mr Flynn, waving at the books as he shuffled his way to an armchair by the fire. 'All yours.'

Maeve pulled a leather-bound volume from the shelf, spreading it wide with both hands. She smelled the pages as if the scent of paper and glue could tell her what kind of book it was. Then she tried another book and another after that — like she was sniffing plants. There were so many, whole rows in crimson and brown covers with gold-embossed titles and shiny spines; it would take a lifetime to read them all. Helen's mother had been a librarian in Clonakilty before she married Mr Flynn and brought a substantial collection to Union Hall with her. There was a fine gilded geology series of the Royal Irish Academy, entire collections of Defoe and Stevenson and even a section called 'Young Ladies' Literature.' But for all Mrs Flynn's hopes, Helen showed no interest in books, preferring magazines like *Girls' Own* and *Harrods' Digest* or cartoons from the *Illustrated London News* on sale at the counter of the grocery. Helen was mad about love stories, especially when they were short, with fancy illustrations and romantic characters she could emulate. Maeve was different, enchanted from the start by literary volumes which she could take home to the island every weekend and read at night when her mother was sleeping. *Wuthering Heights* and *Little Women* were favorites. There were no books or bookshelves at home, nor electricity, which meant Maeve had to use an oil lamp at the kitchen table, breathing in fumes of paraffin and seal oil. But no bother. She read and read for hours until one night Mam, waking from a bad dream, plucked a copy of *The Turf Cutter's Donkey* from her hand and tossed it into the fire. 'Rubbish!' she cried. 'Why waste your time imagining donkeys when we've real ones in the fields beside us!' Maeve tried to save it from the flames. But it was too late.

Mam tapped her skull. 'No harm done — the donkey won't burn if it's in your head.'

A pang of anger shot through Maeve but she said nothing. What could she say? What could she do? She just dipped her head and sobbed into her hands, sad that the same mother who'd encouraged her schooling was now so far gone that she burned her books.

When Maeve lied to Mr Flynn about the book — pretending she'd lost it — he told her not to worry and gave her a copy of *Jane Eyre* instead. Maeve stared at the illustrated cover — a lady in a blue bonnet reading a book — and smiled.

She smiled. 'Can I really have it?'

'Anything you like, my dear.' Mr Flynn held his newspaper in one hand, stroking his moustache with the other. 'The more you read, the more you roam. You won't be on your island forever.'

Maeve hugged the book like a newborn babe, rocking it gently before placing it in her sack. The fire inside the parlor crackled and hissed; and for a moment she imagined it was her own father sitting beside her in that room, smoking his pipe and saying how proud he was to see her reading all those books. She felt safe but also sad that it wasn't her home and Mr Flynn wasn't her father.

Outside the window, the evening sun slid behind the hill of Cathergal.

'Come here!' Helen shouted from the kitchen, interrupting Maeve's reverie. 'We're making Christmas pudding.'

'But Christmas is ages away,' Maeve replied, moving from the parlor to join her.

'Who cares a fig?' laughed Helen, as Maeve entered. 'Mummy likes to start early, don't you, Mummy?'

'I do.' Mrs Flynn was cutting a strip of pastry in half and then quartering the halves to make eight pieces. She powdered each slice with a fizzle of flour as she chanted 'Panis Angelicus.' Helen joined in — perfect pitch — and they both sang like larks, high silky voices drowning out the radio news.

Helen drew Maeve to the sideboard and named each ingredient of the recipe. Nutmeg, madeira, suet, cinnamon, ginger, cardamom and sultanas. They were all new to Maeve — and she wondered if any might help with the cures. What if she mixed a bit of ginger with some of her own island ingredients — *duileasc, pucaí cáis, carraigín*? Different plants, different names, but you'd never know.

Helen lent Maeve an apron and the three worked away between oven and sink. They sliced oranges and pitted dates, scoured pots and cooked apples, weighed butter on one scale, raisins on another. They beat eggs and squeezed lemons, grated peels and almonds and poured out measures of brandy and port. And the more they labored the more Maeve felt utterly embraced, as if there were no doors between them and they could walk in and out of each other's lives. Breathing in the aroma of roasted pears and walnuts, she even joined Helen and her mother singing

John McCormack's 'Macushla.'

Before the song was over, Maeve felt something wet against her ankle. Scamp was licking the back of her leg. With a nod from Helen, she led the spaniel to the pantry and fed him leftover beef scraps, burying her hand in the pelt of his neck. He was an indoor dog, groomed and smooth-haired, not wayward and matted like Bawn. She stroked his fur until he'd finished his food and poked his head high in the air, panting a gravy breath. Good dog, good dog. But nothing compared to Bawn.

Passing back through the hallway, Maeve peeped into the parlor. Mr Flynn was napping in his easy chair, smart as could be in his herringbone suit; his round frame perfectly at rest with two large shoes stretched out on a rug. Mr Flynn's steel-rim glasses hung from the holder of the dial phone, perched on the sideboard, while the *Skibbereen Eagle* lay spread on his lap, open at the business pages. His tummy rose and fell with easy breaths, hands steepled over his belt as he curled one thumb around the other. Maeve wondered what he was thinking. Stock exchanges of barley and beef? The latest prices of grain and fowl? New timetables for shipping and service? He made a faint noise with his throat. Almost a snore.

'Are you asleep, Mr Flynn?' she asked.

'I am.' He lifted an eyebrow. 'Fast asleep.'

'Let's get some air.' Helen threw Maeve a spare coat. They were both giddy from the baking and songs.

The moon cast silver medals onto the bay as they strolled the road to Keelbeg pier. Helen took Maeve's arm and spoke softly into her ear. 'Do you want to know something?'

'What?

'A secret.'

'What secret?' Maeve wondered why Helen was whispering when there was no one about.

Helen stopped and grabbed Maeve's shoulders. 'I fancy him.'

'Who?'

'Seamus Kennedy.' Helen pronounced the name precisely, as if she was acting in a play. 'Gorgeous, isn't he?'

Maeve stared down at her shoes, then at Helen's. She felt a stone in her throat. She gave a small cough before answering. 'You think so?'

'I know so.' Helen patted the space over her heart, fluttering her fingers like butterflies.

Maeve stood still on the road, almost white under the moon.

'Do *you* fancy him?' Helen looked at Maeve through her fringe.

'Of course not,' Maeve lied. 'He's *English*.' She didn't know what to say.

'No he's not,' laughed Helen. 'He just sounds that way because he lived in London. But he lives *here* now. And his father is Irish. Irish as you and me.'

'Not as me.' Maeve pulled at her coat collars, though it wasn't cold. In the silence that followed she could feel the pulse tick in her ear.

She changed the subject. 'Will we go to the pier?'

'If you like,' said Helen. 'But promise me?'

'What?' Maeve raised her hands, gathering curls at the nape of her neck.

'To help.'

'Help how?' Maeve was still dazed.

'To write a letter.'

'A letter?'

'Yes, a letter to Seamus.'

'Why me?'

'Because you write like Miss Collins. Lovely words. Beautiful copperplate.'

Maeve sunk her hands in her pockets, feeling sullen, disappointed, sidelined. But she couldn't tell Helen. Not now. She whistled through her teeth before protesting, 'I can't lie.'

'Why not?' Helen nudged.

'Because I can't.'

Helen pursed her lips. 'I'd do it for you if *you* were in love. You write my letters, you wear my clothes. Fair bargain, no?'

And before Maeve could say another word, Helen had grabbed her by the waist and was whirling her in a circle, their wild hair flying like banshees in the wind.

They stood for a while by the pier after, breathless and silent, still locked together as they listened to a brace of yachts bounce softly in the water, halyards clinking in the evening's breeze.

When they got back to the house, Helen fetched her mother's notepaper and sat Maeve down at her bedroom dressing table. She dictated a letter over Maeve's shoulder.

Dear Seamus,

I am writing to tell you that I fancy you. I saw you at the Glandore Regatta. You are the bravest person I've ever seen. I cannot say who I am. But I hope to see you again soon. Perhaps at the Rowing Club next week?

A secret admirer

Maeve wrote down what Helen said. She didn't like doing it, but felt she had no choice. Helen had acted first, shared her secret, planned her letter. Pipped her at the post. Snap. Now Maeve had written to the boy they both fancied. For Helen. And worst of all, she meant every word.

Helen gazed in the mirror, fingering a pendant in the gap of her breasts. She twirled the beads and bared her teeth admiringly before lowering the glass from her face and passing it onto Maeve who was sitting on the bed. Rain pattered at the window pane, veiled by crocheted curtains. The Rowing Club dance began in three hours. All the teams would be there — including Seamus Kennedy.

'Have a look.' Helen nodded to the mirror.

Maeve shook her head, reclining against the bed frame and tucking her legs back under herself.

'Go on,' Helen insisted, tapping Maeve on the knee. 'You're the belle of the ball.'

Maeve peered into the glass to see a map of freckles and a small pimple to the left of her lip. If only she'd inherited her mother's looks.

'I'm all spots.' She narrowed her eyes, posing the mirror on her lap.

'They'll be gone as soon as you kiss a boy.' Helen took a bunch of Maeve's curls in her hands. She stroked the thick locks with a comb stopping every so often to pluck out strands from its teeth which she curled into tiny balls and placed on the sheet beside Maeve, making a field of little black sheep.

'Do you think Seamus fancies me?' Helen asked.

Maeve nodded, afraid to imagine an answer as she took in her friend's bright features and inhaled her lemony smell. She felt a flutter in her chest and prayed Seamus wouldn't feel the same.

Helen floated to the wardrobe and unhitched a green velvet dress with a silver shawl collar and braided cuffs. She held it out before pinning it to her breastbone. Facing Maeve, she cocked her head. 'Do you like it?' She tousled a lock. 'It's yours if you want. For writing my letter.'

'Not sure it would fit.' Maeve felt a shadow cross her heart. She didn't like writing Helen's letters and didn't feel like wearing her hand-me-downs.

'Suit yourself.' Helen plonked the garment on the bed and reached for a plush cream towel. 'I'm going for a bath.' She flung the towel over her shoulder, tossing the comb to Maeve. 'Use this while I'm gone.'

Maeve flipped her hands open and caught the comb mid-air.

'You'll never get a man with hair like that!' Helen's black-berry eyes flashed.

While Helen was in the bathroom, Maeve played with her comb and lipstick, making little faces in the mirror. After seeing *Gone with the Wind* they'd cast themselves as Scarlett and Melanie. Maeve had been happy to play second to Helen's Scarlett, but alone now she couldn't resist the main role. Plucking the velvet gown from the bed, she held it up, turning like a sixpence from left to right, the hem gleaming like surf in the sun. With Helen's dress pinned to her chest, she waltzed to the papered wall and traced the lyre and lily patterns with her finger, as if caressing Rhett Butler's arm. Gliding back to the dressing table she sampled of Helen's perfume bottles, taking a drop from each, until she caught herself in the mirror, and stopped. Maeve dipped her head and raised it again, the smile vanishing from her face.

'Don't be getting notions now,' she heard Mam mutter in her head. 'It's not your dress and it's not your house.'

She replaced Helen's gown in the wardrobe.

Helen returned from the bathroom wrapped in two towels and smelling of lavender. She sauntered around the bedroom picking things up and putting them down again in different places — a fashion cutting from the *Illustrated London News*, a night powder filched from her mother, a bowl of speckled marbles sent by her Aunt Jane in Galway, a multicolored tin of tea from Madras. Then, turning to the mirror, she flexed her gleaming shoulder blades before slipping into a nightdress and collapsing onto the bed.

'Try doing this,' she said, pulling the top of her nightgown down and breathing onto her nipples.

Maeve hesitated a moment but ended up doing as Helen said, blowing down until her own breasts went taut. She imagined what it might be like to wear a brassière like Helen did with men stopping in the streets to gawk. Maeve envied Helen's full chest and the furry mane between her thighs, showing through her parted dress. Though there was only a year between them, Helen seemed much older than Maeve. Her periods had begun three years before, when she was thirteen, whereas Maeve had to wait until she was fifteen the previous year. But she'd no trouble at all when they came. Periods were celebrated by women on the island as *bláthscaoileadh*, 'bloom release,' and *an t-ádh dearg*, 'the red luck.' But it was not so on the mainland. Maeve was surprised when Helen gave her a special issue of *The Sacred Heart Messenger*, which her mother had lent her, describing monthlies as a blemish inherited from Eve. A 'curse' which could only be 'redeemed,' according to the Pope, in fertile marriages. The same Catholic magazine praised De Valera for giving motherhood a special place in the Irish Constitution. But Maeve was unimpressed, considering it all part of nature's way. She'd seen animals doing all kinds of things on the island: cows birthing calves, rams rutting ewes, stallions covering mares, their flanks bucking and jigging, their nostrils flaring, wild for it. Nothing shocked her.

Sitting down beside Helen on the eiderdown, Maeve smiled about such things while chamber music seeped up from the second floor where Mrs Flynn was reading and resting.

Outside, rain tapped hard against the window pane.

They arrived late at the Rowing Club. 'It's what ladies do and gentlemen expect,' said Helen, taking Maeve's arm.

The dance hall was full of young folk lounging by a food and drinks stand. Helen and Maeve recognized Robbie Rynn and his Glandore teammates chatting beside the band, and beyond them a gaggle of Myross lads, including Con Hegarty and Jim Casey from school, smoking Woodbine by the back door. They exchanged mute glances. There was no sign of Seamus.

The local band was already in swing, alternating between crooning Ink Spots and jaunty foxtrots, as Maeve and Helen hung their coats in the Ladies' and found seats beside Nell Nagle, dressed like a *banbh* for the Bandon Fair. No one was dancing. The floor was empty.

Helen invited Maeve for a waltz and, when she declined, took to the floor on her own. She weaved like a silver trout in a stream, shifting from soft shoe shuffles to fluid jives, imitating Busby Berkeley routines she'd seen at the pictures and proving

Josie Hayes right when she said Helen was the cleverest 'copia-
tor' of them all. But Maeve thought her best was 'The Lambeth
Walk' when she raised her hands in the air and leaped forward
before bending back and clacking her heels, left right, right left,
swaying in an arc, clic clac clic clac. By the time Helen was done
several others had joined the floor.

Maeve put her hands between her knees and mused as her
friend continued dancing with one new partner after another,
darting glances about the hall, obviously waiting for Seamus to
walk in and discover his 'secret admirer.' Maeve sat and mused:
had Seamus ever received the letter? And if so, what had he made
of it? Did he keep the note in a special place or simply frown and
throw it away? And what would he make of Helen right now,
swigging gin from a flask as she swooned on the shoulders of
Glandore sailors?

Maeve gripped the wooden seat. Her hands were sweating.
She was worried Helen might go too far, like Cait McCarthy
when she stole the grog on Corpus Christi and swam across the
sound to Ardra, arriving half naked at the Parish *Feis*. Or Mary
Sheehan who met a travelling tradesman at Skib Market and
ran off with him to Glengarriff. Maeve was tempted to whisk
Helen off home though no one else seemed to bother much. Miss
Collins was dancing with the Presbyterian teacher, while Josie
Hayes sniggered in a corner with some giddy girls from Leap.
Only Robbie Rynn appeared to show interest, standing near the
food stall, hands in pockets, stealing odd glimpses at Helen as he
chatted with his mates about Spitfires and Messerschmitts and
the latest motors in from England — Morrises, Hillmans, Austin
Cambridges. Maeve was surprised he found cars as interesting
as Helen. Silly man.

Then he arrived.

Maeve knew it by the look on Helen's face: she came to a halt in the middle of a dance and stared.

Seamus walked straight to Robbie's group, who greeted him with raised glasses. Maeve overheard him say something about being held up with an emergency at his father's Surgery, but before he'd finished his sentence Helen was there beside him. The group welcomed her too and they were all soon chatting and laughing, recalling the drama of the Glandore regatta.

Maeve wanted to join them, but when she rose from her seat her body froze. She felt awkward in the long navy dress Helen had lent her and was annoyed the way Helen had tied her curls back, exposing her pale neck and freckles. She heard Mam's voice muttering again — 'You're not their kind, you don't belong' — and couldn't help fearing her mother might be right. Maybe she *was* getting beyond herself, thinking she could fit in with these folk? But then she heard her father say — '*Ar aghaidh leat!' Up and Away!* — and she stepped across the floor.

Seamus turned and introduced her to his rowing mates.

'This is Maeve Sullivan,' he said. 'She lives on an island.'

'What island?' asked Robbie, taking a sip of beer. 'I sail a lot around here.'

'Oileán Bhríde,' said Maeve.' The one between Staic Séipéil and the mainland.'

'You mean Rabbit Island?'

'I mean Oileán Bhríde — Brigid's Island.'

Robbie gave a puzzled smile, opening a packet of Gold Flake and offering everyone a smoke.

Maeve declined but Helen accepted.

'Why is it *Rabbit* on the maps then?' rejoined Robbie.

'Because *we* didn't make the maps.' Maeve waved away the

cigarette smoke.

'Who did then?'

'The English. But it's called after Brigid by those of us who live there. We've a well too, for cures.'

'Last dance, ladies and gents,' cried the band leader.

Helen stubbed out her cigarette, flicking it away like a wasp. She opened her flask and waved it around. 'Last drop?'

'Thanks.' Seamus poured a glass and raised it in the air. 'To Oileán Bhríde.'

'To Oileán Bhríde!' everyone replied.

And before Maeve knew it, she was dancing a waltz with Seamus Kennedy.

She'd never danced in public before. The only dances she knew were those she learned in Helen's bedroom and the *casadh* at Island wakes. This was different. The steps were totally new to her; but Seamus was surefooted and was soon whirling her deftly in circles. Maeve gave little resistance as he clasped her palm with one hand and cupped her waist with the other. He was expert and she trusted him, eager to do everything right; she tried not to cling or push, and never to swing her hand up and down as if she was drawing water from a pump. She was following Seamus intently now, relaxing into the motion, anticipating how he'd turn left or right a quarter of a second before he did so; and standing lightly on the balls of her feet, alert and ready for the next step, knowing as she moved it was all in the pulse, at once taught and given, directed and graced — like divining for water or fishing for trout — feeling his hand on the small of her back, tilting her arm back, and then drawing her close as they wove their way round, through shoals of white shirts, without stepping on toes — perfect focus, rapt, keen, attending to the very next turn, the short quick curve of shoulder and wrist, sensing the coming beat of the feet, ebbing and flowing in one great wave. *Súitú.* Like the whoosh of surf on a sandy shore. It was frightening and fun. Every moment and more. And the smell of him, yes — that special tang of hair oil and smoke, of gin and sweat, a smell she'd not smelt from anyone before. She'd never been close to a boy in her life and just couldn't keep her eyes off him, there before her, center of motion, as all about them, walls and lights and skirts and faces whirred like figures in a Halloween parade. She dared not look away for an instant lest she lose her footing, her mooring, her man. Her *fear maith.*

Waltz ended, Seamus drummed his chest with his hands and inhaled deeply; while Maeve stepped back, resplendent, still taking him in. The glistening locks and tight wet shirt, the open collar and ink blue eyes.

Once they'd caught their breath, he asked if she was ready to leave and she said yes. But when they went for their coats and looked for Helen, she was gone.

Out on the driveway, Maeve found Helen's scarf on the ground. She wrapped it around her neck, recognizing the lemony smell. But where was Helen? She inquired from others leaving the club and learned that she'd left with Robbie.

Seamus asked Maeve if he could walk her back to the village and she said yes. She didn't want to be too familiar but had no wish to return on her own.

The air was cool as they strolled the road. They kept a shy distance between them; Maeve was happy to be with Seamus but still shook by Helen disappearing like that without a word. Was her friend playing games again? Peeved that Seamus had asked Maeve to dance before her, running off with Robbie in spite? Was she jealous or drunk? Maeve had no idea and said nothing of this to Seamus as they traded banter about this and that — the crowded Yacht Club, the lively band, how well Helen and Robbie danced.

Passing by the Parsonage, they heard a cry in the air. A distant wail fading to a moan.

They stopped and listened.

'It's coming from the woods.' Maeve pointed towards Leap.

'A bird, I'd say.' Seamus stood still. 'Long-eared owl, maybe?'

'More like a heron, protecting its young.'

'You know your birds,' said Seamus, impressed.

'Seabirds anyway, especially in Irish.'

'You prefer Irish.'

'It's the way I think.'

'What's the Irish for owl?'

'*Ulchabhán.*'

'And for heron?

'*Coráin liath.*'

'Sounds better in Irish.'

'Tell that to your King.'

'He's not my King.'

'Well, you sound very English.'

'I lived there. Does it matter?'

'In a way, yes.'

'What way?'

'I don't know, but when I say things in Irish, I hear them differently. See them differently. Birds. Trees. Fish. Clouds. Everything really.'

'Teach me something.'

'Like what?'

'Like hello. How do you say hello to someone?'

'You say *Nach tú?* Is it you? And you reply, *Is mé*, It's me.'

'*Nach tú?*' asked Seamus.

'*Is mé*,' replied Maeve, poking him on the arm and laughing as they slowly recovered their stride.

They walked on for another spell, enjoying the patter of their own footsteps, until Seamus grew animated about some new discovery.

'Did you ever hear of the Peking man?'

Maeve shook her head.

'They found a skull. Forty thousand years old.'

'Where did they find it?'

'In the Gobi Desert.'

'Where's that?'

'Mongolia.'

'Near China?'

'Yes.'

'Who found it?'

'A Frenchman, a scientist. The bones were wrapped in ancient scrolls and buried in an underground cave. Crania and mandibles. My father read about it in a medical journal and says it changes everything.'

'Everything? Like what?'

'Like who we are. Where we're from. Darwin was right. We're not descended from Adam. We're descended from animals.'

'From birds too, I hope?'

'Of course.'

'And fish?'

Seamus smiled. 'What do *you* think?'

'About what?'

'Where we come from. My father says we come from nature, and I agree.'

'I do too. We come from nature and we come from God. It's really the same thing, isn't it? God's in the earth and in the water, right? Not above us or beyond us. He's beneath us. Like he's moving through us and we're his hands and feet. His eyes and ears.' Maeve felt the heat rising inside her again, the small little flame flickering in her bones. 'There's holiness in everything, that's what I think. Everything. Not just in us, humans, but in dogs and dolphins and plants and weeds....'

'God in a dog?' Seamus grinned. 'That's a bit much.'

'No, it's not. And it's not really about *knowing* anything; it's about touching something, feeling something. You just *sense* it.'

'Do *you* sense it?'

'I do,' said Maeve, walking on. 'God heals things. He works through saints like Brigid and through cures, using ordinary things like water and plants. Brigid is in water and plants. She *is* the water and plants. She's not really a person, though they called her a saint and gave her a name; she's more like a force, or a feeling, something that moves us like currents or clouds. That's what my father taught me and that's what I believe.'

Maeve went quiet then, hoping Seamus didn't think her cracked. They had reached Leap Bridge, with not far to go. She took a strand of hair and put it between her teeth, chewing gently as she thought about what to say next. How could she tell Seamus about the Brú and the healing? Explain to him how she cured some people but not others, how she used a different kind of medicine, the 'old knowledge' few followed any more? Could he ever understand such things?

She decided to talk about the stars instead. 'Do you know what we call that?' she asked, pointing a hand to the Milky Way.

'No. What do you call it?'

'*Bealach na Bó Finne*. The swagger of the white cow.'

Seamus smiled, asking Maeve to repeat the words slowly before turning around to the west: 'And do you know that one?'

'Which one?' Maeve squinted.

'That one, Gemini. Look. It's really two stars in one, beside each other, there, across from the Plough. It's a good story.' And walking the last stretch of road to Union Hall, Seamus told Maeve about the mythic twins who preferred to remain stars than ever be parted.

She loved the sound of his voice — deep and smoky with a strange accent. Everything chimed as they strolled in step, following the Leap estuary as it coiled in silver sheets beneath the road. While over their heads a crescent moon curved like a finger guiding them home.

When they reached Union Hall, Seamus accompanied Maeve to the Flynns' where she was staying with Helen. They were shy as animals nearing the house. They looked about but no sign of Helen. Just the key under the pot.

'Goodnight,' said Seamus, a little nervous.

'Goodnight,' said Maeve, lifting the key. Then she added, 'Would you like to come to my island?'

'When?'

'Soon?'

'Yes.' He fumbled in the dark and took her hands. He leaned in close, as if to kiss her, but held back. 'I'd like that a lot.'

'Off home with you now,' she said, turning the lock.

'How do you say that in Irish?' he asked.

'*Buail abhaile.*'

'*Buail abhaile*,' he repeated slowly, before slipping off to his house up the hill.

IV

CURES AND CHARMS
August-September 1941

Sméar dubh - blackberry

Before Maeve had time to invite Seamus to the island, he invited her for a sail on his ketch. He invited Helen too, promising to take them both as far as Cape Clear and have them back again by nightfall. Maeve imagined he asked Helen because he was afraid Maeve might say no without her. But if so, he was wrong. The ocean was her element and she loved the idea of a day with him at sea.

Helen was another matter. Maeve was a bit worried since they'd still not spoken about the dance, even though they'd already spent a whole week together at school. Helen never mentioned anything and Maeve, though curious, didn't want to pry. She still couldn't believe that Helen had disappeared with Robbie like that, and had no idea if it was not out of devilment or pique at not being asked by Seamus to dance, or simply because she genuinely liked Robbie. Though if the latter, it was a quick change of heart; she'd been so taken with Seamus the week before. Maeve was puzzled by Helen's silence. It wasn't like her. They'd shared most things until then. But maybe it wasn't all Helen's fault. Maybe Maeve was to blame too since she didn't want to confess to Helen her own feelings about Seamus: how her heart flamed when she saw him at Mass and almost stopped when she feared he had drowned, how she leapt for joy when he asked her to dance and trembled the whole walk home through the night. And how she almost died when he took her hand and said he wanted to visit her island. Maeve had shared none of this with Helen. There were two of them in it.

Maeve and Helen arrived at Drumbeg to find the Kennedy yacht rigged and waiting. They were surprised to find Robbie standing at the wheel beside Seamus. Once aboard they weighed anchor. Maeve offered to ship the mooring and hoist the halyards but Seamus would have none of it. He was the captain and passengers were passengers. She thought that silly but said nothing. She watched as he worked his nautical skills, tightening the mainsheet and fixing the tiller. Stripped to the waist, Seamus was much darker and slimmer than Robbie who stood squarely beside him with his thickset arms and sandy hair hanging over his eyes. Seamus reminded Maeve of Connie the morning he'd sailed for America, keen and alert, eyes all set on the ocean before him. Only Connie was sixteen without an Intermediary Cert, whereas Seamus was eighteen completing his Matriculation. Worlds apart.

The ketch was soon tacking from Glandore harbor onto open sea, mainsail, mizzen and jib all stretched taut before an easterly breeze. High above the mast, a brace of gannets sliced the sky. Seamus checked his compass and encouraged the girls to sit back and enjoy the sail — seven miles by sea with a fair wind astern.

Maeve perched at the bow beside Helen, who had no sea legs and was visibly nervous. Pale as a sheet.

'Breathe deep and keep your eyes on the waves,' coaxed Maeve, holding her hand.

While the boys were busy up forehead, winching the spinnaker, Helen relaxed and finally confided to Maeve what had happened at the dance. 'Me and Robbie slipped back to Daddy's bar without anyone noticing. We drank beer and smoked Woodbine before kissing behind the stout barrels. We hid the bottles and butts in the bins.' Helen flushed as she whispered, color returning to her cheeks. 'We're mad for each other, you know.'

Maeve listened but didn't tell Helen anything about her own walk back with Seamus that night. Or her excitement at his promise to visit the island. She hesitated for a moment, but thought the better of it. There was something about Helen that troubled her. She held her tongue, and Helen didn't inquire.

Once moored at Cape Clear, Seamus and Robbie lowered the mains'l, gathering the collapsing sails in their arms before reefing them tightly onto the boom.

Stepping ashore, Maeve stumbled on a flagstone, recalling how, five years previously, on her tenth birthday, her father had taken her to this same island — Oileàn Chléire — the farthest west she'd ever been. She remembered him guiding her gently from the boat onto the pier.

Seamus reached out a hand to steady her.

Then the four of them headed to the harbor bar, brimming with visitors. A group of northerners, down from Belfast, were loud with stories of war: busy naval docks, butter rations and American Air bases set up to fight the Germans. Maeve was amused by the Ulster accents — great *blas* — which she'd only ever heard on Flynn's radio. But she couldn't keep her eyes off Seamus, sitting up on a stool at the bar. Though every time she looked, he seemed to look away.

After a few rounds they took their glasses down to the pier where they admired an elegant three-master in from Baltimore and watched the trawlers landing their catch. As the fishermen weighed the fish on the scales, Maeve reeled off the names for Seamus, singling out their special traits. *Scadán*, silvery herring soft as dulse. *Diabhal dearg*, red gurnet with jutting jaws. *Iasc bran*, bronze bream with thumbprint gills. *Ronnach*, sleek mackerel with rainbow backs. Helen and Robbie soon slipped off to the jetty but Seamus stayed, amused by Maeve's lists; and once, when their shoulders touched for a second, Maeve's heart beat so loud she was afraid Seamus might hear it. But when she turned she found he wasn't listening at all; he was staring at Helen flirting with Robbie by the water. Roving eye? Wandering mind? Or just hoping Maeve would flirt with him like that?

Passing the Stags on a broad reach home, Seamus pointed to a bird at the bow. 'Look! A guillemot.'

'I don't think so,' Maeve screened her eyes against the sun. 'It's flying too slow.'

'A cormorant then?'

'No, much too round.'

'Perhaps a gannet?'

'Too small.'

'What then?'

'A petrel.'

'A petrel? You sure?'

'Yes. See how it glides right close to the waves. Gannets fly high and have wings twice the size.'

Seamus laughed, enjoying the banter. 'Fulmar petrel?'

'Close enough. It's a storm petrel actually. *Gearr Úisc.*' Maeve rose to the occasion; she was back in her element, teasing, knowing, relishing every detail. 'Small and black. See. They flit like bats, and they love wild seas, big rollers, stormy weather.'

'Is that why they're called stormies?'

'I'm not sure.' She stared as the bird veered windward. 'But my father told me petrel comes from Peter. Saint Peter'

'Really?'

'Yes. *Aithníonn ciaróg ciaróg eile.*' It takes a fisherman to know one.' Maeve smiled, imagining her father and Saint Peter hauling in nets with birds flying overhead.

'You're quite the scholar, aren't you, Maeve?'

'If you say so, Sir.' She clicked her tongue and didn't let up, explaining that they were also called Mother Carey's Chickens after Our Lady, Mother of Care. They might be shaggy little things, she said, but they were famous for rescuing people at sea, and guiding lost boats safely to port. 'Sometimes they show up, sometimes they don't. You never know.'

Seamus gave the petrel a captain's salute as it sheared off leeward, then turned to Maeve. 'And what can I teach *you* now, Miss Sullivan?'

'Maybe things learned from *your* father.' She poked him on the chest. 'You know, medical things, your kind of cures.'

Seamus pulled up a sleeve and stretched a palm. 'A bargain.'

'Right so.' Maeve shook hands and leaned on the wheel, lulled by the slap of sea on the hull.

She eyed the billowing sails and felt grand.

Seeing Seamus skipper the boat that day, Maeve knew the sea was in him. *Tá mianach farraige ann.* They were a match.

Maeve held her hat as they drove through the village. She was sitting between Helen and Robbie in the back of Captain Rynn's car, enjoying the comfort of the button-tufted seats. They were headed to the Kennedy's for tea.

It was a close August day and the village glowed in a muggy haze. Local families sat gawking on benches outside Flynn's pub, glasses of orange and porter in hand, loitering after Mass. As the car sped past, a young fellow — Nell Nagle's brother from Reen — threw his cap in the air and hollered 'Up the slack!'

The Captain was proud of his new Model T straight off the Ford assembly line in Cork. Glistening steel grey with a fold-back roof. In spite of the rations — England's war hurt Ireland too — the Captain's car always ran. After all, priests, doctors and solicitors had to get around.

'Henry Ford was a patriot.' Captain Rynn spoke to his passengers over his shoulder, stealing a glimpse in the rear view mirror. His lizard eyes darted between Helen and Maeve. 'Made fortunes in America but never forgot his own. Spent his first million on a factory in Cork. Best patriot the city ever saw.'

Maeve nudged Helen and winked. Patriot? They'd heard the stories of the Captain's 'patriotism' — switching funds from the West Cork Railway to Rhodesian copper mines in order to save the family fortune; not to mention his sympathies for the Black and Tans during the War for Independence when Mr Flynn had to intervene with Sinn Féin to stop the Rynn house being torched to the ground, insisting the Captain was a patron of the Glandore Rowing Club. Maeve also knew from Helen about Rynn's law business — how most big farmers west of Macroom sought the Captain for property cases, estate wills and stamp duties. Helen's father was a regular client. The Captain was deemed the finest solicitor around, master of land transactions and rights of way; and much pitied, it had to be said, for losing his wife to septicemia while giving birth to their only son, Robbie. He was considered one of the most eligible Protestant widowers in Carberry.

And there he was now, sitting at the wheel, dapper as could be in his double-breasted blazer. At one moment, Maeve caught his eye in the rear view and looked away. He was so different from Robbie. Whenever the captain greeted you, his hand lingered that bit too long, caressing like a glove, while his son gave a quick firm clasp. His eyes roved while his son's engaged. They even smoked differently, the father lighting up slowly, inhaling the smoke as if he was swallowing an oyster, the son flicking the butt away after one puff. And they smelt different too — the father oily and perfumed, the son earthy and fresh. Maeve could see Robbie being a good match for Helen; but she could never imagine the Captain being a good match for anyone. Least of all Miss Collins, whom Nell Nagle swore he was courting. The thought of him touching her beautiful skin made Maeve cringe. Nell Nagle was a liar.

But Maeve didn't want to think of any of that just now, sitting between Helen and Robbie in the back of the car. She hoped Mr Flynn was correct when he said that quarrels of money and religion were almost over in the new Ireland, with De Valera and Costello working together in the Dáil, trying to keep the State intact, the ports secure, the people fed. This was the Emergency — England at war, Ireland at peace — and it was important for families like the Rynns and Flynns to get along. Forget the past, do business together, be friends.

Maeve ignored the Captain's leer as they entered the Kennedy's driveway, turning her eyes to the bloom of rhododendrons ablaze outside the window. A flock of starlings wheeled through the air in perfect formation. They had arrived.

Seamus descended the steps to meet them, eyes pure blue in the breaking light. He was followed by his mother, wearing a floral dress and spreading a peach umbrella against the glare.

'Welcome,' said Mrs Kennedy as she glided towards her guests. Her lean, fine-boned face shone. 'My husband is attending a patient in the dispensary. Some unfortunate who broke a collarbone at the Leap Races. But do come in. It's hot out.' She turned to her son. 'Seamus, their coats.'

Maeve and Helen hitched their skirts and stepped carefully out of the car. Seamus was about to take Maeve's coat when Robbie gave him a punch on the shoulder and wrestled him in a circle, laughing.

'Won't you come in?' Mrs Kennedy sized up the Captain.

'Very kind.' The Captain lifted his boater. 'But I must get back. Clients coming for a sail.' He glanced vaguely across the bay, before turning to Robbie and Seamus dawdling by the hydrangeas. 'I wanted the boys to crew, but they've only time for the ladies.'

Maeve winced at the curl of his voice.

'One of those days, isn't it?' Mrs Kennedy waved her umbrella, changing the subject. 'Everyone visiting everyone else. Like Christmas really, these Irish Bank Holidays?'

'Quite so.' The Captain cocked a lidded eye before Dr Kennedy appeared from the dispensary to the west of the house. He looked grand in his striped pepper and salt suit. Such a shame about his missing finger, thought Maeve. Car accident, rumor had it, hard for a doctor trained in what people called 'carriage trade obstetrics.' No cure for that.

'Thanks for driving them.' The doctor reached a palm to the Captain. 'Do come in.'

The Captain shook hands and repeated that he'd guests waiting in Glandore. 'Maybe next time.' He patted his hat. 'I'll be off now.'

'Yes,' said the Doctor. 'And don't worry about Robbie. I can drive him back.'

'Be sure to drop in if you do.' The Captain was already turning the wheel.

'I will,' said Dr Kennedy, tapping his temple in salute.

But Maeve, watching the car snake slowly down the drive, knew he would not. For all the politeness between the two men, there was no love lost.

Dr Kennedy invited everyone to see the fossil collection. But as they were about to follow him to the library, Mrs Kennedy took Maeve and Helen aside. 'You must see my plants first. Not to be missed. "Tropicals" from the Cork Flower Show.'

The three ladies strolled down the garden to a latticed glass house where they admired rows of terra cotta pots hosting rare shoots with neatly written tags: wild crocosmia from the Congo, cashew plants from Madras, blue plumbago from the West Indies, and, further along, a trellis-work of colored, serrated leaves, convolvuli with heart-shaped fronds, wisteria with lacy folds and jasmines studded with snowy white bells. Maeve touched each one by hand, inhaling the pungent odors and wondering if any had healing powers.

Mrs Kennedy identified the various specimens, explaining how the local weather was very suitable for imported seeds.

'You may not know it, young ladies, but you have a "micro-climate" here in West Cork. It's especially hospitable to foreign species. Such a joy to see them bloom. Just look!'

She spoke with precision, moving from one pot to the next, halting every so often to raise a hand to the side of her head, touching her bluish-purple earrings. Maeve wanted to stop and scrutinize every plant they passed but was distracted by Mrs Kennedy's pearls. Her own mother had no jewellery apart from the amethyst brooch her father salvaged from the wreck off Sheeps Head, kept hidden at the bottom of a bedroom drawer.

Maeve marveled at Mrs Kennedy's gait, her light step and delicate voice, and at all the botanical things she knew.

After the glass conservatory, Mrs Kennedy insisted they take a peek at the new arboretum. Maeve walked behind Helen and Mrs Kennedy down through a grove of saplings. Helen, straight-backed and sure, could almost be one of the Kennedy family, thought Maeve as she tugged the straps of a pinafore Helen had lent her that morning, another hand-me-down bought off the racks at the Bandon Sales. And as she watched her friend sauntering easily on Seamus' mother's arm, she couldn't help feeling awkward and freckled. Maeve lowered her eyes to the ground, treading daises under her feet; but she kept lifting her gaze again, enchanted by Helen's soft honey hair, her slim neck and shoulders, her sun-drenched face and amber arms. All that tan olive skin which Helen said came from the 'Spanish Irish' on her mother's side, castaways from the Grand Armada, foreigners who never made it home to Malaga or Madrid, marrying local girls instead and becoming more Irish than the Irish themselves. And the blackberry eyes. Those eyes. What if Seamus too fell under the spell and one day strolled with Helen on his arm?

Maeve felt a creature stir inside, laying little black eggs in the crook of her heart. The sun beat down, uncomfortably hot. She felt sweat on the back of her neck and smelled something sour. Envy. Herself. There was no cure for that.

Back at the house, Maeve and Helen joined the boys in Dr Kennedy's study. Seamus and Robbie hardly noticed their arrival, continuing to inspect fossils through a magnifying glass. It reminded Maeve of how Seán and Connie ignored her as a child when they fished for cobblers in rock pools or hunted after rabbits. Maeve leaned in to study the bones: a bleached spidery ribcage arching from a fragment of spine. She counted six ribs and eleven vertebrae, largest in the middle and smallest at the tail, less than half an inch thick. The size of baby limpets strewn on Trá an Tí.

'What are they?' she asked, pointing to the bone circles with holes in the middle.

'Vertebral pedicles of a fin whale,' Seamus replied, not taking his eyes from the glass. 'Just imagine. The smallest bones of the second biggest mammal in the world!'

Maeve stood waiting for him to turn around and see her. She wanted to tell him all about the bleached bones washed up on her island over the years — basking sharks and conger eels, minke whales and porpoises. She even wanted to tell him about the baby skeleton she found on the rocks off Trá an Tí one day, wrapped in slick leathery weeds which she had to peel away like onions, wondering if it was some kind of treasure, until she spied a little white skull. But she held her tongue, fearing he wouldn't want to hear such things right now; he was off in another world. His father's world of fossils and formaldehyde.

Mrs Kennedy soon arrived with lemonade and neatly cut sandwiches — salmon and egg. The smell of tart salad cream consorted uneasily with the scent of Dr Kennedy's chemicals. As the others ate, Maeve wandered over to a mahogany cabinet on the far wall and inspected a row of labeled bottles. Each bore a notice inscribed in neat blue cursive. Quinine, bromide, iodine, chloroform, eucalyptus and morphine. She rolled the names off the tip of her tongue, whispering the sounds to herself, and for a moment she was tempted to take the glass containers from the shelves and uncork each one, sniffing the contents as if she were Bawn sniffing *púcaí*. She couldn't help wondering what might happen if she mixed some of these medicines with her own plants on the island. Quinine with meadowsweet? Iodine with dulse? She wished she was standing in the Brú with Seamus right then, showing him all her herbs, fungi, berries and roots. But what would he think? What would he say?

Before leaving the Kennedys, Maeve found herself alone with Seamus in the hallway.

'I've fossils on my island too, you know. In my curing shed.' She turned and faced him. 'Would you like to see them?'

'I would,' said Seamus, looking her in the eye for the first time that day. 'I'd like it a lot.'

'When would you like to come?'

Seamus mused before replying, 'What about tomorrow?'

'Grand so,' she said, moving towards the door before he had time to change his mind.

'*Buail abhaile*,' he said.

'*Buail abhaile*,' she replied over her shoulder.

'We missed it.' They watched the ferry vanish from sight. Tadhg McCarthy was on duty that run as Dan was busy in the village; he never waited for anyone.

'I should have pedaled faster.' Seamus bent and undid the bicycle clips from the hems of his trousers.

They'd stayed too long at Helen's and were late for the five o'clock sailing.

'It's not your fault,' Maeve said. 'We were laughing so much we forgot the time.'

'Helen's quite the actress,' said Seamus.

Maeve watched a brace of red shanks hopping along Squince

shore and wondered what Seamus meant. *Quite the actress?* His tone was normal, but what was he thinking? Was he praising Helen's antics or annoyed that she'd delayed them? Was he impressed by her show or wary of her charms?

'What's that?' Seamus pointed to a rock at the mouth of the bay.

'Malachy's Staic.'

'Who was Malachy?'

'I've no idea.'

'So there are some things you *don't* know!'

She chuckled and stared at the bay. Two boats dawdled at anchor, no skippers in sight.

Seamus turned to her. 'How will you get home?'

'I can always swim.' She said, peering across the sound.

'That far?'

'It's less than a mile. I've often done it.'

'Really?'

'Yes.'

'I thought islanders couldn't swim.'

'My eye.' She poked his arm and smiled. 'I swim all the time. But if I swam home now, would you follow me?'

'Of course not. It's freezing!' Seamus shivered.

'Don't worry. Dan will take me once he's done in the pub. He rows quicker with a few pints taken.' Maeve pointed to the end of the strand. 'That's his yawl on the mooring.'

'Like a dog waiting for its master.' Seamus rested his bike against the slip. 'A loyalist.'

'Loyal as they come.'

'The village pubs are open 'til ten.' Seamus glanced at his watch then stared across to the island, spread out wide like a beached whale. 'You'll have a long wait.'

'Two hours. But haven't I loads of books to read?' Maeve unlatched her satchel and took out the almanac of planets that Seamus had just bought her. He'd given a copy to Helen too. Always the gent. Maeve put it to her chest and rocked it gently.

'By the time Dan comes, you won't need it,' said Seamus. 'The stars will be out.' He raised an eye to the sky. The light was thickening. 'Meanwhile, maybe we could walk the headland?'

'Why not?' said Maeve. 'Do you know Cuas na Manaigh?'

'I don't,' said Seamus.

'Well come on then, I'll show you.'

They left Seamus' bike at Squince and walked up to Myross headland. They took a shortcut through the graveyard into a field of drystone walls, patched with bracken and gorse, until they reached the cove.

'Cuas na Manaigh,' Maeve announced, patting a grassy ditch. 'Monks' Cove.'

'So where are the monks?' asked Seamus.

'Gone. Hundreds of years ago.' She plucked a bunch of black berries from the bank, careful not to prick herself on the brambles, and handed a few to Seamus, who cupped his hands to receive them.

'Monks actually lived here?'

'Yes, there was a monastery in the old days. And before that a *lios*.'

'A *lios*?'

'A stone shelter, from pagan times, when people worshipped Brigid as a goddess and ferried their dead across to Staic Séipéil. It's sunk in the grass now.' She tapped the ground with her feet.

'Right beneath us.' They both looked down then up again, gazing out at the distant rock rising like a burned scone on the horizon. 'My father brought us here when we were little, my brothers and me, after school. Grand spot for birds.'

They scanned the waves until Maeve spotted something. 'Greater blackback.' She pointed to a dot on the waves. 'And those further out — see? — lesser blackbacks.'

'How can you tell?' Seamus squinted.

'The greater have pink legs, the lesser ones yellow. They both have black feathers. And yellow eyes with red rims and little spots in the middle.'

'How many kinds of gull are there?' Seamus was amused by her bird games and played along.

Maeve knew she was a bit of a know-all, but she couldn't help it: she loved her lists of birds and plants, all those names she'd learned by heart and written down in her father's book. In Irish and English. She was happy to be alone now with Seamus in this special place, but a little worried she might appear forward, like Helen, or say the wrong thing.

'How many kinds?' Maeve repeated Seamus's question. 'Lots. But most around here are herring gulls. They're not as big as the blackbacks and make terrible cries when they hunt. Pure scavengers. Like starving cats!' Maeve scrunched her face and let out a screech through her nose and throat. 'The smallest are common gulls, though they're actually not common at all. You'd be lucky to see a few in a year.'

'You're a talking dictionary!' Seamus sat up on the ditch and laughed. 'Enough!'

Maeve did the same, careful to avoid the prickled gorse.

'I love dictionaries. But I learned birds from my father before I ever opened a book.'

'Your father taught you lots of things.'

'He did. Things that mattered anyway. Birds and plants and weeds and roots. Healing things. Good things. He loved birds and knew every sort. And he had his own favorites; one for each season. He called me after them when I was small.'

'Like what?' Seamus cocked his head.

'Like *Spideóg* in spring because he said I blushed like a robin when he teased me. *Fuiseóg* in summer because I sang like a lark. *Druidín* for autumn when I hopped like a starling….'

'And in winter?' asked Seamus. 'What did he call you then?'

'He called me *Dreoilín*. The winter wren.' Maeve brushed a mist of midges from her face as she recounted how she'd dress up as a wren girl every Stephens's day and go knocking on neighbors' doors asking for money and singing a song:

> *The wren the wren the queen of all birds*
> *On Stephen's day got caught in the furze*
> *Up with the kettle and down with the fell*
> *And give us a copper for singing so well….*

'I like *Dreoilín*!' said Seamus, clapping loudly until he was interrupted by a low moan. Two heifers poked their heads over Driscoll's ditch, steaming and big-eyed. One had a guilty air, like Dan Daly's I've-stayed-too-long-at-the-pub look; while the other resembled a Garda Siochána scolding trespassers.

Maeve made her Brigid sign, sending them ducking and padding up the field.

'I bet you know your cattle too.' Seamus chuckled, watching them go. 'Brown and black. Friesian and Hereford. You'd make a grand scientist, Maeve Sullivan.'

'Would I now?'

'You would.' He seemed to be teasing, until he turned and added, 'But you'd have to give up your *piseógs*.'

Maeve frowned. '*Piseógs*? What do mean?' She slipped down from the ditch and stared straight at him.

'Nothing.' He avoided her look, peering out to sea. 'That's what my father calls them anyway. Wives' tales. Superstitions. All that stuff about weeds and wells.'

Maeve winced. 'So that's what your father thinks, is it?'

'It is.' Seamus kept looking at the waves.

'And what do *you* think?' she asked, hands tightening into fists. 'Have you no mind of your own, Seamus Kennedy?'

Seamus shrugged.

'Well?' Maeve persisted.

'I think a lot of it is made up. Magic and make-believe. It does no harm, I'm sure, but for *real* cures you need science. One has to go to College. Study medicine. It takes years.'

'Like you, I suppose?'

'Yes.' He paused. 'And *you* could too.'

'*Me*?' Maeve fixed him with a glare. 'That's where you're wrong. You've no idea. No one finishes school on the island. No one goes to University. No one. There's no money. There's no way.'

'Maybe there is.' His eyes softened. 'I could help with the science and mathematics exams.'

'Mathematics? What do sums have to do with it?'

'Everything.' He rolled up a sleeve and bared his wrist. 'Think of it now. Pulse and temperature.' He tapped a vein. 'It's all about counting.'

'But it's not what counts.'

'What counts, then?' Seamus lifted his face.

'The *way* you listen, the *way* you touch….'

'…with water and weeds?'

'Why not?'

'Because it's not real, Maeve. Can't you see? It's all in the mind.' He tapped his skull.

'Aren't bodies minds too?' She patted her heart. 'Mine is.'

'Well, my mind cares about things that exist. Magic wells are all very well…'

'You sound like Father Kehoe.'

'Father Kehoe believes in Mass. I believe in medicine.'

'And I believe in plants.' Maeve plucked a blackberry from the ditch and popped it into her open mouth. 'They're good enough for me.'

Maeve fell silent then, chewing slowly. She wished she could explain things better, about the water and sea wracks and how the remedies worked if you believed in them, if your body believed even if your mind didn't. She wanted to tell Seamus about the animals and the islanders she'd already cured — her mother and the Dalys, and even Helen, though she wasn't sure Helen would want him to know about her warts. And what matter if some of them got sick again after getting well; it nearly always worked for a time. Yes, Maeve wanted to tell Seamus that healing was something she *had* to do even if she didn't want to. It was stronger than her, like a river inside her waiting to surface, a tide of the blood she couldn't resist. But something that only really worked if other bodies responded. How could she share such strange things with Seamus, when she couldn't even tell her own family, when no one but she any longer believed? And Áine Daly who some said was already half cracked. Perhaps Seamus needed to know her better and one day actually *see* for himself. He might think differently standing in the Brú and watching her work a real cure. They'd missed today's sailing, but there'd be other times. For now, she'd let the hare sit.

After the moment of silence, Maeve suggested a swim and Seamus was game. In no time they were clambering down the rocks and facing into the maw of the cove. They approached the edge of the deep purple pool, full of waving seaweeds. Maeve removed her shoes and without thinking, dived right in. Like all islanders, she swam in clothes; in fact, she'd never seen a naked islander until the day she spotted the white moon of Dan's behind as he squatted in the fuchsia bushes.

Seamus was more hesitant, but eventually followed suit; he stripped down to his underclothes and joined Maeve in the silky water. They swam out to the mouth of the cove where they paused and treaded the waves together, their legs cycling perfectly, chins above water, looking out to sea. Maeve flipped under after a while, keeping her arms straight by her sides as she dived like a cormorant beneath the swell, holding her breath for as long as she could before surfacing again, the ache in her chest melting as air rushed back into her lungs. She spouted water, rolling and snorting like a seal, and kept dipping under and rising again, swimming further each time, daring Seamus to do likewise, to follow her out into open sea. And he did, all the way, plunging when she plunged, surfacing when she surfaced, noisily emptying his lungs and inhaling deep again every time, until he reached Maeve a good league out and they floated together, side by side. They rose and fell on the swell of the waves, head to head, in unison, almost touching. They were both in their element, fearless and free, their bodies buoyed by the current, their faces flushed by the breeze.

Back ashore, Seamus offered Maeve his coat and they tarried for a spell, watching barn swallows and sand martins flit in the gloaming until, as light dipped, they became indistinguishable from bats and dragonflies. And as they looked further out, onto the horizon, they could see the slow unrolling of blue, deep blue, under a lowering sky.

'We should go now,' Maeve said, pulling Seamus's coat about her, and climbing back up over the rocks. 'Dan will be sailing soon.' On the bluff above Monks cove, she picked a bunch of sea campions and slipped them into her pocket. Handy cures.

'I like this place,' said Seamus as they returned through the Myross fields.

'I'm glad,' she said.

'You know, I'll really miss it all when I'm gone.'

'Gone.' She stopped and turned. 'Gone where?'

'To boarding school.' He paused beside her. 'I thought Helen told you.'

'Helen? You told Helen? Before you told me?'

'I didn't. My mother did, when the Flynns came for tea yesterday. Our mothers are friends. Helen was upset when she heard the news.'

'Of course she was.' Maeve couldn't hide her hurt. 'What school? Where?'

'In Dublin.'

'Dublin. Why *Dublin*?' She shifted her sack from one shoulder to the other, the books digging into her ribs.

'It's a school run by Jesuits. They teach physics and chemistry and mathematics. It's important for medicine. And more open…'

'More open to what?' Maeve swiped at an invisible horsefly.

'…to the world, to different kinds of people, to boys like me from mixed marriages. That's what my father thinks anyway.' He took a breath. 'You don't know what it's like here sometimes, Maeve. Father Kehoe thinks he has God in a bottle.'

'I know.' She was close to tears. 'But not everyone's like Father Kehoe.' She slipped a crushed sea campion into his hand. 'I'm not.' She wanted tenderness, to be close again, like minutes earlier in the water. To touch him.

'What's that?' He unfurled the blossom in his palm.

'Smell it and see.'

He sniffed. 'Goldenrod?'

'Try again.'

'Evening primrose?'

'Again.'

He put his nose right up the flower, inhaling deeper now.

'Sea campion.'

'Yes. It's all about smell in the end. Science just names what you already know. Believe me, these leaves are healers.'

By the time they got back to Squince, Dan was heaving in the mooring, his frame blurred in the half-light. He was tipsy from porter but still well able to handle a rope. The boat hit shore — a soft swish of pebbles as he motioned Maeve aboard. *Súitú.* The sound was always best at dusk.

'Get in there, girleen,' he coaxed. 'Home with you now to where you belong.'

Seamus moved to take Maeve by the waist and help her over the gunnel, but Dan was there first. Maeve was disappointed and hoped Seamus was too; but it was too dark to read his face.

As the boat drifted into the night, Maeve clutched the almanac to her breast and glanced back at Seamus standing alone on the shore.

Buail abhaile.

That night Maeve lit a lamp in the Brú and leafed carefully through the Astronomers' almanac. Her gift from Seamus. She widened the wick of the oil lamp so that light spilled, soft as flour, onto the centerfold: the chart of stars for that night, fifteenth of August, 1941. She recited the title to herself — *The British Nautical Almanac and Astronomical Ephemeris* — before letting her eyes pour over the map: planets and moons spangling the universe like a scatter of plankton. Bright little flares all over the page. *Tine shionnaigh.* She ran her fingers across the chart pronouncing the names of her favorite stars, first in Irish then in Latin — Cassiopeia, Rigel Kentaurus, Proxima Centauri, Orion-Cygnus. Her tongue tasted the syllables as her ear savored the sounds, the same stars she and Seamus had seen just hours before in the evening sky. Night writing. Brigid signs. But how could she read them? What were they saying? Time would tell.

When Maeve went to school the following Monday, Miss Collins took her aside. She spoke solemnly into her ear, 'Your friend Helen is sick. Very sick. You should see her right away.'

Maeve left her sack at the school and ran straight to Union Hall village.

When she knocked at Helen's door, Mr Flynn answered. He said Doctor Kennedy was with Helen running tests and had insisted there be no visitors. Mr Flynn's brow was wet, his eyes full of fear. Maeve was frightened by his fear. One nail driving in another. 'Come back tomorrow,' he said. 'We'll know more.'

When Maeve returned next day, after school, Mr Flynn invited her into the hall. He was even more haggard, his normally laundered clothes shabby and creased. He had an awkward set to his mouth and had difficulty speaking at first, starting and stopping sentences without finishing them.

'... fever… terrible fever…three nights….'

He fingered his sideburns as if scratching an invisible scar.

Maeve took his hand and nodded. He calmed down and spoke again, more clearly now: 'Helen. She lost consciousness on Sunday, crying out terrible things in her sleep. She's covered in rashes and can hardly swallow. Dr Kennedy thought it was flu at first, then some infection or food poisoning; but when he saw the rash last night, and the swollen mouth — "strawberry tongue" he called it — he knew what it was. Scarlatina.'

Mr Flynn cleared his throat and coughed. 'If we can't get her temperature down, she'll have to go to the fever home in Bantry. For quarantine.'

Mr Flynn spoke so quietly Maeve had difficulty following. But two images stuck like hooks in her brain. *Quarantine* and *strawberry tongue*. She had visions of Helen trapped in a ward with sick people dying all round her. She squinted past Mr Flynn up the stairs, as though Helen might come running down.

'Can I see her?' she begged. 'Just for a moment. I won't stay long. Please….'

'I wish I could, Maeve.' He bowed his head, exposing a bald spot she'd not noticed before, running his hand back and forth over the parting. 'Dr Kennedy says no visitors. She's hardly conscious, she doesn't know anyone.'

Mr Flynn took a step back from the door, retreating into the hallway. 'It's in Dr Kennedy's hands now. And God's. You must leave now, Maeve. We'll let you know when we've any more news. I promise.'

Maeve nodded and turned away.

She waited for word, unable to sleep that night or to concentrate at school next day. But no message came. Two days, three days, and still nothing. Maeve grew so desperate she was about to go to the Kennedys' to speak with Seamus, to see if he knew anything, when, on the fourth day, Miss Collins handed her an envelope after class. A handwritten note from Helen's mother.

Helen worsening. Too weak to be moved to hospital in Bantry. She woke briefly from her fever this morning and asked for you. Dr Kennedy has sent for new medicine from Dublin, but she may not have long. We're all praying.

- Mrs Flynn

Maeve folded the note and put it in her pocket. Awful news, but at least Helen was at home and not halfway to Bantry. Maeve would go to her, but first she must fetch a cure from the island.

When Maeve reached Squince, Joe Driscoll, sorting pots, offered to ferry her across if she promised to help his slow daughter, Máire, with her writing. He rowed her over to Trá an Tí and waited while she hurried to the Brú for a flask of well water and a mix of samphire and dulse. She strapped the flask to her belt, placed the plants in the tobacco tin and was back at Squince by lunchtime. She was soon scrambling up the Ballinatona road, a short cut to the village which she hadn't taken since accompanying her father to cure Paddy Casey's stroke five years ago. The climb was steep and overgrown as Maeve beat her way through brambles and bindweed. She had to cross a row of ditches covered in lichen and liverwort, careful each time not to slip and drop the tobacco tin. Cresting the hillock, Maeve cursed aloud, realizing she'd lost the water flask and had to return. She found it eventually half a mile back, snagged on a tangle of spikey gorse. Stopping to catch her breath, she could hear her heart beating in her ears and the shriek of a crow flapping low over a whitethorn. She reattached the flask to her belt and beat her way back up the hill. She had to get to Helen before it was too late. For all her shifts in moods and tones, Helen was the one who'd taken her in, the friend who'd opened the door when she'd lost her father and sought shelter beyond the island, the person who introduced her to another way of life. Despite her whimsy and willfulness, Maeve loved the way she laughed and played, her warmth, her smell, her spiritedness. She needed her. She'd not let her die.

By the time Maeve reached Flynn's, it was dusk. She peered through the window of the living room where Mr and Mrs Flynn were sitting by the fire, talking earnestly with Dr Kennedy. She didn't knock, knowing they wouldn't approve of her cures. So, careful not to make any noise, she stole around to the back of the house and made her way in through the kitchen. Scamp met her as she slipped through the door, but did not bark. She patted his head and fed him scraps from the larder before making her way up the back stairwell.

Helen lay stretched on the sheets as Maeve entered. She was sleeping, her face a pale moon pocked with patches. Her mouth and lips were puffed and chapped.

Maeve approached the bed slowly, careful not to wake Helen

or disturb the medicine bottles on the bedside table. She touched her temple and felt her pulse, a soft flutter. She took the water flask from her belt and, adding six drops to the cure, rubbed it gently onto Helen's tongue. Lifting her head slightly, Maeve made sure Helen could swallow; then, sprinkling water on her own palms, she placed them flat against Helen's forehead before running her fingers down her cheeks, caressing her neck and shoulders, up and down, as she whispered softly into her ear: '*Faoi Bhrat Bhríde sibh*. May Brigid mind you.'

At the sound of the words, Helen opened her eyes for an instant. She tried to say something, but Maeve put a finger to her lips, shushing her gently, before kissing her forehead and placing her hands together on the sheets. Then she slipped quietly out of the house without saying another word. Dr Kennedy and the Flynns would be up again soon. It was all now in the lap of the gods.

Next day, Maeve received a note from Helen's mother saying the fever had broken during the night. Helen had recovered consciousness and was over the worst. Dr Kennedy's new medicine had arrived in time. She'd need to convalesce for a week, but she was on the mend.

Once Helen was fully recovered, the first thing she did was visit the island.

She stepped off the ferry at Trá an Tí, carrying a parcel wrapped with taffeta and ribbons.

Maeve brought her straight to the house and when Mam saw the fancy box, she wiped her hands on her apron and frowned.

Maeve sat Helen at the Ship's Table — fine piece of Sullivan salvage — and unwrapped the gift, slowly undoing the ribbons, one after another. She lifted the lid.

'What's that?' asked Mam as if a rat might jump out.

'Can't you see, Mam? It's a *císte milis*, a sweet cake.'

'And my scones! What about my scones?' Mam pointed to the griddle.

'We can have cake *and* scones,' Maeve said, stroking her mother's arm.

Helen paid no attention, continuing to speak to Maeve as if her mother wasn't there. 'Lemon sponge with almonds. Me and Mummy made it for you.' She lifted the cake from the container and reached into her pocket. 'I brought this too — here! — Jasmine tea. All the way from India.'

Maeve took the tea tin and handed it to Mam, who smirked at the jeweled princess on the cover.

'The best tea comes from Madras,' Helen piped. 'That's what my father says. Don't you agree, Mrs Sullivan?'

'Madras!' exclaimed Mam. 'What's wrong with Myross?' Mam hadn't been further than Cork in her life.

Helen carved the lemon sponge into pieces, offering the first to Mam. 'Will you try some, Mrs Sullivan?'

Mam shook her head, taking the knife from Helen. 'Soda bread's enough for me. Away with you now, the two of you.' She shooed them off like a gaggle of geese.

Maeve slipped a slice of cake into her sack as they stepped gingerly out the door.

Maeve scurried ahead, embarrassed by the stench in the yard — a mixed whiff of puck goat, rancid cream and rotting herring flung on the manure heap; odors that never bothered her before smelling them now through Helen's nose.

They hurried along until they were out on open land, heading for the well on the far side of the island. Maeve regretted her mother's carry-on but was excited to be finally showing her friend the cave. Approaching the east meadow Maeve began to relax, the sweet grassy breeze filling her lungs. Scores of Meadow Browns flitted over clumps of red and white clover, resting every so often on the bright bells of ragwort and bladder-wort before rising again in a flurry of wings. *Féileacáin*. Shifty little creatures with their gossamer sails and caterpillar torsos. One moment motionless cocoons, the next exploding for their day in the sun.

Crossing the west pasture, Helen became fussed of a sudden.

'I can't believe it.'

'What?'

'That he's leaving.'

Maeve paused and turned. 'You mean Seamus?'

'Yes, Seamus. It's awful. We're not good enough for him, apparently. Heading off to Dublin like that, fancying himself a cut above.' Helen flung her hands in the air then put an arm tight around Maeve; she pulled her close. 'Well good riddance, that's what I say. We'll manage just fine without him.'

Maeve was about to defend Seamus — saying it was his father's doing — when she spotted Dan and Tadhg at work in Gort an tSaighdiúra. They rose from their spades as the girls approached.

Dan shook Helen's hand, green eyes gleaming through his leath-er-beaten face, while Tadhg stole a hooded glance.

'How's Miss Flynn today?' said Dan. He downed his tool, waxing lyrical about the many grand visits he'd made to Flynn's pub over the years, times when he'd be ashore for hurling matches or cattle marts, and especially the day the whole village knelt on the road outside the pub listening to the blessing from the Eucharistic Congress in Dublin. A big foreign voice bellowing out from Flynn's radio placed on a first-floor window over the grocery. Celebrating Saint Patrick's coming to Ireland more than a thousand years before. Stamping out paganism and the snakes and all that.

'Imagine!' said Dan, lifting his sleeve to wipe his face. 'And your father, Florrie Flynn, God bless him, serving the best pints in the county and not charging a penny.'

Helen smiled and pointed to the tool by his side. 'What's that?'

'That? That, young lady, is a hoe for mending ditches.' Dan poked a stack of stones and elbowed Tadhg. 'This side, my oats. That side, his beets. Good neighbors, good fences. Know your place, that's what we say. Blue murder otherwise. People have been killed for less around here.' He grinned. 'Amn't I right, Tadhg?'

'Christ you are,' winked Tadhg. '*Tuigeann Tadhg Taidghín*. Two of us in it. We've been at it all week, fetching stones from the beach below, hauling them up and stacking them tight. Digging's work. Handy too sometimes. Never know what you'd find.' They were in Gort an tSaighdiúra — Soldier's Field — where an English officer, sent to collect rents, had been robbed and buried a century before.

'No indeed,' sighed Dan, taking a spade and plunging it deep. He stabbed, heaved and hoisted, tossing a wad onto the ditch before letting the spade down again, resting on the handle. 'Patience and endurance will take a snail to Jerusalem.' He doffed his cap and sang the saying. 'We're almost done. Then it's harvesting and composting for tillage. Just the few of us left on the island now, God knows, but we'll not starve. *Le cúnamh Dé.*'

Helen warmed to Dan and ignored Tadhg as she traded village

gossip and news about the foreign war — Japan bombing China, Hitler invading France.

Dan's eyes filled with movement as she spoke, dancing to her words. He was more interested in her than the war.

'May I pet the donkeys?' Helen asked after a while, nodding to the animals hitched to the cart.

'No bother,' said Dan. 'But they're not donkeys.'

Helen wrinkled her nose. 'They *look* like donkeys.'

'Well, come closer for a proper look.'

Helen stepped forward, careful not to get dung on her shoes.

'Do you notice anything?' asked Dan, winking at Tadhg then back at Helen.

Helen shook her head.

'Well believe me, they're not the same. And they're not donkeys.' Dan lowered his voice as if confessing a secret. 'Look here. Do you see? One is a mule and one is a genet.'

'What's the difference?' asked Helen, bemused.

'This one,' said Dan, patting a hairy mane, 'has the head of a horse and the body of a donkey. He's the mule. That one there has the head of a donkey and the body of a horse. That's the genet.'

'How so?'

'Because a mule is sired by a donkey and a genet by a horse.'

Helens's eyes widened. 'I never knew that.'

'Well you do now,' laughed Dan.

Then Tadhg shifted his feet and spoke. 'The mule's our own. The genet's on loan. John Sheehey swam him out from Ardra and left him here 'til the job's done. When it's over, we'll unhitch him and he'll swim back home. Some creatures never stay long. Quick visit and off they go. Shots from a shovel.' He scooped an empty spade in the air and looked straight at Helen. 'Clever

ones, those genets, devils for work and demons for breeding.'
He gave a quick smirk, wiping his mouth with the back of his
sleeve. 'And fierce loyal to their own....'

'We're off to the well,' interrupted Maeve, sensing the drift
and not wishing to follow.

'Pray for us so,' said Dan.

'And pray for yourselves while you're at it,' added Tadhg,
not lifting his head from the spade as he cleared his throat and
spat in the ditch.

Following Bawn into the pasture, they spotted a clump of púcaí
growing near cow pats and Maeve explained to Helen how they
were cures for the sadness. But Helen wasn't listening, continuing to hum a song she'd heard on the radio that morning. They
plucked strands of grass and rolled them through their fingers
as they strolled on through heather and gorse until they reached
the path to the cave.

'Let's see your famous well, then,' said Helen, 'but I can't
catch a cold. Still under doctor's orders.'

'Dr Kennedy's a good doctor,' Maeve nodded.

'I know,' said Helen. 'He cured me.'

Maeve gave a wounded stare. 'He cured you?'

'Yes, Daddy said it was the extra draft of morphine Dr
Kennedy ordered from Dublin. Arrived just in time. One more
day and I'd have been off with holy God. That's what Daddy said.'

'And my cure?' Maeve felt a pang in her chest. 'You opened
your eyes. You saw me. You drank the water. You got better.'

'I was in a fever, Maeve. I didn't know what was happening.
But maybe your water and weeds helped too? And why not?'

'But the cake? You brought it specially to thank me....'

'...Yes, to thank you for being my friend. For helping me with Irish. Mummy says you're a "perfect saint." That's why we baked the lemon cake.'

Maeve's tummy tightened. She could feel bile rising inside her. 'It was my cure, I know it.'

'Well, maybe.' Helen looked about, unflustered. 'But Seamus thinks otherwise.'

'Seamus? What has Seamus to do with it?'

'He says your cures are all *piseógs*.'

'He said that?'

'Yes, he did. But look Maeve, it doesn't matter what he said. He only repeats what his father says. *My father this, my father that.* You know that. Forget Seamus. He's not worth it. I know he took us out sailing and brought me roses when I was sick. But none of it matters. What matters is that I'm better now — and I am here with you. We're still best friends. That's what matters.'

Maeve looked out to sea then back to Helen. She was furious with Seamus too right now. But she couldn't be angry with both of them. Her heart would empty. She gnawed at her lips.

'And what do *you* think?'

'Of what?'

'My cures.'

Helen shook her head. 'Sometimes I don't know what to think.'

Maeve sucked in the salt air, holding her breath until it hurt. She'd wanted Helen to visit for so long, to show her the well and tell her everything. But now it was ruined. What was the point?

After a long silence, Helen peered wistfully up at the sky. 'I shouldn't have said anything about Seamus. I'm sorry. It wasn't fair. He probably didn't mean it. And now he's off to Dublin.' She turned towards Maeve. 'We'll miss him, won't we?'

But Maeve did not reply. She watched a schooner on the horizon catching wind, its sails folded like collapsing lungs before luffing again, nudging on.

'We'll go back so,' Maeve said, turning on her heels.

'Yes,' said Helen. 'Before we catch cold.'

Walking home through the fields, Helen said she was starving.

'Have this,' said Maeve taking the slice of cake from her sack.

Helen ate like a hungry bird.

Bawn ran ahead, disappearing beneath barley stalks for long moments before surfacing again. Maeve watched him leap and dive, waiting for the swish of his tail. She knew that Helen was already elsewhere. Back in the village or off in Madras. Neither of them mentioned Seamus again.

The day before Seamus left for Dublin, he invited Maeve for a last sail. Despite her mixed feelings, she didn't want to decline, no matter what Seamus had said about *piseógs* or how many roses he brought Helen when sick. In spite of it all, Maeve was still mad for him. She couldn't help it. And maybe Helen was making things up? She was always changing stories — saying a lie was only a lie when the truth was worse; she loved drama.

So Maeve decided to sail with Seamus.

They left Glandore harbor reaching westward under a steady wind. Once free of the bay, they tacked all the way to Castletownshend where they had lunch at Gallagher's bar before sailing home in the evening.

As they passed the island on the way back, Maeve told Seamus she'd like to land. Just for a bit. She'd something to show him.

Seamus eyed the sun's angle. Descending slowly. 'All right,' he agreed, 'but we can't be long.'

They lowered the mainsail and paddled in between the rocks. Folds of copper kelp rolled back and forth beneath them, underwater petticoats welcoming them ashore.

Once landed, they reefed the sails and heaved the boat up to the tide line. Crossing Gort an tSaighdiúra, smelling of seed grass and dung, they were met by Dan's mule. He snorted aloud, black eyes shining, as he paddled the air with a hairy hoof. His nostrils flared, exhaling noisily, when Maeve approached and stroked his mane. 'You're all right,' she whispered, 'It's only us.'

'Does your mother know we're coming?' Seamus asked as they neared the house.

'She's over in Myross. We've the place to ourselves.'

'And your dog?'

'Mam tethers him to the settle when she's gone.'

She took Seamus's arm and guided him to the Brú.

'My father's place,' she said, opening the door and spreading her arms. 'Where he smoked fish and made cures. Now it's mine.'

Seamus bowed to avoid bumping his head on the lintel. The door was six foot — same height as Michael Sullivan — and Seamus wasn't an inch under. Loose thatch trailed like hair from the rafters, veiling empty nests where recent swallows had left mounds of droppings and fluff. The bare whitewashed walls were stained from years of smoking. Fish and tobacco. A smell of dried wrack filled the air. Thong weed, bootlace, carrageen.

Maeve dipped a finger in the font before moving swiftly about the room. She was back in her lair, sure in her skin, scenting things, touching things, saluting everything about her.

Maeve placed a hand on Seamus's shoulder, then removed it gently.

'I've things to show you,' she said, pulling him by the sleeve towards the corner of the shed. She lifted the peg of the lobster pot and started emptying its contents. First the Petersen tin, gleaming in the half-light, then the well water flask, followed by coils of bind weed and bugle blossom, clusters of fleshy-leaved samphire and curling stalks of kelp, shrunk and leathery as an old man's hands. She caressed each of nature's gifts, eager to display her goods, impress her guest, win him over at last. Her bafflement abated, she was back in her element, sure of her powers.

'My cures,' she whispered, as if someone besides Seamus might hear. 'It's mine now,' she boasted. 'All mine.' She wheeled in a circle, hand in the air. 'Mam hasn't darkened the door since the drowning.'

Maeve glided her finger along the ledge until she came to a row of globed shells. 'My father gave me these for my tenth birthday.' She took a shell in each hand and lifted them to the light. 'Urchins. Sea hedgehogs. *Crainneoga thrá.* You know them? They're not great for eating but are bright as rainbows when covered with water.' She dampened the dimpled carapace with drops from the font until the shell turned suddenly pink and purple, like a creature returning to life. 'See?' she said, flipping the shell to reveal the hole where the mollusk once lived.

On a higher shelf, above the urchins, fishing tools were spread out beneath a coil of rigging and a man's tattered sou'wester hung on a spike.

Seamus followed her step by step, inspecting each item until he came to the thatch on the wall.

'What's that?'

'That's a Brigid cross,' She unhooked it from the nail and handed it to him.

He weighed the straw in the palm of his hand before pressing the knot where the dried reeds meshed. Then wagging a finger, he mimicked Father Kehoe. 'That Brigid one was a right pagan! Ruling the roost 'til the Christians came.'

'You can say what you like, Reverend Father,' Maeve replied, grabbing the thatch and holding it safe. 'But I tell you this — she heals all ills.'

Then, taking the tobacco tin, she raised it in the air. 'If you're sick, come to me!' she sang. 'Come to my cave and I'll find you a cure.'

'A cure for what?'

'That's up to you.' Maeve jigged the tin and gave him a wink. 'Maybe we could start with your faith.'

'You can try if you like, but there's no cure for that!'

'There's no cure without faith.'

'Is that so? And the plants?'

'It takes both.' Maeve stroked a sprig of samphire hanging from the shelf.

'And the water?'

'Of course,' she continued. 'But, you see, they're all one. Water and plants — they *are* the faith. It's not what you think, it's what you touch.' She raised a finger and tipped her tongue. 'It's all in the nerves.'

Maeve poured some water into a mug, and added some powdered pucaí. Then she took out her father's clay pipe and filled it with old tobacco.

'Try this,' she said, handing the pipe to Seamus

'What is it?' he asked.

'My father's pipe. You can smoke it.' She gave him a match. Seamus sat on the stool and lit up.

'And take this,' she added, passing the mug.

'What's in it?' He peered through a plume of smoke.

'A cure for the faith,' she laughed. 'Try it.'

He took the mug in his free hand and peered deep into the murky water.

'Maybe Josie Hayes was right. Maybe you *are* possessed!'

'That's why they call me Biddy the witch!'

They both laughed at that and went on to talk about witches and weeds, and saints and cures, while Seamus smoked the pipe and drank the mug, until they eventually fell silent. They sat there together then in the darkening hut for a long time — though it seemed but a moment — without saying another word, looking through the window as waves rolled past in lazy billows, until Seamus finally put the pipe and mug aside and, rising from his seat, stepped forward.

Maeve turned and moved back against the table as if trying to escape him; but she didn't move away when, after a moment's hesitation, he came closer and ran his thumb along her eyebrows, closing each eyelid, one after the other, and then traced the bridge of her nose all the way down to the curve of her mouth; as if to say shush but also to invite her, as he lifted his thumb away, to open her lips. And she was taken by his tenderness, his sureness, all the while breathing in his breath, taking him in, trusting him, believing him. And then she took his hand and placed it lightly on the base of her throat before gliding it down along her collar-bone, over her cotton shirt, and further down onto her sternum between the gulley of her breasts. Until something deep inside her stirred and with a quick intake of breath she pulled him to her. Their lips met; her heart rose like a wren. *Dreoilín*.

By the time they left the Brú, the evening star was high in the sky. *Réalt an tráthnóna*. Maeve pronounced the name in Irish and Seamus repeated it. Other planets would be out soon, but they had no need of more light to guide them.

'*Tabhair aire, mo chara*,' said Maeve, as they stepped into the boat. 'Take care, Seamus. Take care of yourself in Dublin. And remember to come home.'

V

LEAVINGS
September 1941-January 1942

Neantóg -nettle

'Not bad for a *ciotóg*.' Mam tapped Maeve on the wrist as they sat together at the kitchen table. They were writing to the boys in America: Connie in Dayton, Seán in Boston. Maeve was transcribing her mother's words patiently — the local news, the miserable fishing yields, foxes swimming the Sound and biting off chickens' heads in the night, the endless rain, the bitter storms, the damp.

'Tell them they're well off out of it,' Mam concluded her litany of woes. 'The place is cursed!' She slapped a palm on the table. 'Write your brothers that!'

Maeve nodded calmly, composing her own version of things in perfect copperplate, adding different phrases and stories, knowing Mam wouldn't read a word and that this letter, like all the others, would likely never be read. Every letter sent went unanswered. But Maeve never told her mother, knowing the monthly ritual kept her going. And Maeve made up letters from the boys in turn which she read to Mam, sitting by the half-door, her mind dawdling as she mended old shirts or polished battered boots in hopes her sons might return. She even knitted scarves she never finished, insisting each time on new double-cross rib patterns which she would ravel and unravel until they were almost perfect — which they never were. And even Maeve had hopes for a while that Seán and Connie might actually write one day saying they were coming back to look after Mam and the house. But they never did; and the continuing silence fed dark fears in Maeve that they might be sick with some incurable disease or missing in action in the Pacific Ocean, having signed up for the faraway war. And she felt anger, too, that they never sent money orders home like the Daly and McCarthy children, who'd also gone abroad to find work. Not a penny to feed their ailing mother or put oil in the lamps.

Before the ink was dry, Mam rose from the table.

'Jam,' she said. 'I want jam.' And taking a bowl of black berries from the sink, she thrust it towards Maeve. 'Boil 'em quick before the devil spits on them.'

Maeve held her tongue, obliging Mam with colanders and pots, stoking the fire and pouring out measures of carrageen and sugar. She too had a *grá* for blackberries, the only edible fruit on the island, with their stubby red snouts poking through brambles in early summer before turning black and sweet under the August sun. Hardy survivors of the island's salty winds and welcome apologies for the thorns growing rampant in the untilled fields. Maeve loved Mam's blackberry jam, even more than the exotic marmalades the Flynns made from Seville oranges and thimblefuls of Scotch whiskey — fine gold strips in smooth see-through jelly, so bright compared to the tar-black jars lining the Sullivan shelves.

As Maeve was stirring the berries in the pot hung over the fire, Mam suddenly changed her mind.

'Come!' she said, grabbing a comb and ushering Maeve toward the brass-braced chest. 'To hell with jam. Sit down there and I'll flatten your curls.'

Maeve sat and Mam set to work. She took Maeve's hair tight in one hand, placing a line of hairpins between her lips with the

other. She then pulled the curls into a bun which she fastened
with a band, proceeding to shape it with one hairpin after another,
which she drew from her clenched teeth, moving her fingers back
and forth as if mending nets. As she worked busily, plucking
pins out and putting them back again, she began to mutter away
to herself.

'What use is *she* to any of us? The miserable few of us left
here anyway. What good did she do us — that Brigid one —
only take my Michael and never give him back. Bad cess to the
bitch!' Then staring at Maeve: 'And she took you too, she did!
She stole you from me and gave me back a stranger — just look
at you now. A perfect changeling!'

Mam flung the hairpins into the hearth before rounding on
Maeve and grabbing her necklace.

'And this' — she whispered — 'more stolen goods. *Tarrthálas*
filched from a drowned woman's neck.'

Maeve clutched her chain but Mam pulled tight. 'Don't think
you can hide from me, young lady. All the mad rubbish in that
head of yours. Slinking off like a thief to the Brú. Quick as a
ferret, cute as a fox. But I know. I do. I know about your "cures."
And your sly carry-on with the doctor's son.'

Maeve freed the chain from her mother's grip before rising
suddenly up from the chair.

'What carry-on?'

'You know what I mean. We all do. Nóra McCarthy saw you
at it in the shed. You and the boy. The two of ye. She told me.
And you probably think he loves you, don't you? Poor fool.
*Súil na circe i ndiaidh an ghráinne, súil ainnire i ndiaidh a grá
geal*: Like a hen after grain, a lass after love. You'll soon find
out. You've a lot coming. He'll play you like a sprat and throw
you back. That's what they do with island girls.'

'*Ciúnas*!' Maeve shouted, grabbing Mam's comb. 'Stop it! Right now! What's wrong with you?' She hissed the words at her mother's face. 'You never let me alone, ever since the drowning. You never want me out of your sight! You can't bear anyone else to love me — Helen, Áine, Miss Collins, Seamus. No one's good enough!' Maeve tore off her apron and threw it to the ground. 'But I'll not lose my friends, and I'll not abandon the cures. Never.' She glanced out the window at her father's shed. 'And you think I don't see what you're always at? Sneaking about and spying all the time, envying everything I have. Even *this*' — she held the chain in the palm of her hand — 'And why? Tell me why? You know right well and so do I. Because it was given to *me*!'

Maeve sat under a bruised sky and stared across the sound to Ardra. Sitting on the Daly's upturned hull, she buried her fingers in the scruff of Bawn's neck, loosening out burrs. A cold black wind blew in from the sea — *an ghaoth dhubh* — its coldness a relief from Mam and the overheated kitchen. Maeve knew it was the Sadness fed her mother's sickness — her sour breath and fevered grasp, her trembling bones and bitter words. Unbearable loss. *Diadhánach*. She knew it, she shared the loss, but she still hated her. Connie and Seán were well gone, fleeing the misery and the solitude, the squalor and the damp, like all young islanders before them. Sullivans, Dalys, McCarthys and more. Like goslings in spring and swallows in autumn. Fly-away-Peter, fly-away-Paul. Only Maeve was left.

She bared her face to the bitter wind and thought of the sparrow she'd saved that morning — trapped in the shed, battering its wings against the window pane. She'd cupped its body in her hands and held it, feeling its warm silky frame, feathers opening and closing, its tiny webbed claws paddling in her palms, before she opened the door and released it.

Maeve knew she had to leave; but how could she leave Mam?

A fresh squall swirled in off the sound. Gulls swooped from the air as Maeve bent her head and tossed curls over her face. Buffeted by the breeze, she clenched her teeth and stared out at the water where shallow rocks showed through the surface like bruises on a corpse.

She stroked Bawn hard before removing her fingers from his pelt, rubbing her hands together as if brushing off pain. Worries assailed her, buzzing in her head like bees in a jar. And the biggest worry was Seamus.

He'd left for Dublin first week of September. Almost two months gone and she wouldn't be seeing him again until the following summer. How could she bear it? How could she wait so long? Stuck there on the island with no more school. That made it harder: no more school. She'd begged Mam to let her go on for the Leaving Cert, like all the other girls in her class; but Mam refused. Even when Jane Collins came to the island pleading to give Maeve the extra chance, for more education, a better life, Mam said no: there was no money left for education and Maeve was needed at home. And the neighbors weren't much better. The Dalys, who'd normally do anything for Maeve, were at their wits' end, having lost their harvest to rain and sold their nets and pots for a pittance. They needed Maeve too to help feed the cattle. And the McCarthys — no surprise — swore they hadn't a farthing with dwindling crops and meager fish yields. It was all hopeless; and Maeve had to admit that even if Mam had said yes and offered to sell their last possessions — the copper bell, the brass chest, her amethyst brooch, her knitted coat — it would still not be enough to pay for the school books and fees.

There was no way out; and the truth was there never had been. It had always been so for young islanders: abandoning school, halfway through, to help their families with fishing and farming, and more often than not, emigrating after. It was how it had been through the generations. Seán and Connie were now in America, the Daly boys working as dockers in Trent, the McCarthy girls maids in Manchester. Partings and departings, regular as turning tides, ever since Myross lost half the Parish to the hunger a hundred years before, when those who didn't die in local poorhouses fled to England or crossed the ocean to foreign lands. Ellis Island, Grosse Isle, Van Dieman's Land. Miss Collins had taught them all about that. Faraway names remembered while local names were forgotten. The hunger ended back then, to be sure, but not the loss and the leaving. Island children never finished school. That was the way. And despite all Miss Collins' efforts, there'd be no exceptions for Maeve.

So, having turned seventeen that September, Maeve found herself trapped. The last young person left on the island, she kept house for Mam and tended the animals — the few remaining hens and goats — for a daily subsistence of eggs and milk. She missed Helen and her classmates, but above all she missed Seamus. Every single day she missed him; more and more the longer he was gone. He did write, from time to time, short letters once or twice a month which arrived in wafer-thin envelopes with the stamp and motto of the boarding school — Belvedere College, Dublin: *Per Vias Rectas. By Straight Ways.* Chatty letters with news of rugby and tennis, of outings and exams, of foul weather and stodgy food; but scarcely ever an intimate word. No 'Sweetheart' or 'Darling,' no signing off with 'hugs' or 'love.' No real response to Maeve's letters to him: large folded white pages which she wrote and rewrote with the greatest care and detail every week, always adding warm terms of endearment. Maybe the Jesuits watched over the post, checking the letters? Or maybe Seamus was just too busy with studies for his final exams? Maeve clung desperately to every new note, treating the physical envelope as some kind of proof that their feelings were real. She would take each letter to the Brú and kiss Seamus's handwriting since she could not kiss his hand. And sometimes it was if he was there in the shed for a moment. Sitting beside her, stroking her arm. But he wasn't. She couldn't deny the bitter truth: Seamus was gone for the whole year and Mam was sinking more into madness. The cures, it seemed, were no longer working. The nettle teas and samphire brews, the Water and the liberty caps, all useless now. Her mother was declining every day.

Maeve bowed her head and cursed her lot — her sick mother and her failing gift.

But enough. Maeve opened her eyes and peered over the sound. Tide on the turn. The shore still grey. She pulled the scarf over her head and slipped down off the boat's keel. She must go back and see Mam.

Maeve walked with Bawn round the bowl of the bay, hugging the shoreline. The ragged flight of terns announced rain. She shivered, inhaling whiffs of dead cuttlefish and feeling the pinch of scallop shells under her feet. She looked across to the Fastnet for yawls returning to port, but no sign. Maybe they'd spied herring off the Stags and were trying a last trawl. Or maybe they were sheltering in Schull for the night? Or were already home, safe at Keelbeg, with Helen and Robbie watching them dock — taking a moment from their studies to admire the gleaming catch?

Helen Flynn. Maeve missed her too. Greatly, in fact, hardly seeing her at all these last few months as she prepared for the

Leaving with the Sisters in Clon and rode the same bus home as Robbie, who was doing his A Levels at Bandon Grammar. Helen had written to say that she and Robbie were studying hard in her house every night now. And Maeve couldn't help imagining the blazing fire in Flynns' parlour where, for two whole years, she'd worked with Helen after class, sitting at the table where Robbie sat now.

Maeve buttoned her gansey and quickened her step. Across the sound, the mist was thickening into cloud, creeping down the potato drills of Ardra. Bawn ambled along, sniffing at cockles and rotting kelp. She followed him, thinking what it would be like to live with Seamus and one day travel the world and help heal the suffering and the sick. Maybe the two of them might go all the way to China and deliver babies to poor mothers. The Gobi desert. Working cures together?

By the time Maeve raised her head, she was already in Soldier's Field, inhaling smells of damp grass and dung. She looked up to see a break in the clouds. A ray of gold on the wrong side of the sun. *Buailteóg*. The sky, pierced by a shaft of light, opened and blazed, before closing again, sucking the brightness back into itself. Her heart flooded and ebbed. She tapped her necklace, repaired after the tussle with Mam, and begged for something, anything, to speed up time and bring Seamus home.

Instead of returning to Mam, Maeve decided to drop by the Brú. Cold and tired, she wanted to rest before facing her mother. Fastening the latch behind her, she wrapped herself in a sheepskin and lay down on the earthen floor.

Before dawn, she woke with a fever. Her shirt was soaked and her breathing ragged. Maybe she'd caught a bad chill sitting too long on the Daly's hull, the dampness creeping into her bones; or maybe, God forbid, it was the first signs of scarlatina? She swallowed, checking her tongue for swelling, and put a hand to her forehead; but it was hard to tell if she had a temperature. She rose from the floor and struggled to the shelf. Best remedy, she knew, was a dose of nettle and samphire. Wiping sweat from her face, she chopped the dried leaves hurriedly, fearing the fever was worse than she thought. Her body was on fire, eyes streaming and fingers shaking so badly she dropped her knife onto the ground. She recalled Helen shuddering as she slipped into a coma. She must take the cure without delay. All that was missing was the water. But when she stumbled to the font it was almost dry. Just a few drops left which she quickly swallowed before everything went black. She could see nothing in the dark, smell nothing in the air, feel nothing on the ground. Nothing.

'*Ná bíodh eagla ort*,' a voice said. 'Don't be afraid, girl. Your heart is broken. You're sick with sadness. *Diadhánach*. Like your mother before you and hers before her, caught in the tides, circling the hole. Talk to your mother and ask her the truth. Break the spell and live again; for until you do you'll never be well. *Buail abhaile*.'

Next morning, Maeve felt better and went to her mother. She found her on Trá an Tí, sitting on a rock picking algae from the nets. As Maeve approached, Mam raised a hand to her mouth as though she was seeing a ghost, then continued to clean a coil of hemp mesh, dropping bits of dulse to the ground and wiping her skirt after.

When Maeve stepped closer, Mam bristled and shied, gathering the nets about her like a shabby gown. Maeve paused a few feet off and knelt on the sand. Hands on her knees, she spoke to her mother: 'I want to know, Mam. Where you came from. I want to know everything.'

Mam hesitated at first, fingers searching the nets as if they were hauling some forgotten catch. Her head seemed shrunken, eyes smaller, lips thinner, as though she'd grown older and younger at the same time. *Cailleach*. A hag searching her past, a child searching her future. Then, pushing the nets aside, Mam cleared a space for Maeve beside her, and spoke.

A river of words streamed from her tongue. Names proper and improper, distant and near, an untold story suddenly undammed, unfurling of its own accord, in a voice graver and surer than anything Maeve had ever heard from her mouth. As soon as Mam started she couldn't stop. She told of Noreen Ryan of Raheen marrying Seán Ó Duinn of Leap, giving birth to Máire Ní Dhuinn who wedded John Driscoll the Shoe from Traguma, raising three children all since gone to America, then a late fourth, Úna, who stayed home and married her neighbour, Conn Casey, with whom she bore six infants, three dying of the bad times, two following their uncles to Newfoundland, and the youngest, Kit, surviving long enough to wed John Donoghue of Ardra with a herd of heifers and a prize piebald mare, and she the belle of the entire Casey clan from Myross all the way to Reenagreena. Married at eighteen, pregnant at nineteen, she drowned at twenty. Swimming to Oileán Bhríde with a baby strapped tight to her back. 'Me,' Mam said, pointing to herself. 'That baby was me.'

Maeve reached out a hand, but Mam didn't notice. She continued to speak — keening almost — as if talking to someone in another world.

'My mother, my mother, my long lost mother. Kit Donoghue. Twenty years old. Why did you drown while I was saved? They found me still breathing, wrapped in a blanket, tied to your body washed up on the tide. No one knew and no one could say why you took to the water that bitter day, a dark wild evening with no one about. Why did you do it? What took you at all? No one spoke about it for years after, though I heard many rumors growing up. Some said it was "the nerves" that got you; others that I wasn't my father's child, and the shame was too much; others again that you'd been drinking in the village that afternoon and fancied you could brave any weather, even a gale blowing in from the east. I heard all the stories, every one of them different. But whatever it was, everyone said it wasn't natural. Even the parish priest at the time, Father Murray from Leap, forbade your poor body a Christian burial. The mother I never laid eyes on. My mother. Instead of resting in Myross graveyard with all the other "decently deceased," there you are still, to this day alone, hidden away in a nameless grave. A sunken stone by Brigid's Well.'

Mam lifted the nets and continued threading them between her fingers, stitching and unstitching, until she stopped again of a sudden and looked up towards the sky. Low cloud was turning back into mist. She breathed in hard before looking down at her wizened hands, splayed open on her lap. And she smiled to herself as, lapsing back into reverie, she spoke about a grand handsome man she'd met one day on the strand at Cooscroneen — more handsome than the Big Fella, Mick Collins himself — and how she went walking with him on Myross hill and was smitten for life by the time she got home. His name was Michael Sullivan and she was that mad for him she left her life on the mainland and came to live on his island — her *fear maith* forever. She gave him all she had to give, only to lose him to the sea. The same savage sea that swallowed her mother.

'I bore him three children and now they're all gone,' Mam repeated, pronouncing each name, one after another — 'Seán

to Boston, Connie to Dayton, and Maeve to God knows where.'
She paused and stared at her daughter, as though she was seeing
her for the first time. 'My third one, my lost one, my Maeve.'

Then Mam fell silent, returning to her nets, as if she'd never
said a word.

Maeve sat with her mother for a long time, helping her with
the nets and humming childhood songs, before rising up and
going to the well. She knew in her bones where the body lay: a
covered stone on the bluff above the cave, a place where Bawn
often loitered and pawed, circling the mound as he sniffed the
ground. Once she reached the spot, she stood with her dog, eyes
squinched against the salty wind and for one fleeting moment
felt that she, Maeve Sullivan, *was* her mother Eileen Donoghue
and her grandmother Kit Casey. All three thrown back from the
sea. And she stayed there, not feeling any cold, looking out at
the same wild waves, watching a black cormorant rise up on
outspread wings.

By Advent, Maeve was so worried about Mam that she hardly
left her side. She didn't leave the island for weeks on end. She
missed Seamus and Helen so much she tried not to think of them,
which meant she thought about them all the time. But worst of
all was what happened to the Dalys. Maeve was inconsolable
when Áine suddenly passed away with smallpox, third week of
Advent. An easterly gale blew so hard Dan couldn't make the
crossing to fetch Dr Kennedy from the mainland, so he asked
Maeve to do what she could. And she did: giving Áine the water
as she sat by her bed, bathing her burning forehead and rubbing
boiled kelp on her rashes and scabs. She soothed her itchy skin

with thong weed and lanced the milky ooze from her blisters. Maeve tried everything in the book, but nothing worked. All she could do in the end, was take her hands and hold them tight, as Áine went raving into the dark. And soon after, Dan followed, taking to the drink without cease and sucking madly on his empty pipe as if it was his very last breath; he cursed the world at every turn, neighbor and doctor, priest and God. *Goin an míol, airg an míol, maraigh an míol!* 'Wound the beast, harass the beast, kill the beast,' he swore in the night. He cursed everything about him too — the failing crops and famished cattle and endless gales that battered the shore. Nothing could quiet him but the drink, and he drank without fail to the last drop. Until one day he rose from the bed and took a wild lunge at Maeve in the yard, before stumbling down to Trá an Tí, where he stood for hours hooking mullet and rass — shoving their heads into his mouth until the quivering creatures were dead. It was no longer Dan Daly, the Dan Maeve knew, her father's best friend and gentle guide. He too was gone. Gone in the head. Gone with the storms with no coming back.

Two days after Dan's mad fit, Dr Kennedy crossed from Squince and took him to Bantry hospital. The Daly cottage was empty by Christmas, which Maeve spent alone with her mother who thought she was Mary feeding Jesus in the hen coop. They didn't go to Mass in the village and Maeve didn't visit the well. She was too bruised with loss and doubts. How could Brigid have failed them like that? Letting Áine and Dan disappear from her life — the sun and moon of her island life? The cures should have saved them, but they did not. Maeve wrestled with her grief through those long grey days; she questioned Brigid, she complained with bitter tears; but she never cursed her to hell the way her mother and Dan did. How could she? With Seamus off in Dublin and Helen busy at school, she had no one else to turn to. She was all she had left.

As the year turned, Maeve smelled fear in the air. Not just in the houses and yards but all around. The few visitors from the mainland — Father Kehoe, Dr Kennedy, the odd fish and fowl merchants — brought darker news each time they came. It was a bad time, early 1942, with Hitler threatening England and Churchill threatening the Irish ports, shipping lanes patrolled by submarines and bombers, food exports rotting on the quays of Wexford and Cobh. De Valera had kept Ireland out of the war, but when Maeve looked out to sea she couldn't be sure whether it was Jerries or Tommies she should be more afraid of. Warring vessels crossed each other in the night. And the woeful weather didn't help. Since Christmas, the water had grown so cold the lobsters weren't running and the few pulled from the pots had no claws or feelers. Even the few cod caught off the Copper Rock had nothing in their bellies when gutted. *Faic*. And on January 6th, *Nollaig na mBan*, the well froze over for the first time ever.

Things were so bad on the island by Brigid's Day that Dr Kennedy was soon called back. He came right away and his counsel was clear: Mam needed permanent medical care in a mental home — for chronic dementia — and Maeve should move without delay to the mainland. At seventeen, she was too young to handle a house on her own. And the McCarthys couldn't be trusted. There was no future on the island, Dr Kennedy said. Things were unmanageable. It was time to go.

The following day, Dr Kennedy talked with Mr Flynn about finding Maeve a suitable job in Skibbereen and arranged a car to take Mam to the Cork asylum. The Sullivans would leave by the end of the month.

In those last few weeks, Mam never left her bed. The Dalys' next door was empty and everywhere Maeve turned the McCarthys seemed to be waiting. Scenting opportunity in misery, Tadhg and Nóra filched all they could from the vacant households, hovering about with greedy looks, squabbling like gulls over leftover scraps — utensils, drink, furniture, tobacco; they sold off the remaining livestock and never wanted for gleanings from the odd sunken war vessel. 'Floating corpses have deep pockets,' Tadhg said with a grin.

Maeve knew Dr Kennedy was right. They had to go. Mam required constant attention — much more than Maeve could manage — and the thought of living alone beside the McCarthys was too much to bear. Besides, Maeve would be much closer to Helen on the mainland; and to Seamus when he returned from school for the summer — only four months to go. She'd miss the Brú but could bring some cures with her: dried plants and púcas, the black book and water font. But there was something Maeve knew she couldn't bring along. Her beloved Bawn. As she packed her curing things into a sack, Bawn lay at her feet without stirring. Eyes shut, with his snout on his paws, he lay so still Maeve thought he was sleeping until he lifted his eyelids whenever Maeve passed close by, following her with his gaze. She knew he knew. And in the end he stopped eating altogether and had to be coaxed out of doors for his needs.

On the eve of the departure, Maeve brought Bawn to watch Tadhg McCarthy and two Myross men, Tom Sullivan and Joe Deasy, fasten the last remaining heifer to the back of a yawl — to row it across the Sound. The beast was hauled bellowing and rearing into the water, halters about its neck and shoulders, until its head dipped under and, after a few seconds, surfaced again, nostrils flaring as its front hooves pounded the waves. It got so agitated that Joe Deasy had to grab it by the short horns and push the head right under again — until, half drowned, it went quiet. It swam fine after that and made it across.

Later that evening Maeve brought Bawn to the well. The sea was like pewter under low cloud. No wind. No birds. Entering the cave, she sat with Bawn in the dark, running her fingers through his pelt before dipping her hand deep in the pool and sprinkling water over his head. She put her face to the scruff of his neck, smelling his deep animal smell. But Bawn did not move or raise his snout; he just lay there listening to Maeve's breath.

Tá brón orm, tá brón orm: I'm sorry, Maeve repeated. But there was nothing for it.

When they got back to the house Maeve fetched a tether and led Bawn to the McCarthys' yard. She handed the rope to Tadhg, nodded twice and turned around. Her dog was put down in the usual island way.

Next morning, Maeve watched Mam run her fingers down the window pane and pull the curtains for the last time. They were waiting for Tadhg to come for the trunks: the brass-braced storage chest for Mam's stuff and the one pine crate and lobster pot for Maeve. It was all they could manage as Maeve moved to new lodgings in Skibbereen and Mam to Our Lady's Home for the Mentally Infirm in Cork.

Maeve was ready but Mam still stalled. She shuffled to the half-door and stared into the yard, her features bleached by the last few weeks of sorting and packing, her stray words salted with black mutterings. Maeve was the one who did everything in the end, folding ganseys and blankets into a bag, and hiding the rest in a fish box in the loft, in case someone might return one day.

'We'll be going so,' Mam said finally. 'They can burn the rest.' She waved a hand at the remaining things — the high-backed settle and pine dresser, the oak trestle table and Captain's Chair, the black iron kettle and butter churn. Maeve knew by her look she no longer cared. The only thing Mam clung to was the copper bell, the last piece of salvage hanging by the door.

Tadhg arrived at eight o'clock sharp and, tipping his cap, heaved the chest onto his back. His bracken-brown hands moved briskly to secure the ropes, peaked ears sticking out as he bent and lifted. He cast a furtive glance at the bell, gull eyes narrowing at the vanishing prey.

'Are you ready now?' he said, a hint of glee in his voice.

Mam nodded vaguely, fidgeting with her shawl as she took Maeve's arm and walked from the house.

An hour later, Tadhg rowed the Sullivans across to Squince, clinging to their boxes and bronze bell. Curlews keened and skittered overhead as Maeve looked back across the Sound. *Diadhánach.* From a distance, in the morning light, the potato drills gleamed like ribs of a corpse. Beneath their serried rows, Maeve caught a last glimpse of the well. A small black hole receding into gorse.

VI

SKIBBEREEN
January-July 1942

Hawthorn - sceach Gheal

Dr Kennedy and Mr Flynn were there to meet them at Squince. The beach was deserted. They escorted Mam to Dr Kennedy's car for the eighty-mile ride to Cork, then packed Maeve's things into Mr Flynn's boot for the drive to Skibbereen.

Before parting, Maeve took Mam in her arms and held her, mute and shaking, for a long moment. She clasped her loosely at first, inhaling the damp aroma of her coat, the uncombed hair, the stale whiff of illness, and then tighter until she could feel her thin shoulders, tucked in like a goose, and the tiny nubs of her sloping spine. Mam pulled back and gasped for air, staring at Maeve with blurred eyes as if she didn't know her at all. Her mouth moved but there was no sound. She said nothing as their bodies parted, simply opened and closed her lips as she clutched a handkerchief like a crushed bird in the knot of her fist.

Dr Kennedy drove Mam to the Asylum in Cork, while Mr Flynn accompanied Maeve to her new 'suitable placement': Minehan's Drapery and Haberdashery, 68 Main Street. Skibbereen.

Mr Flynn carried Maeve's bags from the car and introduced her to Mrs Joan Minehan, standing by the shop door to greet them. She invited Mr Flynn in for tea but he politely declined.

'Look after her well.' He smiled at Mrs Minehan, then at Maeve.

'Oh, I will, Mr Flynn,' said Mrs Minehan, taking Maeve by the hand and leading her inside.

Maeve liked her employer from the start. Her quick eyes and hearty handshake, her no-nonsense voice and Protestant precision. Everything about her was nice and neat, from her widow's black dress to her braided hair raised up by a comb.

An attic bedroom, spare and clean, with a skylight and simple brass bed were her new lodgings. Ten shillings a week, Mrs Minehan explained, including board, deductible from Maeve's monthly earnings of three sovereigns for staffing the shop — selling women's clothing and haberdashery. Ten hours a day, six days a week, Sundays off.

Mrs Minehan then left to make tea while Maeve unpacked. She pushed her bags to one side and placed the pine trunk at the foot of the bed, covering it with her overcoat. Now that she lived in town she'd have to be careful about the cures, though she was already thinking of a remedy for the rash she'd spotted on Mrs Minehan's calf. She needed to keep to herself for a while, not wishing to be labelled 'a stray from Biddy's Island,' 'off with the fairies' or 'soft in the head.' Enough of that. Catching a glimpse in the wardrobe mirror, Maeve saw her mother staring back, pleading to slip inside her like a stowaway. She turned away, vowing things would be different now. Her mother, God help her, was safe at last with the nuns in Cork, and Maeve was ready for a new life.

Maeve hung the water font and Brigid cross beside the door. She turned the trunk around to use as a desk and placed her pile of precious books — gifts from the Flynns and Miss Collins — on a makeshift shelf along the window sill. Plenty of good light for reading. And before she did another thing, Maeve took a sheet of paper from her bag and wrote to Seamus. She licked the tip of her pencil and bent over the page:

Dear Seamus,

How are you? I'm grand here in Skibbereen but I think you'd hardly recognize me. I'm a 'mainlander' now, a right townie, making my own living, renting my own room — imagine! It may take a bit of time to settle, but I'll manage. I'll have steady wages from Minehan's Drapery — two sovereigns a month — and my books for company. I'll be kept good and busy until you get back from Dublin in June. Five months seems so long! I'm already counting.

I'm hoping to meet Helen and Robbie on Sundays when they're free. They've promised to take me out for a spin. Helen always makes me laugh.

I must go now as my boss has tea for me. She's very kind and I think you'd like her. I wish you were here beside me now.

Write me soon. And never forget, Ta grá agam dhuit,

Your Dreoilín forever,

                    Maeve

Maeve didn't say anything about her mother and Bawn. Or about her feeling of *diadhánach* leaving the island. There were no words for it in English. Besides, she wanted Seamus to imagine her happy with her new life.

Maeve settled in quick. She worked the till and counter while Mrs Minehan inventoried stock and arranged new fabrics in the window display.

They both got on grand until Mrs Minehan caught her reading a book when things were slack in the shop one day and wasn't a bit pleased. She plucked the copy of *Jane Eyre* from Maeve's hand and, raising it in the air like a soiled handkerchief, said that the only Eyre she knew was Eyre square in Galway — and that's where it belonged. Maeve had never been to Cork or Limerick, not to mind Galway; in fact she'd never been to a city in her life, Skibbereen being the biggest town she'd ever seen, finding the half-mile of houses a boring walk, without a single stretch of ocean in sight. But she got the message and promised never to bring a book to work again. Seeing how hurt she was, Mrs Minehan gave her a pat on the arm, warning that though she was normally calm, if something went wrong — an order delayed, an invoice mislaid, a fabric torn, or any other class of malingering — she was fit to be tied. She mimed a little temper fit for Maeve there and then in the shop, rubbing the flats of her hands up and down her sides as if they were burning and she wanted to put the flames out. Then she gave a small little laugh before going serious again as she turned the knob of her radio, perched on the counter, and released a wave of BBC voices. They all sounded loud, deep and clear. Strange foreign names filled the shop floor — Rommel, Montgomery, Benghazi, Agheila. Wars were the greatest curse, Mrs Minehan said, recounting how she'd lost her father in the Boer war, her husband in the battle of Ypres, her brother in an ambush by Dev's men — and now here she was longing for word from her beloved son, Willie John Minehan, First Corporal in the British Infantry Division, still fighting in Libya. Her poor darling boy stuck in a siege. But he'd be home soon, she prayed. He'd be home soon.

Maeve soon got used to her employer's ways and found her a decent and generous soul. What made things hard, though, was that Maeve had no real interest in clothes. She thought pounds and pence, if you had them, should be spent on more important things than cotton and silk. She couldn't believe the number of folk who travelled there from all parts — as far away as Glengarrif and Clon — to browse the racks of skirts and hats. One rich lady, Mrs Raftery, came all the way from Mallow to have her daughter fitted with a lace and taffeta wedding dress when she could have as easily gone to Cashes in Cork. Word had it Mrs Minehan was one of the best seamstresses in the county.

But worse than Maeve's indifference to clothes was the *waiting*. Waiting for one day to end and another to begin, folding garments neatly on the counter, pinning and ironing, tucking and pleating. Waiting for Friday wages so she could send a few shillings to Mam in Cork and deposit the rest in the new account she'd opened in the Munster Provincial Bank, on the advice of Mrs Minehan. Waiting for Helen and Robbie to come visit on Sundays and take her on drives to Schull or Castletownsend. But above all, waiting for Seamus. Her Seamus. Her one and only *fear maith*. Waiting for his letters with the latest news and stories of school, rereading the pages over and over, hunting between the lines for hints of longing, and often surprised, even ashamed, by her own neediness. She couldn't help it. She found his letters so short and matter of fact, as if he was afraid of being caught by some Jesuit and having his words read out in front of the class. Maeve hoped it was something like that, and not something else. Whenever an envelope arrived, she'd steal up to her bedroom and put the thin blue paper to her lips, sniffing for a whiff of Sweet Afton, recalling their last kisses on the island and the bold secret things he'd whispered in her ear. Each remembrance lit more little flames in the pit of her chest — a fire she never wanted to burn out.

In early March, a month after Maeve's move to Skibbereen, she received a visit from Miss Jane Collins. She was in her room sorting plants when a knock came to the door.

She opened it to find her teacher standing on the landing with an arm full of books.

'May I come in?' Jane Collins smiled. 'I've something for you.' She looked gorgeous in her green tweed coat and wool hat.

Maeve blushed, stepping back to let her in. 'Oh, Miss Collins, you're welcome. But it's small in here.'

'No bother,' said Miss Collins. 'All the more cosy, and I won't be staying long.'

'Please.' Maeve offered her a chair by the trunk which served as a desk.

Miss Collins placed the books on the desk and sat down.

'So you're settling in fine,' she said, looking at the neatly arranged shelves and tidy bed, before patting the bedspread. 'Come here and tell me how you are.'

'I'm grand.' Maeve sat beside her teacher, peering at the books she'd brought.

'You're wondering what they are?' She raised her brows. 'Well, I'll tell you. They're papers for the Mater Nursing exams.'

'Nursing? How kind. But I'm working full time now. I'm not free to study for any exams.'

'You'll be well able, and won't I help you?' She took Maeve's hands in hers. 'I've already spoken with Mrs Minehan and she says if I come on Fridays, when I'm done in the village, she'll give you a half-day off.' Miss Collins reached for a volume in the pile — *The Mater Nursing Academy Handbook* — and opened it on her lap.

'See here,' she said, running a finger down the Contents. 'If we take a chapter a week and practice the exercises, you'll be ready for the scholarship tests by August. You're the cleverest girl I know, and if you want to be a healer, this is the way.'

'I do,' said Maeve, taking the manual onto her knees. 'But you see, Miss' — she paused for a moment before continuing — 'I already am a healer, I have my cures.' She nodded to the bottles of dried plants and fungi lining the shelf. 'The ones my father taught me.'

'I know that, Maeve,' Miss Collins put an arm around her. 'I know that. But your father is gone. And you're no longer living on an island now.' She patted the Mater Manual. 'This is the new way, real science, a kind of medicine they practice the world over. It's the future, and you can do it.'

'You think so?'

'I know so.'

Maeve glanced over at the water font and wondered what the Mater Hospital would say if they found her slipping drops into a patient's medicine while reading a medical chart or mixing samphire with chloroform. They'd think she was touched and throw her out. But she didn't share these thoughts with Miss Collins. Grateful for her teacher's kindness — arriving out of the blue to help her — she'd give it a go and see what happened. She'd nothing to lose, and knew Seamus would be pleased. She'd find a way to combine the cures. Brigid and Hippocrates.

'When can we start?' she asked

'Why not this Friday? No time to waste.'

'Friday it is,' she said, rising from the bed and placing the manual flat on the desk.

As Miss Collins made to leave, she squeezed Maeve's hand tight, saying, 'You learned cures with your father, and writing with me; now you'll learn medicine with nurses. You'll manage, I know you will. And never forget, you're young, very young.'

In the months that followed, Maeve studied for the scholarship, worked hard in the shop and continued to long for Seamus. She relished her Friday meetings with Miss Collins, busy full hours when they would spread out the copybooks on Mrs Minehan's parlour table, sharing pots of tea as they revised for the papers she'd be sitting in August. Mrs Minehan called them a 'grand pair of heads' and they'd often pause to calculate together how the bursary, if Maeve got it, could cover three years of nurse training and lodgings in Dublin once added to Maeve's savings from work. Miss Collins was practical and attentive and seemed to grow lovelier each time she came, wearing new tweed skirts and fragrant perfumes, one week verbena and lavender, the next orange and geranium, as if she was dressing differently for every visit, always bringing little gifts of journal articles and books which Maeve read every night tucked up in her bed.

They worked away diligently, week after week, until one Monday in May Maeve received a letter from Miss Collins announcing she would not be coming. Not that Friday or any future Friday. She said she was terribly sorry but could not explain. Maeve wept silently for days but, egged on by Miss Minehan, redoubled her efforts, more resolved than ever to sit for the scholarship, speaking to Miss Collins in her head as if she was still sitting there beside her.

And every night she spoke to Seamus — lying there in her bed, wild with fantasy and desire, until sleep crept upon her like an island tide.

During all this time, Maeve felt blessed to have Helen.

Once Helen had completed her Matriculation in May she was free at last to see Maeve again. On Sundays, she and Robbie would collect Maeve from the corner of Market Street in Skibbereen, and the three would drive off in the Captain's car for picnics on the Ilen river. They'd play whist and twenty-one on checkered picnic rugs, drink flagons of cider — Robbie and Helen were devils for drink — and devour thick slices of Mrs Flynn's pork pies. Once the three of them went as far as Lough Hyne, where they swam in brackish water and searched for sea anemones which Maeve listed in her notebook before storing away in her tobacco tin.

But it wasn't until they went to Schull, during the Bank Holiday, that Helen and Maeve got time to talk alone. They sat in Moran's Pub in the Square while Robbie was rowing with his mates in the bay. Helen ordered a flagon of Magners, just in from Clonmel, and darting her eyes around the lounge, told Maeve she had 'news.'

'What news?' Maeve poured two glasses; one for Helen, one for herself.

'Our teacher,' said Helen.

'Miss Collins?' Maeve pictured her pretty button nose and sleek neck, her fulsome mouth and belladonna eyes. She expected good things. 'What about her?'

'She's gone.'

'*Gone?*' Maeve sat back, as though scalded.

'Yes.'

'Where?' Maeve gripped the edge of the table.

'No one knows. I overheard Father Kehoe talking to Daddy in the shop yesterday. He said she'd just packed up and left….'

'…why?'

'To avoid "scandal." That's what Father Kehoe said. And when I asked Josie Hayes, she said it was because she'd been caught red handed.'

'Red handed?'

'Yes, in the act. Imagine! With the Presbyterian! Father Kehoe found them at it in the classroom after the Feis.'

'No.' Maeve put a hand to her chest. 'And what business is it of Father Kehoe's?'

'Everything's his business. Especially when it comes to scandal. Mightn't be so bad if the man was Catholic. That's what Josie says anyway.'

'But it's not fair. Miss Collins is a great teacher, everyone loves her.' Maeve clenched her fists. 'What does your father say?'

'Not much. He just looked sad and kept repeating that everyone should forgive and forget and not mind who digs with the other foot. He said he wished Miss Collins well wherever she went.' Helen breathed in and thought for a moment. 'Daddy's right. But we must be careful. We must *all* be careful.'

Maeve stared at Helen, wondering what she meant. 'You and Robbie? You're careful, aren't you?'

'Me and Robbie? Yes, of course, we're careful. Robbie's a gentleman.' Then Helen added after a pause: 'Though I have to admit he did try it once; he's Protestant too, remember, and had a drop taken — but I told him where to stop.' She looked about and lowered her voice. 'We went a bit far — but not *that* far. I'm saving the rest for "wedlock."'

Maeve was relieved for Helen but very upset about Miss Collins losing her job like that. Maeve prayed she'd be happy with the Presbyterian, and that he would love her. As Robbie loved Helen. As Seamus loved her.

Seamus. Her Seamus. Maeve took a swig of Magners, the

fizz stinging the back of her nose. She sat back and swallowed deeply. Maybe it was time to tell Helen about Seamus? Why, she wondered, had she waited so long? Laying her palms on the table, she recounted everything; and once she got started she couldn't stop. The first night walk after the dance, their sail to the island, their kiss in the Brú, the exchange of letters during the long dark winter and their secret vow to live in Dublin together — Seamus going to Surgeons, Maeve to the Mater. Just imagine how wonderful it would be, she told Helen, nursing the sick, delivering babies, no longer having to hide her healing in caves or sheds or lobster pots. But of course — she concluded, waxing practical as she replenished their glasses — it all depended on her passing the exams. She needed the scholarship to cover the fees, and enough money for lodgings in Dublin.

Helen listened to Maeve's every word, chewing on a bit of pastry, before sitting back and folding her arms. She mustered her thoughts, looking older of a sudden, her face serious and birdlike.

'So you love him?'

'I do.'

'Really?'

'Yes.'

'And what about your mother?'

'My mother?' Maeve was taken aback. Helen never inquired about Mam before, but was clearly weighing things in her head.

'She's in a Cork hospital. Dr Kennedy said there's nothing I can do anymore. That's why we left the island. It was too much.'

'I'm sure she misses you.'

'Mam doesn't know me anymore, Helen. It's terrible. Her mind's gone.'

'And Seamus?' Helen let the name hang. 'Does *he* miss you?'

'Of course he does. He writes every week saying how much he misses me. How he longs for us to live in Dublin together.' Maeve was exaggerating but wanted Helen to believe her.

'Are you sure?' Helen tilted her head. She gave Maeve one of her slanty looks, her blackberry eyes growing blacker. 'You know boys.'

'Boys?'

'Yes, boys. How they say things.'

'Say things? Does Robbie say things?'

'Of course he does, all the time, but I know what he means. I see him every day, on the bus, for homework, for tea, for cards. We're in and out of each other's houses. We *know* each other.'

Maeve frowned, not sure where Helen was going with this.

'Robbie's like family,' Helen went on. 'Like a brother.' She paused. 'More than a brother.' Helen peered down at the table, chasing a crumb across the oilcloth with her thumb, before looking up. 'Whereas you hardly know Seamus, do you? You haven't seen him for ages.' She paused. 'Was it September? Eight months ago, no? Think of it, Maeve. How could you know?'

'Because I do.' Maeve flushed. 'You've no idea, Helen. All the things he's told me.'

'Why did you never tell me, then?'

'Because Seamus said not to, until we were ready.'

'Ready for what?'

'To go to Dublin.'

'So you aren't ready yet?'

'I *am!*' Maeve clenched the edge of table and was about to leave when Helen's face suddenly altered, her features softening.

'Listen, Maeve.' Helen lowered her voice. 'I believe you. I do. Really. I just want you and Seamus to be happy. Like me and Robbie. That's all.' And leaning across the chair, she put her face so close to Maeve's it seemed like she was going to kiss her. 'You'll manage, Maeve,' she said. 'I know you will. You're a real friend. And a real healer. You healed *me*. Didn't you?'

Then taking Maeve's hand, Helen stroked the scar on her wrist, caressing it gently. 'I'll help you, Maeve. And I'll tell you this.' She gazed in her eyes. 'You'll pass the scholarship. You'll find the money. You'll be with Seamus and go to Dublin.'

Maeve looked back at Helen, not knowing what to think. She could never tell when her moods shifted. Now she was saying she'd healed her when before she'd denied it. Yet Maeve wanted to believe her.

'I've an idea,' Helen said, opening her purse and dropping a shilling on the table for the drinks. 'Come with me.'

When they arrived in Skibbereen, they drove straight to Mr Flynn's office. Helen asked Robbie to wait in the Ford while she and Maeve entered the redbrick Rail Station on Bridge Street.

Maeve stood in the vestibule full of hanging hats and long coats, while Helen went to speak with her father.

After a few minutes, Helen opened the door and beckoned Maeve in.

Mr Flynn was seated at a large teak desk, laden with clusters of papers. He rose to his feet, peering through half-moons.

'Helen tells me you're in need of a job.' He knit his brows then slackened them. 'As it happens, we are looking for someone to help with the ticketing. So what do you say!'

'Thank you, Mr Flynn. That's very kind. But I couldn't leave Mrs Minehan.'

'Of course not, Maeve. There's no call to leave anyone.' He tapped the pocket watch on his herringbone waistcoat. 'This will be an *extra* job, one day a week, handling fares for the new trains to Baltimore. Sundays and Bank Holidays. A temporary arrangement, just for the summer. July and August. Ten shillings the full day, from 10 in the morning to 8 at night. If you like?'

'Oh, I would like that very much, Mr Flynn.'

'Excellent.' Mr Flynn shook Maeve's hand and sank back in his chair. 'I gather you'll need it — every penny — for the nursing in Dublin.'

Maeve smiled, feeling great love for Mr Flynn at that moment, sitting there in front of him, the best of men, kind and diligent, 'good to his workers and honest in trade,' as Mrs Minehan always said. He was doing it for her, a needy young islander; but he was also doing it for Helen. Behind all his jovial gestures, Maeve noticed the deepening lines of worry in his creased forehead: signs of concern about his daughter's flightiness and shifting moods. The Flynns could not manage her anymore; she was too spirited for them, skittish and nervy as a headstrong filly. They needed someone to watch over her, to keep an eye, to care. Which was one reason, Maeve felt, she was being offered the job. To stay close to the family. And God knows, Maeve was willing. She would do anything for Helen. How many times had she not rallied with excuses when asked about Helen's whereabouts or the missing keys to the pub or shop? How often had she not nursed Helen's hangovers with nettle brews after trysts with Robbie in the rowing club? She'd always been there for her and knew few sweeter rewards than to feel her silky hair upon her neck as she whispered mischievously into her ear, 'Where would I be without you, Maeve? What would I do without my Biddy Island girl?' Maeve needed Helen as much as Helen needed her. And in spite of all the moods and turns, Helen was the person Maeve loved most in the world after Seamus. She'd opened doors for her, taught her how to dress and dance, to use telephones and knives and forks, and borrow books from the family library. And here she was now, arranging a job so she could go to nursing school in Dublin. Yes, Maeve knew the Flynns wanted her as a minder for Helen, especially since they'd found gin bottles in her bedroom that summer and were worried about her headaches and late nights with Robbie. They fretted about the courtship while not wanting to forbid it, for Robbie was a kind boy and the Flynns and Rynns were good neighbors now, grocers and solicitors engaged in trade. An eventual marriage — though mixed — could be a blessing for all concerned. If only Helen could be minded.

Maeve stood as Mr Flynn took a pen from his breast pocket and composed a note of employment. As he wrote carefully, he kept raising his head from the desk to sing the praises of Ireland's railway — how it was reuniting the country with new steam locomotives arriving down from Belfast — 'harbingers of times to come' — connecting countless Irish towns, north and south, traversing parishes and counties, borders and boundaries, to the four corners of Ireland. Its rail links were equal to India's best, jewels of the British empire! At which grand comparison, Mr Flynn poked his pen at the atlas beside him — India, Britain, and Ireland out on its own!

Maeve nodded approvingly, well used to Mr Flynn's recitations about the West Cork Railway and flourishing nations. When he'd finished signing the note of appointment he handed it to her with a smile. Then reaching for his bowler, he patted it like a puppy before escorting the girls to the door

'Be good now,' said Mr Flynn with a wave. 'And if you can't be good be careful!'

Two weeks later, a Wednesday, Maeve received a note from Helen suggesting they meet at the Eldon hotel.

The Eldon was busy when Maeve entered, its lobby humming with guests as she passed the portraits of local martyrs, Mick Collins and O'Donovan Rossa.

Maeve spotted Helen right away, sitting beside a gilt-framed Edwardian mirror which made her look double. She was chatting to a bellboy and stroking white lilies arching from a pewter vase.

As soon as Helen saw Maeve she ignored the boy and waved to her. 'Come here to me.' She patted the chair beside her.

'What is it?' Maeve asked.

'You won't believe it.' Helen twisted a curl before pushing it away. 'Robbie.'

'What about him?'

'Guess!'

'I can't. Tell me.'

'He wants to marry me.'

'Marry? Why so soon?'

'Soon? We've been courting for years. I'll be eighteen next month.'

'I know. But are you ready for babies?' Maeve frowned, not sure why she was unsettled by Helen's announcement.

'Who's talking about babies? We're planning to go to London, Robbie will pass the Bar at King's Inns while I'll do drama at RADA.'

'RADA?'

'Yes. The Royal Academy of Dramatic Art. Best theatre school in the world. Imagine! That's what they say in the *Illustrated London News*. Robbie wants to rent a little flat in Chelsea.'

'Do your parents know?'

'Not yet.'

'And Captain Rynn?'

'God, no. We'll wait for the Leaving results, then tell everyone. We're keeping it to ourselves for now. Like you and Seamus.'

Maeve didn't know what to say. She looked about her as hotel guests signed in at Reception, lifting trunks onto trolleys, stroking their hats, coming and going. She knew Helen was a born actress, trying on roles since the day they first met. Always making things up, so many different faces that Maeve sometimes wondered if she knew her at all. Was she serious? She could imagine straight away how the London plan might work — Robbie was practical with a wealthy father and Helen was eager for anything; she could travel, she could act, she could begin a new life and be happy in another country. But Maeve was surprised to find herself hesitating for some reason, holding back approval and joy. Why the caution, she wondered. Was it because she didn't want to lose her friend — miles away in England where they'd never be able to meet or talk, share their feelings or take long walks? She'd so miss the dance of her blackberry eyes and the lemony-oniony scent of her breath. Or was it because she feared that telling Helen of her plans for Dublin might have given her ideas about London? *Is maith an scathán súil charad* — friends' wants mirror each other? Or simply that she worried Helen wasn't yet ready for such a move, and was acting on impulse, after too much gin?

Isn't it great?' said Helen, miffed by Maeve's silence.

'I suppose so,' Maeve muttered finally, staring down at the lilies in the vase.

'You suppose!' Helen sat forward in the chair. 'You *suppose?* So it's fine for you to elope with Seamus, but not for me to marry Robbie?'

'I know. I don't know.' Maeve fumbled with a white lily leaf before adding. 'Maybe you decided when you weren't thinking… when you were drinking?'

'Drinking? My Lord, Maeve, you sound like my parents! Don't you trust me?' Helen raised her voice then lowered it again quickly. 'Don't you?'

'I do,' Maeve said finally, wanting to mean it.

'Good.' Helen straightened her skirt as if the matter was settled and that was that. She reached over and touched Maeve's wrist. 'You'll keep my secret?'

'Of course I will.'

'Promise?'

'I promise.'

The following Monday Maeve received a note from Seamus telling her he was down from Dublin. A week earlier than expected. He suggested they meet straightaway at Keelbeg for a sail.

Maeve took off work and quickly changed into her summer skirt. She pinned her curls back and took the next bus to Leap, not thinking about what Mrs Minehan might say or what the Kennedys might think about their son heading straight out to sea and him hardly in the door. She dropped everything and went.

'Maeve!' Seamus opened his arms as she stepped from the bus. 'You made it.'

'I did,' she laughed, sinking her head onto his shoulder.

'You're home!'

'It's a neap tide,' he said. 'Let's catch the boat while she's still afloat.' He stepped towards the saddle of his bike, patting the crossbar for Maeve to jump on.

Maeve sat sidewise onto the bar, gripping the handlebars as she leaned back onto his chest.

'Hold tight,' Seamus pushed the bike out with one foot, pressing the pedal down with the other. 'We'll be there in no time.'

'We're off.' Maeve waved a hand in the air.

A flock of sparrows burst from a tree widening out like a spread umbrella.

When they reached Keelbeg, the fishermen were busy sorting fish into barrels. A couple of herring gulls looked on, heads sunk deep in fat bodies, posing lazily on skinny legs. Maeve spotted the Kennedys' dinghy, the *Rachel*, on its mooring to the east of the pier. It was already afloat on the ebbing tide, its mainsail ready for hoisting. Seamus hauled in the mooring and ushered Maeve toward the stern. They raised the gaff-rigged canvas together. All set.

There was a light breeze in Glandore harbor, enough for Seamus to swing the bow windward and veer the boat into a broad reach. The *Rachel* nosed steadily into the bay, Union Hall receding as Glandore rose larger on the opposite shore.

But it was not, Maeve soon realized, to Glandore they were heading. It was due south to the mouth of the harbor and then further out past the mossy crags of Adam and Eve in the direction of Staic Séipéil. Maeve swallowed salt air into her lungs, thrilled to be back in her element, surrounded by ocean. It was ten months since her last sail with Seamus. Three hundred and four days. She'd counted every one.

Rounding the rock of Adam, they sighted the Rynn two-master, *Jeroboam*, bearing down from the east, its crimson spinnaker in full bloom.

'Starboard must give way to Port,' boomed Captain Rynn, perched at the helm, sporting a dapper braid cap and serge vest. Maeve winced. The *Jeroboam* was just yards off, goose winging on a brisk breeze, assisted by an inboard engine.

'Motor must give way to sail,' replied Seamus, raising a hand over his head. But he relented and jibed just in time, not risking a brush with a vessel twice his size. As the boats came level, Seamus cupped his hands and shouted to the Captain, 'Where's Robbie?'

'Home studying!' roared the Captain, tippng his cap. 'Where you should be?' His voice rose to a nasal snort as he swung his schooner to the north, leaving the *Rachel* bobbing in its wake.

Maeve glanced up at the luffing sail, keen to banish the Captain's leer.

'Lee-Ho!' said Seamus, tacking west and pointing the dingy towards Staic Séipéil which now loomed low across the strait, scarce a mile off. 'I think we'll make it in a single tack.'

Maeve was assured by his confidence. Her shoulders slackened as she leaned against the gunwale, jib sheet in one hand, the other shielding her eyes as she watched a low-slung trawler power by. They waved at the skipper, John Joe Nolan, standing at the wheel of his cabin, proud as punch of his recent catch.

They soon passed close to the Belly Rock, best spot around for mackerel and sprat. Her father had exact bearings for it, which she shared with Seamus. You knew you were over the fishing rock when Malachy's Staic masked Squince coastguard house to the north with a line running east to the Galley head. Sink a line of feathers and you were sure of a full house. Never failed. And sure enough, as they passed the mark, mackerel shoaled to left and right, rippling the surface like flung pebbles.

But Seamus wouldn't stop for a second, his sights fixed firmly on Staic Séipéil, rising larger now, all grey and yellow with slate and gorse.

'Tell me about school,' said Maeve as they rode the waves.

'I hated it,' said Seamus.

'Why?'

'Miserable food. Detention. Bullying in the dorms. They mocked my London accent and put frogspawn in my sheets. How's that for a life?'

'Really?'

'Yes.' Seamus nodded, peering up at the sails. 'But I got my own back on the rugger pitch — crash tackled the buggers, broke their knees.' He smiled. 'That stopped them.'

Maeve was hoping Seamus might say something more intimate, like how sorely he'd missed her and was glad to be with her.

'Did you hear about Jane Collins?' she asked after a while.

'I did,' said Seamus, pulling at the tiller. 'My parents told me. They were furious with Father Kehoe. Called him a bigot and said it was wrong she was expelled like that. My mother was angry with him about the war too. She'd asked Father Kehoe to pray for my Uncle Bill in the RAF — but he said he preferred to pray for De Valera to keep Ireland neutral than to bless British officers. My parents believe in the war against Hitler. So do I.'

'I know.' Maeve stared at the swell. 'But I hate fighting.'

'I do too. Everybody does. But we have to fight sometimes, stand up to evil. We should be sharing our ports with the English and letting them set up airfields in Cork, like in Belfast. That's the right thing to do. We're in this together. All of us. Ireland and England on the same side. No matter what your country or creed, Catholic, Protestant, makes no difference. Hitler's destroying everything, everywhere. No one's safe on land or sea. Even right here. We have to do *something*.'

Maeve stared down into the waves. She'd never heard anyone speak like that about the war before, except on BBC radio. Not even a Unionist like Mrs Minehan. Seamus was fierce when he got going; she liked that about him. Though she still hated war.

As they neared the Staic, Maeve spotted seals in the wake. *Madraí na farraige*. Sea dogs with whiskers and snouts, almost human. She remembered her father's stories about the caves and graves and phantoms of the sea. *Port na bPúcaí*. And what Mam said about her after the drowning, that she was a *púca* cast back onto the shore, a changeling returned from another world. But what did such stories matter now, she was with Seamus, after all the waiting, far out where kitty wakes filled the air and porpoises crossed their bows. She gazed up at the billowing sails as waves cast spray onto the deck, salting her lips, and she recalled the many times she'd sailed these same waters with her father and Dan as a child. How they'd haul and land the slatted pots, sorting out crabs and lobsters, crayfish and urchins, as they chewed on slabs of thick buttered batch before baiting the pots with salted cod strung through the gills with thin black twine. The slap of surf on the tarred hull. The clatter of claws on the wooden deck. And everywhere a haze of sweet tobacco.

Maeve drew her cardigan closer about her — a cool spring nip still in the air — as Seamus sat astern, eyeing the blue shale crest of the Staic. His landmark. He steered the boat towards Cuas an Oileán — a cloistered bay to the south of the tip.

She gazed at his tanned face and shoulders, his thick lashes and bushy hair. She loved Seamus in a boat, the way he could handle things like her father, setting moorings and hosting halyards, splicing ropes and weighing anchors. He could rig a mast in no time and was canny at reading currents and clouds. Like he was doing right now beside her, matching tiller and mainsheet to catch a stray breeze, staying on course, riding the waves. They were two of them in it right then sure enough, herself and Seamus, breathing the wind, cruising the sea. And Maeve couldn't help imagining that one day they might sail other seas together and heal the sick in foreign lands. She gazed at her wind-blown skipper and, in that instant, felt deeply blessed.

Entering the lee of the land, Seamus lowered the sail and rowed. And as he pulled back and forth with his lovely hands, he asked Maeve to sing one of her Irish songs; and she did, leaning right back and lifting her throat.

> *Siúil, siúil, siúil a rún*
> *Siúil go sochair and siúil go ciúin*
> *Siúil go doras agus ealaigh liom*
> *Is go dté tú mo mhúirnín slán*

> *Come my love, quickly come to me*
> *Softly open the door and away we'll flee*
> *and safe for aye*
> *may my darling be*

Maeve let the words roll over them as they navigated the last stretch of rocks. Closer to shore, she stretched over the gunwale and gazed down into the water below. Sheaves of kelp swayed beneath them, shimmering skirts courting the light, as wavelets lapped in the clefts of the rocks, flooding and eddying, heaving and sighing. Sounds which might seem strange out swimming alone at night with nothing but phosphorescence to guide you, thinking that if you peered deep down you might see a face peering back up. Sea creatures. Drowned sailors. Ghosts from the past. *Púcaí*. But in daytime, now, beside Seamus, there was nothing to fear. Her feelings were his feelings, her islands his islands, the watery wild their watery home.

Oyster catchers screeched overhead as they moored. Seamus offered to help Maeve ashore, but halfway in they slipped on kelp and Maeve let out a sudden cry, clinging so tight to Seamus they could hear their hearts beat.

Once ashore Maeve led the way, guiding Seamus up a shingle path. They soon arrived on a flat green ledge, a wild grassy acre looking west to the Stags. She hollowed out a circle and sat down. 'Come here to me,' she said, patting the space between them. She pulled a crab apple from her pocket and rubbed it on her sleeve before handing it to Seamus, who sat down beside her. They stayed like that for some time, chewing slowly, until Seamus took the apple core and flung it over the ledge to the sea. A gull swooped swiftly out of the sky, hovering on wings until, seeing its mistake, it flapped sulkily away. Laying back onto a clump of thrift, Seamus put his palms behind his head and closed his eyes against the lowering sun; while Maeve, still sitting, gazed down at his raven hair and the faint shadows under his armpits, inhaling his scent, sweet and strong. All was calm, all was still. And she felt she could stay like that forever, in that hollow crease of land, watching his chest rise and fall, his legs stretched out onto the grassy sheets.

'*Tóg spailp dom mo rún, tóg spailp dom.*' The words fell slowly from her lips. She wanted Seamus but she didn't want to say it in English. He kept asking what her words meant and she kept saying she couldn't say. And eventually Seamus sat up and moved closer to her and the two of them were almost one, gently melding in the soft air. There was no hurrying as he slipped the cardigan from her shoulders and laid her down on a blanket of grass. Her body shook like a gannet as Seamus kissed her arms and neck. And soon a tide was coursing through her and she did not know if it would ever cease. She floated on her back, listening to the call of curlews chime with Seamus's voice as he began saying things that nobody had ever said to her before — simple things, ordinary things, like how he loved her small button nose and the way her mouth pursed when she mused; how her hazel eyes flashed when she laughed and went dark again when she saddened, showing dark brown flecks amidst the green and blue, long enough for him to count the tiny spots of her iris — one, two, three, four — like he was doing now; and the slight shy cast when she looked away. And he told her how he loved the freckles on her forehead too and her scalloped ears and chipped front tooth and the way she used Irish whenever she cursed or was overcome by joy, or went mute when a mood visited her from nowhere and she turned inside herself for a while — quick as a vixen — and the way she sang to him, her island songs, even if he didn't understand a word; and how she got excited when telling him about some new book she was reading, or listened intently when he told her something he was doing, as if it were the most important thing in the world, even if it was nothing at all. Yes, he loved all that, he said, and taking her left hand he kissed the scar on her inside wrist, the burn between the blue veins where she'd once been scorched by a candle as a child. The faint wax stain that saved her from harm.

'It's alright to be a *ciotóg*,' he said, whispering into the shell of her ear. 'It's no shame, no matter what people say. You'll be a great healer with a hand like that. The best Cork nurse Dublin ever saw.'

And all the while Maeve looked into his face and wondered if it was really him speaking those words. Was it Seamus speaking to her at all? But she didn't ask, she only said — 'Be careful' — as she wrapped her hands around him and the dark roiling tide flowed deeper and faster inside her until her watery body opened and she gave him all she had to give.

When they sat up after, Seamus was starving. He asked if there was something to eat. All practical again, as if nothing had happened. Maeve took a piece of soda bread from her sack and broke it in two, then broke the halves in half again, one piece each for now, two bits for later on. She then took a bottle of milky tea from her sack and, unstopping the cork, took a swig — cool and sweet — before passing it on to Seamus. As they drank their tea slowly, without a word, they watched a family of seals swim close to shore, the bull protecting the mother and a bob of speckled pups. The family tumbled and curled, making little puffing sounds, until the cow slid onto a flat rock and shuddered her way along the edge after a stray pup. Then they were gone.

When they'd eaten, Seamus lit up a cigarette, drawing in deeply before blowing out smoke in a single stream. Then fishing something from his pocket, he turned to Maeve and opened his fist. A silver bracelet.

'I got it in O'Laoghaire's,' he said. 'It's not gold, but I hope you like it?'

'*Tá sé go hálainn*,' she said. 'It's beautiful.'

'Here, let's put it on.' He held out the shiny thread.

She nodded, letting him fasten it to her wrist. Then removing the chain from her neck, she asked, 'And will you wear *this*?'

'I will if it fits.' He smiled.

'Here,' she said, slipping it carefully over his head.

He helped her fix it around his neck, before arching her gently down onto the grass.

'How do you say those things in Irish?'

'What things?'

'You know.'

'Those things?' She tilted her head.

'Yes.'

'*An luífidh tú liom, a chroí.*' She spoke the words slowly, deliberately.

'What does it mean?'

'It means *An luífidh tú liom, a chroí.*' She kissed him.

Seamus laughed, leaning over her, eyes soft with light.

'Are you mine so?' she whispered up to him.

'I am,' he said.

The sky around his head was vast as the sun slid sideways out of a cloud. 'And are you mine?'

'I am so.'

Two nights later, Maeve had a dream. She was stumbling through a warren of caves, looking for an infant which black-hooded nuns had taken away. 'My baby, where's my baby?' she kept calling in the dark, louder and louder, her feet slipping on silt and mud, stretching out her hands as she sank into a hole.

Maeve threw the blanket from her and reached for the trunk at the foot of her bed. She unfastened the latch and rummaged for the flask. Tearing at the cap, she spilled the water onto the floor, but managed to save a few drops in her hand. She wet her forehead, making a Brigid sign, before lowering her fingers to her neck, then her breasts and then lower down again to her thighs, whimpering, moaning, weeping big tears, as she dabbed the water onto her sex. 'Please Brigid,' she cried. 'I can't have a baby. Not now, not yet. Whatever happens, I can't have a baby.'

Maeve said nothing to Seamus and the following week they were back at sea. This time they sailed to Glandore, across the bay, hugging the north shore, staying closer to home. She had the day off from Minehan's and since there were no oar races that Sunday — in the lull between the Ross and Schull Regattas — Seamus was free. Helen and Robbie were cruising with Captain Rynn off Baltimore, so Seamus and Maeve found themselves alone again.

Before they reached the rock of Adam — passing Kilfinnan House to the East — Seamus said he had something to tell her.

'I've a job,' he announced, pushing the tiller as they went about.

'What sort of job?' she said, dipping her head under the boom.

'A summer job, volunteering.'

'Volunteering?'

'Yes.'

'For what?'

'The RNL.'

'What's that?'

'The Royal National Lifeboats.'

'*Royal?* You mean English?'

'No. Irish. Royal *national*. It can be English or Irish. There's no difference when it comes to saving lives.'

Maeve flushed. She wasn't one for politics, but this wasn't politics, it was their summer. And as for saving lives? That's what *she* wanted to do too. She looked down at her lap, not knowing what to say, but knowing she had to say something.

'So that's why Mick Collins and O'Donovan Rossa died?'

'What do you mean?' Seamus had a baffled look. 'Collins and O'Donovan Rossa? What do they have to do with it?'

'They died for Ireland…'

'Many people died for Ireland.'

'…so we could be free.'

'Well, we're not free.' His eyes narrowed. 'We're not free of fear and hate, are we? We're not free of Hitler.' He pulled hard at the main sheet, tacking to windward. 'You see, it's not about *us*, Maeve. It's not about Ireland. It's about the world. Doing something for the world.'

Maeve shivered, hurt by his words. She felt scolded, diminished, an offshore island girl again. She hated him putting her down like that and was gutted at the thought of him going away again so soon. Just days before, on Staic Séipéil, she was ready to give the world for him, everything; and she still was. But now he seemed ready to give her up for the world. And while she shared his wanting to save people, she couldn't help remembering Helen's warning. *Do you know him? Do you really know him?* Suddenly, Maeve wanted to strike back, explain what she meant about freedom, defend herself; but the nugget in her heart melted. She was too smitten. She couldn't fight now. She couldn't lose him.

'How long will you be gone?' she asked after a silence, staring into the waves.

'Not long,' said Seamus. 'A month or so. I'll be starting in Cobh on Monday.' His eyes grew intent, scanning the horizon. Maeve sensed there was no use protesting; he was already somewhere else. 'German subs are stalking the shipping lanes, Maeve, they're all over the place, attacking fleets crossing from Halifax. They're sinking boats not far from here, ships with women and children aboard. Passenger ships, cargo ships, full of innocent folk. It's on the radio every day. You've heard it, haven't you? The *Lusitania* all over again. Only worse. We have to do something....'

'I know. I know. I know what you're saying. But why *you*?' She felt fiercely sad. 'Because your mother's English? Because your uncle's in the air force?'

'No, Maeve. Because I've a mind of my own. A conscience. That's why. And because I want to be a *real* doctor.' He stared hard at the headland. 'I'll be working with medical officers, brave men, trained men who can teach me important things.'

A real doctor. Important things. The words smarted. Maeve too wanted to do important things, to cure the wounded and heal the ill. She wanted it so much in fact that she'd have abandoned everything right there and then — job, salary, lodgings, everything — and gone with Seamus to Cobh, to join the Royal Lifeboats and save drowning sailors, working by his side in dangerous seas. If only she could; but she knew she could not. They'd never accept a girl like her; and even if they did, she couldn't abandon her work without notice. And the scholarship exams? And her mother in Cork? Who would support her if Maeve was gone? It was cruelly clear: Seamus would go and she would stay.

Maeve felt bile at the back of her throat and silently swore at the bitter sea. 'When will you return?' she asked after a moment.

'End of July,' he said. 'But time flies. I promise, Maeve.

You'll see. I'll write and tell you everything, every expedition, every seaman lost or saved. I'll be back before you know it.'

Maeve clutched the seat and trembled. Tears stung her eyes. 'And Dublin? What about Dublin?'

'Of course,' said Seamus quickly, as though suddenly aware of Maeve's hurt. 'I haven't forgotten Dublin. Of course not.' He loosened the sail and fixed the helm, sinking to his knees as he took Maeve's hands and kissed them repeatedly, her fingers and wrists, her knuckles and palms, turning them over and back again, covering them with his lips, his chin, his nose, his hair. 'We *will* go to Dublin. As soon as I'm back and settled in Surgeons. As soon as you've got your scholarship exams. We'll go to Dublin. I promise.'

'You always promise.' She heard Helen say *men say lots of things*, recalling all the long months of yearning, on the island, at Minehans, at the Rail Station, the post office, endlessly waiting for letters, preparing for the Mater exams, counting the days to Seamus' return.

'I promise because I *mean* it.' Seamus looked Maeve straight in the eye. 'We'll go as soon as summer is done. Just like we said. You and me. Together.'

Maeve wanted to believe him, and to also believe she'd get the exams, the place in nursing, the extra money for lodgings in Dublin. She had to believe it. She raised her head. 'And where will we stay?'

Seamus looked down at the lines of his palms, swallowing, considering. 'We'd have to live separately at first of course — my father would insist on that — but we could get digs beside each other. Perhaps by the Grand Canal? You'd love it there, Maeve. It's beautiful, and quiet, with leafy banks. The water and gulls will remind you of home. We'll walk out each evening after work.'

And closing her eyes Maeve could already see the water streaming through the canals and hear the cry of the Dublin gulls and smell the city scents of the air. She took Seamus's arm. 'And when we're finished studying can we travel the world? Can we go to foreign places together?'

'Of course we can. What place would you like?'

'India maybe.'

'India?'

'Yes. Perhaps Madras. Where the medical missionaries went, to help mothers and babies, the poor and the sick...'

'Madras, why not? Helen swears it's where the best tea comes from.' Seamus laughed.

'And after that China.' Maeve's mind wandered, lost in her thoughts.

'And see the skull of the Peking Man? Why not?'

'Just the two of us.'

'Just us.' And taking Maeve's hand, Seamus placed it on the hollow of his throat, then lowered her fingers gently onto the chain around his neck; and leaning forward, he ran his other hand behind her ear, brushing back a curl so he could nestle his palm on the nape of her neck, as he drew her closer, until forehead to forehead, nose to nose, mouth to mouth, he whispered softly, 'me and you.'

'You and me — *Tusa agus Mise*.' she whispered back.

They rowed the last stretch home to Keelbeg, the water flat as a dover sole. The hills above Union Hall village, mirrored in the bay, glowed purple with heather. As they approached the pier, a shadow crossed the bow to port. Maeve frowned. Cloud shade? Stray squall? A clump of drifting wrack? But no, as they looked closer, they saw it was a shoal of hungry mackerel — gobs, fins and tails thrashing madly as they chased sprat down to the bottom of the sea.

VII

RETURNS
July-October 1942

Láracha - sea wrack

Maeve peered about the tea room, her buttered scone untouched. Large families were crowding Fields after Wednesday Market, faces blank as big-eyed calves. She fidgeted with her bracelet. No sign of Helen. She was late again and Elevenses were almost up. Helen was always tardy, but forty minutes was too much, and Maeve wanted to tell her about Seamus' letter. Maeve took the envelope from her sack and, removing the thin blue page spread it flat on the table. She read it to herself for the tenth time.

RNLI Coastguard Station
Cobh
Co Cork
Thursday
July 15, 1942

Dear Maeve,
I hope you are fine in Skibbereen. I wish I could say the same about the sea. Our boat's been busy with rescue missions, some in very stormy waters off Wexford. But I'm still in one piece and learning a lot about first aid recovery. I assisted with emergency surgery today. Mangled limb of a seaman rescued from the waves after a frigate struck a mine. The work is brutal but the doctors on board have asked me to stay. They want me to sail with them

to Belfast next week, where we're badly needed. All the damage Jerry is doing — shipping lanes a mess, cargos going down by the day. It means prolonging my posting for another two months, until I start my studies at Surgeons. I'm so sorry. I know it seems long, but I can't say no.

I miss you, Maeve, and wish I could take a few days off and come see you right now — tell you all the news, go for walks in Myross and make a trip to the islands.

I may not be able to write very often if things get any busier or we're billeted in small Antrim ports. But I'll send word whenever I can.

Meantime, work hard for those exams and rest assured it won't be long before I'm back. I'll come for you first week of October. Then we'll go to Dublin.

I think of you all the time, Maeve, my one and only dreoilín.
   - Seamus

Maeve lifted the envelope to her mouth and glancing about, kissed it quickly along the seal where Seamus had wet it with his tongue. She imagined their lips touching. Then she placed the featherweight paper back in the envelope and inhaled, her chest rising and falling, before staring out Fields' window at the bruised sky. Seamus. At sea for another two months! Heading off to Northern ports. To godforsaken Antrim for God's sake. Three hundred miles away. Maeve wanted to believe all he said — she really did — that he missed her and wanted her, that he was fighting Hitler and saving lives. But what if he drowned and never came back? What if her hopes were all in vain and Helen Flynn was right after all? What if she ended up like her mam, alone in a madhouse talking to walls?

Maeve pushed her curls back and had a good mind to get a

train for Cobh before Seamus sailed. But she knew she'd never make it in time; and if she did, what would she say? What would she do? Seamus would never change his mind. It was useless. She'd just have to wait another two months, filling each hour in the shop by day and preparing for the exams by night. Waiting, more waiting. She'd not give up and she'd not give in. And Helen would always be there for her, to lift her spirits and offer advice, to give her a hug and make her laugh.

But where was Helen?

Maeve cast another look about the room, taking a sip of cold tea before pushing the cup away. What was wrong, for God's sake? Had Helen got sick or had an accident? Or run off with Robbie without saying a word? Not one week ago she'd been sitting at this very table in Fields, aping Barbara Stanwyck with a cigarette — 'I have my man and he has me.'

Maeve had never smoked in her life but she craved for a cigarette now. Part of her wished she was like Helen, never worrying, never torn between what she was and what she might be — what she still always wanted to be.

Maeve flipped the envelope and read the address one more time — *Miss Maeve Sullivan, Minehan's Drapery, Skibbereen, West Cork.*

For all her cures, she'd no cure for this. The missingness.

Whistle and hiss. Wail of a steam engine from Bridge Street. Morning train from Cork. Maeve glanced up at Field's clock. Past midday. Helen wasn't coming. Rising from the table, she knew she should return to work; but she didn't. Instead, she turned north outside Fields and hurried to the bus. She must see Helen.

The driver was a terrible talker, blathering on with the passengers about this and that scrap of gossip or news — the storm damage to Cleary's chemist, the latest price of beef on the hoof, the sickly face of the curate in Leap, the Japanese invasion of Java.

Maeve swore under her breath, wishing everyone would stop nattering and settle in their seats. Halfway to Leap, by the turn for Raheen, the bus ran into a line of lorries ferrying heifers to Dunmanway, while a huge lady sitting beside Maeve snorted away like a sow in her sleep. The bus kept stopping and starting, letting school children on and off at every turn — Drinagh, Colla, Manch, Reenagreena — little pale faces with eyes blank as saucers, mouths gaping like waifs in the pictures. When they arrived at Leap, Maeve looked down at her fists to find Seamus's letter in a twisted knot.

Once off the bus, Maeve walked the two mile stretch to Union Hall, not pausing once to inhale the honeysuckle wafting from the hedgerows or gaze about her at the foxgloves and wild daisies. She didn't even hear the birds.

When she reached the village, she went straight to Helen's.

Mrs Flynn answered the door and, seeing it was Maeve, pulled her quickly inside. She retreated a step, eyes blurred with grief. 'It's terrible,' she said.

'What?' Maeve put a hand to her throat.

'Helen. She's been drinking and won't leave her room. I brought her tea but she won't touch a thing.'

'What happened?'

'He's gone.'

'*Who's* gone?'

'Robbie.'

'Gone where?'

'To London.' Mrs Flynn beckoned Maeve further into the hallway. 'Captain Rynn discovered they were about to marry, behind his back, without saying a word. He says they're far too young and that Helen put Robbie up to it; and he doesn't like the prospect of Catholic grandchildren. He's furious and won't let his son see Helen again. He's taken him off to England. They left Saturday on the Fishguard ferry. Helen went after them, followed them all the way to Cobh. She was desperate, poor child, but the boat had left. She came back in a frightful state. She hasn't left her room since.'

'Can I see her?' asked Maeve, feeling her legs weakening.

Mrs Flynn stood aside, pointing to the stairs. 'Go knock on the door. She might open for you.'

Maeve knocked and, when there was no reply, entered.

Helen was sitting on the side of her bed. She didn't look up.

'I'm so sorry.' Maeve rushed to her friend's side and hugged her, shocked by how bony she felt in her mother's crushed dressing gown, collarbones exposed above the neckline. There was a stale odor from her hair and Maeve could scent gin off her breath. The lemon-oniony smell was gone.

Helen let herself be held but did not lift her hands from her lap nor return the hug.

'Your mother says you're not eating?'

Helen shook her head, staring at her bare feet as if they would somehow do the talking. In the background, the radio announced the British routing of Rommel at El Alamein.

'You've been drinking?' Maeve looked for clues but could see nothing apart from a chamber pot half-tucked under the bed, speckled with what looked like vomit. No trace of a bottle or glass.

'Drinking?' echoed Helen, toneless as a telephone operator. 'Not enough.'

'Here.' Maeve sat in close, pulling the flask from her sack. 'Take this.' She lifted the container and, reaching for a cup on Helen's table, poured in four thimblefuls of the water along with a sprinkle of dried *púcaí*. She handed it to Helen.

Helen took the cup between her hands and gazed at it as if she was reading tea leaves, then put it aside without drinking. She reached over and turned off the radio.

Maeve clasped her friend's two hands and listened to her breathe. Helen's room had been altered since her last visit: the ceiling was repainted cornflower blue, and the old skylight had a brand new window with a thin lace curtain filtering the light. Helen had also changed the quilt of her bed, replacing the fleur de lys pattern with crimson roses. On the desk lay a pair of scissors that Helen had been using when Maeve entered the room. What had she been doing, Maeve wondered? Trimming her hair? (Her fringe was crooked.) Shredding the photo of Robbie with his braided jacket and white flannels? (The album had disappeared from its usual place by the bedside, but there were no cuttings on the floor.) Was she planning to injure herself? (God forbid.) Maeve kept searching for clues, though it was hard to see, mid-afternoon, with half-drawn curtains veiling the light.

Helen's cat slunk into the room and leaped noiselessly onto her lap, his marmalade tail rising as he settled into a purr. Helen stroked the arch of his spine.

Maeve thought of Bawn, how he'd comforted her on the island when she was down. On the dressing table, beside the mirror, she spotted a jar with a stone inside. A perfectly smooth sandstone with a spot in the middle, shaped like a star.

'What's that?' she pointed to the jar.

'A birthday present,' Helen muttered. 'From Robbie.' It was the first time she'd uttered his name. 'I'll hit him with it if I see him again.'

'Do you want to?'

'What?'

'See him again.'

'No.' She raised her voice. 'For God's sake, Maeve…. How could I?'

Maeve sat upright. 'Robbie had no choice, you know. Your mother said so. The Captain forced him.'

'No choice,' Helen repeated. 'That's what Robbie said in his note. Imagine! He couldn't even say it to my face. But I don't believe him. Not a word. In the end he just cringed like a pup. *Stick to your own and mind the locals. Good for bed, bad for betrothals*. That's what the Captain said, I heard him. My father was good enough for business but I wasn't good enough for his boy. A Catholic upstart, a Fenian lush. That's what he thought. I know it. I hate him. I hate them both.'

Helen grabbed the cat with both hands and flung it, screeching, onto the floor. 'Robbie swore he'd take me to London. But he hadn't the guts to face his father. He promised the world and slunk away. I never want to see him again.' Helen threw a glance at the jar.

'Don't talk that way.' Maeve pressed Helen's wrists. 'It does no good.'

'*Don't talk that way. It does no good.*' Helen mocked Maeve's island accent. She pulled away and glanced out the window. 'That's what Seamus said too.'

'*Seamus?*' Maeve felt a thud in her chest.

'Yes. Seamus. *Your* Seamus.' Helen paused.

'How do you know what Seamus said?'

'Because he told me. Because I met him.'

'When?'

'Last week. In Cobh. I followed Robbie but he'd already sailed. Seamus was there, about to ship North.'

Maeve shot a hand to her mouth. 'Seamus met you? He never told me.' Maeve reached for the letter in her pocket. 'I got this today. Look. Right here. He says he was leaving for Belfast.' She handed it to Helen.

Helen took the letter and, glancing at the postmark, handed it back to Maeve. 'See. There.' She pointed to the date. 'July 25th. That was Thursday, the day before we met.'

Maeve stared at the envelope. With the weekend it had taken five days to reach her.

Helen rose from the bed and padded to the curtains, pulling them back to reveal a tumbler of gin. She picked it up and waved it in the air. 'Don't worry, Maeve Sullivan. You're the lucky one.'

'Why?

'Because he loves you. He really does. He loves *you* the way I thought Robbie loved *me*. Robbie left me. Seamus won't leave you. I know it. He told me. That's the difference. I made the wrong choice. You made the right one. Here's to you!'

Helen took a long swig, raising her glass in the air. Then she took another before going on. 'Seamus was kind to me in Cobh. So kind.' She knotted her brow. 'I was drunk, very drunk, making a terrible show of myself, screaming things in the street, mad things, awful things, about Robbie and his father, my parents and Father Kehoe, everyone. Seamus took care of me. He talked to me, calmed me down, got me medicine and a room for the night. He even paid my train fare home.' Helen sat back on the bed and sobbed. 'You're lucky, Maeve. You're so lucky to have him.'

Maeve felt her chest loosen. Helen was right. Seamus loved her and she was indeed blessed. She felt glad that Seamus had looked after Helen.

'What will you do?' Maeve asked after a bit.

Helen leaned back, rubbing her palms up and down her knees. She thought for a while before replying. 'I don't know. I don't know anything anymore.'

'What do your parents say?'

'Nothing. They say it's for the best. That we were too young. They worry about my drinking. They want me to go to university.'

'And what do *you* want?'

'To get away.' Helen shot a look about the room, eyes big as a hunted hare. She fidgeted with the gin in her hand, spilling some onto the woolen rug. 'Anywhere.'

Maeve took the tumbler from Helen and, moving closer, caressed her skinny shoulders and arms, as if she was warming her up after a swim. She could feel her body shudder all over, like her mother before she left for the asylum. She knew she must help her, the friend who'd taken her in and opened all kinds of worlds for her. Now it was her turn to rescue Helen.

'Why not Dublin?' Maeve lifted Helen's chin with her finger. 'When me and Seamus go to Dublin, you could join us.'

Helen didn't respond, as if she hadn't heard, letting her head sink down to her chest and staring hard at the patterned mat. Her birdlike frame visibly shook; shivering with cold, or weeping, or laughing, Maeve couldn't quite tell.

'Why don't you?' Maeve ran her hand over Helen's hair, matted and damp, gently unraveling a twisted strand and curling it back around her ear. 'Even for a while, maybe, until you find your feet, until things settle. We could share digs, the two of us.

Like sisters.' Maeve touched Helen's forehead, running her palm down her cheek, stroking the side of her wet face as if she was stroking an island filly, calming, comforting. Something like joy stirred in her breast. 'We could study together during the day and walk with Seamus in the evenings.'

Helen raised her eyes and looked at her friend for the first time since she'd entered the room. 'You're *so* kind, Maeve, my Biddy island girl. You know that?' Helen let her hands fall to her lap, peering down at her own skinny knees, before looking back up. 'Do you think it could work? Do you really think so?'

'Of course it could work.' Maeve passed Helen the unfinished cup. 'Now drink this. You'll feel better in no time.' She watched her take a slow sip. 'And when you come to Dublin we'll find someone special for you, someone far better than Robbie.' She poked Helen on the breastbone, trying to coax a smile. 'You'll see. Everyone loves Helen Flynn. It'll work. We'll be grand, the three of us. Me and Seamus will look after you. We'll look after each other.'

Helen pushed the fringe from her face and looked as if she was going to cry. But she didn't. She drank the cup, every drop, and reaching over, hugged Maeve tight in her arms.

'We will so,' said Helen with a sudden laugh. 'We'll look after each other.'

Later that evening, Maeve accompanied Helen for a walk to Keelbeg. Trawlermen were sorting the day's deep sea catch, weighing the fish on scales before fixing the price. The girls stood and stared. Six-pound cod and ten-pound ling, boxes of haddock and John Dory, scores of plaice and three enormous skates, their wings spread out like giant bleeding bats. The buyer, Bill Glanton, strutted about the quays between coils of mooring rope and tackle, eyes darting from the catch to the girls and back. Maeve had always liked Glanton from the times he'd be buying lobsters from her father, spitting on open palms before smacking hands and trading grubby pound notes. She watched him now as he totted up sums, scribbling things down in a small padded book. Maeve recited the names of the fish. *Ronnach. Deoraí, bradán, cnúdán dearg*. The Irish sounds soothed her soul.

Meanwhile Helen peered wide-eyed at sleek conger eels hung up on iron scales, while local boys betted on the biggest prey.

As the last batch of fish was being stored in crates, someone shouted — 'One more!'

A Reen trawler, back from the Stags, was casting its mooring onto the pier. Bill Glanton called — 'Grand catch' — sucking in his cheeks as he eyed the booty over his nose. A monstrous black fish was being hoisted ashore.

'Mako?' Bill ventured, staring at the five striped gills.

'Mako,' the skipper nodded. 'And not a pound under ninety.'

And there it was, stretched out like a corpse, black glassy eyes staring and still. Helen turned away but Maeve stood firm. A waft of urine and iodine caught the back of her nose. She gazed at the shark's slit gullet, a comb of razor-tipped teeth, gouts of blood clotting the gills where steel barbed gaffs had entered and hacked. Flung on its back, belly up, exposed. Maeve recalled her father saying that makos would eat anything — sprats, salmon, seaweed, seals — even drowned mortals. 'Nothing too big or small for them,' he swore. But Maeve skipped a breath when Glanton grabbed the dorsal fin and something slipped through the long tail slit — a silvery shape all covered in slime, coiling slowly back and forth, its tiny gob mouthing a cry. A shark child. Drowning. *Diadhánach*.

August and September ambled by like slow ewes. Seamus sent notes whenever he could, postmarked Belfast, Portadown, and other Antrim ports, giving his news and repeating his promise to come for Maeve in October. She loved getting word, however short, but she couldn't stop worrying about him out there on the whiplashed sea. She often woke with nightmares of strangled cries and tangled limbs wrestling with the waves. And the fretting was worse with Helen gone. No sooner out of bed — shortly after Maeve's visit — Helen was whisked off to Galway by her parents. To visit a tee-totaling Aunt for the rest of the summer. 'A change of scenery,' they said, before she started university.

Maeve understood why they did it and knew that even if Helen had stayed they'd have had precious little time to see each other with her two jobs, at Minehan's and the Railway. But with Seamus and Helen both far away, the loneliness was unbearable. The only thing for it, Maeve decided, was work and more work — busying herself in the shop by day and spending her evenings reading for the scholarship. Minehan's was bustling with end of summer sales. No let up, not for a second, from noisy customers queuing up for orders — lengths of linen, lace and silk — toying with spools of sewing thread or inquiring about the glorious wedding dress displayed in the front bay window: the order made specially for Alice Raftery of Mallow. Enough! Maeve swore if one more person asked for a serge sample or a box of fish eye buttons she'd leap over the counter and choke them. But what could she do? She needed the wages, every shilling, for the coming move to Dublin, with some left over for her mother each month. Maeve did the best she could, settling her nerves with nettle brews and talking away with Miss Collins in her head as she learned the exam tests off by heart, and then, before going to bed every night, always saying a prayer to Brigid — that she'd get the scholarship, that Seamus would come, and they'd both be in Dublin before autumn was out.

Last Monday of September, Maeve was helping Mrs Minehan unpack new rolls of linen when the post arrived. It was a letter from the Mater Nursing Hospital in Dublin. Maeve sliced open the envelope with a scissors from the counter and read the contents aloud:

To Miss Maeve Sullivan:

The Mater School of Nursing is pleased to inform you that you have been awarded a full scholarship to our Training Academy. The annual stipend, renewable for three years, is valid from October 15 when studies begin. Please bring your birth certificate and a complete Nursing outfit as indicated in the enclosed registration document, payable by cash or postal order. Our teaching staff look forward to welcoming you to the Mater in keeping with our motto: cura personalis in corpore sano.

Maeve almost devoured the letter as she tapped her breast and gave a big holler. She rushed to hug Mrs Minehan and would have done likewise with the postman if he wasn't already out the door. Drawing back her shoulders, she let big breaths out of her as she waltzed around the shop floor, curtseying before the dress dummy, as though inviting it to dance. And when Mrs Minehan stepped forward to protect the nuptial garment, Maeve grabbed her by the waist and spun her in a circle, making her hoot as loud as an owl. Exhausted, Maeve finally sat up on the counter and handed the letter to Mrs Minehan, asking her to read it again, a second time, as witness. She could feel her heart unfurling like a bird. *Dreoilín*. Her wings soared. She'd done it. She couldn't wait to tell Seamus.

As she slipped off the counter, a customer entered the shop. It was Mrs Raftery come all the way from Mallow for final adjustments to her daughter's wedding gown.

'You're in grand humor,' she said as Maeve straightened her blouse.

'And why wouldn't she be?' said Mrs Minehan, 'and she after receiving a scholarship for Dublin.'

'For what?

'For nursing. She's been studying for months. I never saw the likes of it, making lists, rehearsing questions, learning everything off by heart. She passed with flying colors.'

Mrs Raftery walked to the dummy and stroked the silk tresses and folds. 'It's well for some,' she said, 'heading to Dublin for the fancy life.' She curled a length of hem between her fingers before pulling it tight, testing the fabric, making sure she was getting her money's worth. 'But, you know, I often say there's a better life to be had at home. All the young ones nowadays running off to this place or that. But what's wrong with Cork, I ask you? At least for those who can find a good husband and rear a decent family....'

'Like your Alice,' Mrs Minehan finished her sentence, pushing a linen roll a little too quickly onto the shelf.

'Like *my* Alice.' Mrs Raftery wagged her chin. 'My girl never had notions, thank God. Not a one. She never got too big for her boots or thought of leaving her own kind behind, gallivanting off to big towns. She's a grand girl, she is, my Alice, and she'll be around to look after me when the time comes. She's more than happy with what she's got, a fine dairy farmer with ninety acres right adjacent to our own. Counting the days to the wedding, she is, God bless her.'

'God bless her indeed.' Maeve folded the Mater letter in two and popped it into her pocket. 'I'll be thinking of her when I'm in Dublin.'

On the sixth day of October, Maeve was arranging things in the display window when Mrs Minehan called. 'He's here, Maeve. He's here. Your gentleman's arrived.'

Maeve put a hand to her mouth then her tummy. Little shivers ran through her. *Sceitimíní.* He'd come, like he promised. He hadn't failed. She still had many things to pack: her chest and cures, her rug and coat, her font and almanac and Petersen tin, the letter for the scholarship. All upstairs in her room, waiting. But she couldn't wait, not a second longer.

'Where is he?' Maeve dropped a strip of lace to the floor.

'At the front door. I told him to wait.' Mrs Minehan brushed her skirt down and smiled. 'Fine looking man, I must say. And lovely manners. Shook my hand and asked for Miss Maeve Sullivan, if you please.'

'Can he come in?' Maeve glanced at the shop mirror, tidying a curl.

'Of course he can, child. I'll show him the way and make some tea.'

Maeve saw Seamus before he saw her. She ran to him before he had time to move from the threshold into the store, a shaft of afternoon light around his head as he looked about the room, between drapery dummies and scrolls of fabric, bewildered, not knowing where to go. She threw her arms about his shoulders and sank into his chest.

'Seamus,' she whispered.

'Maeve.' He didn't stir; he simply closed his arms around her and breathed. She could feel his hands on the small of her back, and his heart pounding; and she could hear the sound of her name coming from his lips like a wave filling the whole room, pouring over her as everything rose and floated, the cottons and silks, the tweeds and tresses, all dissolving in a happy blur.

They stood together like that for a moment, not saying another word, not moving from the open door to the inside of the store, until Maeve raised her head. She looked up into Seamus's face, his eyes still shut, and, lifting her thumb, ran it gently down his features from the top of his forehead over his lips to the small fine crease at the base of his chin. It was as though she was blessing him, thanking him, teasing him, as she traced a sign of Brigid, before sinking her face back onto his chest. She brushed her nose down the side of his neck, wishing she could inhale his entire being into hers, swallow him up and keep him forever. He was here. He was hers. He had come to take her to Dublin at last.

'I'm ready,' she whispered, as they stood locked together, not stirring. 'I got the scholarship.'

'I know you did.' He nodded. 'Well done.'

'I've been waiting all week.'

'I know,' he repeated.

'Are we going now?'

Silence.

His voice faltered. 'We're not going anywhere, Maeve.'

Her body went slack for a second before gripping his arms with both hands. She peered up, searching his face. 'Not going anywhere? What do you mean? Why aren't we going anywhere?'

'Because I have to get married.'

'To *me?*' She released her grip, pulling back slightly, so she could see him better, hear better what he was saying.

'No, Maeve. No, not to you.'

'What?'

'I have to marry someone else.' He shifted his feet.

'Someone *else?*'

'Yes. I have to marry Helen.'

She pushed him away and grabbed her belly, trying to suck air into her lungs. She pitched back and forth several times, a white roar pounding her ears, before raising her head and opening her mouth. A scream stuck in the back of her throat, her eyes darting about the store until they fixed on his long pale face, unbelieving.

'Helen?' Maeve repeated.

Seamus stepped back, nodded, avoiding her gaze.

'No,' she screamed. 'It can't be. She wouldn't. She knows you love me.'

'I know, Maeve.' Seamus covered his face with his hands. 'I'm sorry, Maeve. I'm sorry. I do love you. I always will. But I have to marry Helen….'

'Why?'

'Because she's pregnant. And I'm the father.'

Maeve bent and moaned like an animal. She curled in two, blocking her ears, unable to listen to another word.

'This can't be.' Maeve lifted her head and crossed her wrists, pausing for a moment, before rushing at Seamus. She clawed fiercely at his collar and shirt, tearing the silver chain from his neck. 'How could you? How could you?'

Seamus took the blows without moving, then pulled her

firmly back into his arms. He clasped her tight as her fingernails dug deep into his ribs.

'Listen to me now, Maeve.' Seamus spoke slowly. His body trembled. 'I have to tell you exactly what happened. When Helen came to Cobh, she'd lost Robbie, she'd lost everything. You know that. I tried to calm her, comfort her. I don't know. It only happened once and as soon as it did I knew it shouldn't have. It's you I love, Maeve…'

Seamus broke off, swallowing hard, before continuing. 'I was in Belfast when I got the news that Helen was pregnant. I took a train straight to Dublin. My parents were waiting, the Flynns too, with Helen and Father Kehoe, all sitting there in Buswells Hotel. It was hell. I wanted to run, escape, to go right back to the bloody war.' He paused for a moment to clear his throat. 'But I had to stay and marry Helen. My father said it was the right thing to do, the only thing…

'…Your father said' — Maeve raised her head and stared him in the eye — 'Your *father* said. What did *you* say?'

'I said I couldn't, that it was you I wanted, I told them about our plans for Dublin, our….' Seamus shook his head. 'They were all crying, saying I had to save Helen, from shame, from scandal, from the wrong I'd done.' He shuddered. 'It was terrible. I said yes in the end because I had to. Every child needs a father. You know that, Maeve.' Seamus hugged her closer. 'I'm so sorry. I've ruined everything.'

Maeve broke his hold and freed her fists. 'Go, Seamus, go away from me now. I never want to see you again.' She pushed his chest and flung herself towards the display window, tearing at the fabrics and drapes as she pulled the wedding dress to the ground. There she lay panting for some time, not saying another word, her body tangled in a mess of veils.

When she opened her eyes she could see boots through a

scramble of lace, but did not look up. She could hear her heart pounding, and Seamus's breathing above her, ragged and raw, and, in the distance, a faint rattle of carriages, and the bells of the Angelus from up at St John's. And through the tolling of bells she heard Mam's voice again, ringing in her brain. *He'll never stay with an island girl. He'll hook you like a sprat and throw you back.* And a sudden image flashed before her mind: the time, just months before, when Seamus stared at her wrist on the island and read the future in the lines of her scar. 'You're my *dreoilín* and I'll not let you go,' he'd said. 'We'll go to Dublin and be healers together.' And then Maeve heard other things, wild things, tumultuous things further away again, tumbling through her head like drowning voices, her fathers and brothers, and mothers and grandmothers, and others before them without face or name, all disappearing, all disappearing down into the hole. *Diadhánach.*

Maeve woke to feel hands behind her head, touching her hair, taking her pulse. Two palms slid beneath her, clasping her knees and shoulders, coaxing her gently onto her feet. Someone was speaking close to her ear. 'It's all right. You're all right, Maeve. It's me. I'm here.' Silence. 'He's gone. The young man's gone. Sure you're only a child. There'll be others.'

It was Mrs Minehan.

Maeve let herself be lifted from the floor and, standing, thanked Mrs Minehan and said she needed to be alone.

Gathering up the wedding dress, Maeve replaced the dummy in the window. She didn't bother to wrap the silks or pin the robe back onto the torso; she just folded the wedding slip under her arm and made her way quietly upstairs.

Back in her room, she took her trunk from the cupboard and completed her packing. The books and papers for nursing school.

Skirts, blouses and underwear. And the cures. She took some dried *púcaí* from the Petersen tin and chewed them carefully before placing the tin in the trunk along with bundles of dried wracks, the scalloped font, the Brigid cross and flask of water. But when she weighed the flask in her hand she discovered it was empty. She turned it over but not a drop. So she sat down on the edge of the bed and cried with the bottle in her hands, cried for herself, for Seamus and for Helen, for the ruined plans of their lives together. Gone, all gone, everything gone. She rocked and wept in the still of the room, big salt tears, bitter and hot, until there were no more tears to weep. She shook the flask and rose from the bed. She must go to the well and get more water. Return to the cave with its candles and shells and breathe in smells of seaweed and tobacco. She needed the water and needed it now; she couldn't go to Dublin without it. It was dark already but she wouldn't wait.

Maeve closed the lid of the trunk and placed it flat beside the bed before stealing down the stairwell and out into the night. She mounted her bicycle and rode to Squince.

Toes, soles, ankles, shins. It was cold, so cold, and black as only the sea at night is black. The tide at Squince was turning as she waded out, one step after another, the water rising around her, hands paddling the waves. There were no boats on the strand she could borrow and she didn't want to wait until morning. No more waiting. No more wanting. She patted the empty flask at her hip. She could hardly feel anything now, only odd little bumps from shells beneath her feet and the quick tightening of her chest as the water rose around her, only the neck and head to go. The head, always the last to go under, the worst sting of cold at the tip of the skull where the skin was thin and the bones were soft — like the dent on the top of a baby's head where the soul slipped in at the start of life and slipped out again at the end. The fontanel they called it in the nursing books. But Maeve didn't want to think of babies now. Not Helen's, not Seamus's, nor the ones she'd never have with Seamus, nor all those left behind at the Convent of the Good Shepherd; poor little things all alone in the dark. All over now as she swam to her own — following the wind to Brigid's cave.

She moved out further into the surf, curling like a cormorant, going under and surfacing again. The soaked hem of the wedding slip — she'd never worn silk things before — swelled under her palms like the wings of a gannet spreading wide before collapsing back around her again. Pale and soft in the watery dark.

Gusts grazed her temple but there were no waves to stem her motion, no moon nor stars to stay her eyes. Only low cloud clinging to the water. She could not see the island as she swam towards it, like a seal to its den, going back to where she came from, one last time before leaving for good. *Púca, púca, buail abhaile*. Off home with you now. She turned on her back for twenty long strokes, then flipped right over onto her chest. Born and bred amongst seaweeds and fish, she could feel the drag where her father went down, down with the others into the hole. Same draw, same tide, same dark, same deep. She dipped and went down, sinking fathom by fathom into the black, through spumes of surf to the currents beneath, to the weeds and the whelks where her father once lay. She flailed and went limp, no more strength, no more air, almost there. When a sudden swell rose up beneath her, lifting her arms and opening her eyes. She saw a flare of phosphorescence scattering in circles around her, so bright and quick she did not know if she was still falling into the hole or rising up toward the light, like a trout buoyed on by a flooding tide, a glut of bubbles flowing from her mouth. A surge was pushing her upwards now, urging her, coaxing her, pulling her, guiding her, until she breached and gulped air.

The clouds had lifted. She looked about under a shawl of stars — *Bealach na Bó finne* — feet treading water as she took in the distant arch of the Galley head, then the mare's mane of Ardra hill before settling on the Island, still a way off. A dim light seemed to gleam from the well. A flicker scarcely visible over the waves, as if a small fire was burning inside, or a first glimmer of dawn was glancing off the mouth of the cave. Or maybe she was imagining things. Maeve heard a sharp cry and peered up to see a storm petrel above her head. *Gearr úisc.* Its tiny wings stirred the air, as it flitted in circles, closer and closer, so low it almost brushed her brow. She raised her eyes and swept hair from her face, turning around in a single stroke — *an deiseal*, like the rising sun. She knew what she must do. She lay on her back and floated to shore, letting the tide carry her in, until she could see the white sands of Squince beach beckoning and the ribbon of Myross road winding upward. She'd carry the island inside her forever. She'd find the well wherever she went. She knew now. The water is everywhere.

ACKNOWLEDGEMENTS

I am grateful to many people for help during the writing of this story.

First, my friend Fanny Howe for her wise and careful guidance over the years from first paragraph to last. Also, other good friends here in Boston for their encouragements and comments: Sheila Gallagher, Susan Brown, James Morley, and Michael and Kathy Fitzgerald.

Moving back across the Atlantic, I would like to thank the following Irish friends and writers who read various drafts of the book and offered expert counsel and corrections: Catherine Fitzpatrick, James Ryan, Paul Freaney, Patrick Hederman, Ronan Sheehan, Kevin Barry, and Claire Anderson-Wheeler, amongst others.

For their generous assistance in checking the accuracy of Gaelic phrases and folk cures, I am grateful to my Boston College colleagues: Joe Nugent, Seán Cahill, and visiting Burns Chair Elís ní Dhuibne who put me in touch with the National Folklore Collection at University College Dublin, as well as Nóirín Ní Riain, Seán Ó Duinn, and Manchán Magan whose celebrations of the Gaelic language and culture were a constant inspiration throughout.

I am also deeply indebted to my family — my wife, Anne, and daughters, Simone and Sarah, for their art work in this volume and for tolerating my long spells in the imagination with the perennial excuse — 'I am in the middle of a sentence,

I'll be there in a minute' — as well as my sister, Sally, and five brothers who provided invaluable advice about plants, wracks, sea birds, and cures.

Not forgetting the neighboring families of Myross and Cooscroneen, whose sayings and memories are scattered throughout this tale — the Burns, Neals, Jennings, Dineens, Donovans, and Browns.

A fulsome thanks to my Boston College assistants for their indefatigable energy and beady eyes: Matt Clemente, Sarah Horton, Peter Klapes, Stephen Artner, and Jeronimo Ayesta Lopez. And, from the bottom of my heart, my deepest gratitude to the team at Arrowsmith Press: Askold Melnyczuk, Ezra Fox, Catherine Parnell, and Rebecca Pacheco, who graciously shepherded this manuscript into being.

Books by
ARROWSMITH PRESS

Ric's Progress by Donald Hall

Return To The Sea by Etnairis Rivera

The Kingdom of His Will by Catherine Parnell

Eight Notes from the Blue Angel by Marjana Savka

Fifty-Two by Melissa Green

Music In—And On—The Air by Lloyd Schwartz

Magpiety by Melissa Green

Reality Hunger by William Pierce

Soundings: On The Poetry of Melissa Green
edited by Sumita Chakraborty

The Corny Toys by Thomas Sayers Ellis

Black Ops by Martin Edmunds

Museum of Silence by Romeo Oriogun

City of Water by Mitch Manning

Passeggiate by Judith Baumel

Persephone Blues by Oksana Lutsyshyna

cont...

The Uncollected Delmore Schwartz
edited by Ben Mazer

The Light Outside by George Kovach

The Blood of San Gennaro by Scott Harney
edited by Megan Marshall

No Sign by Peter Balakian

Firebird by Kythe Heller

The Selected Poems of Oksana Zabuzhko
edited by Askold Melnyczuk

The Age of Waiting by Douglas J. Penick

Manimal Woe by Fanny Howe

Crank Shaped Notes by Thomas Sayers Ellis

The Land of Mild Light by Rafael Cadenas
edited by Nidia Hernández

The Silence of Your Name: The Afterlife of a Suicide by Alexandra Marshall

Flame in a Stable by Martin Edmunds

Mrs. Schmetterling by Robin Davidson

This Costly Season by John Okrent

Thorny by Judith Baumel

The Invisible Borders of Time: Five Female Latin American Poets
edited by Nidia Hernández

Some of You Will Know by David Rivard

The Forbidden Door: The Selected Poetry of Lasse Söderberg
tr. by Lars Gustaf Andersson & Carolyn Forché

Unrevolutionary Times by Houman Harouni

Between Fury & Peace: The Many Arts of Derek Walcott
edited by Askold Melnyczuk

The Burning World by Sherod Santos

Today is a Different War: Poetry of Lyudmyla Khersonska
tr. by Olga Livshin, Andrew Janco, Maya Chhabra, & Lev Fridman

ARROWSMITH is named after the late William Arrowsmith, a renowned classics scholar, literary and film critic. General editor of thirty-three volumes of *The Greek Tragedy in New Translations*, he was also a brilliant translator of Eugenio Montale, Cesare Pavese, and others. Arrowsmith, who taught for years in Boston University's University Professors Program, championed not only the classics and the finest in contemporary literature, he was also passionate about the importance of recognizing the translator's role in bringing the original work to life in a new language.

Like the arrowsmith who turns his arrows straight and true,
a wise person makes his character straight and true.

— Buddha

Ingram Content Group UK Ltd.
Milton Keynes UK
UKHW010150200323
418728UK00004B/55

9 798986 340173